CALL THE NEXT WITNESS

"Call the next witness," said the King. He added in an undertone, "Really, my dear, you must cross-examine the next witness; it quite makes my forehead ache."

—*Alice in Wonderland*

CALL

THE

NEXT

WITNESS

Philip Mason

THE UNIVERSITY OF CHICAGO PRESS
Chicago & London

Reproduced from the first American edition, published by Harcourt, Brace and Company in 1946 in a larger format.

The University of Chicago Press, Chicago 60637
The University of Chicago Press, Ltd., London

95 94 93 92 91 90 89 88 87 86   5 4 3 2 1

Library of Congress Cataloging-in-Publication Data

Mason, Philip.
   Call the next witness.

   I. Title.
PR6025.A7926C3   1986   823'.914   86-7122
ISBN 0-226-50955-9 (pbk.)

To
_____

E. A. M.
_____
❖

CONTENTS

Part One

•:•

THE PEOPLE

IN THE STORY

❖

$P_{Y\acute{A}R\acute{I}}$, or PYÁRAN, the Flame of the Forest
   GOPÁL SINGH, her husband
   KALYAN SINGH, Gopál's father
   NANNHE SINGH, a leader of the Congress party
   HUKM SINGH, a leader of the supporters of Government
   *All these four are landholders of Anantpur in Ramnagar
   District.*

   The following come from Galthána in Sháhábád District:
   SÁHIB SINGH, Pyáran's father
   THE THÁKURÁNI, Pyáran's mother
   BITIYA, Pyáran's sister
   BHOLA NÁTH SINGH, Bitiya's husband
   RÁM KALLÁN SINGH, a servant of Sahib Singh
   JEHÁRAN, a Bráhmani, Pyárí's old nurse. *The First Witness*

RÚP SINGH, Constable, of Gosaini police station, near
   Anantpur
SHEO DAT PARSHÁD, a Brahman of Anantpur
PREM RÁJ, a servant of Kalyán Singh
GHULAM HUSAIN, Sub-Inspector, of Gosaini
MOHAMMAD 'ISHAQ, Inspector of Police, of the circle con-
   taining Gosaini
SALÁMATULLAH, Sub-Inspector of Police in Ramnagar city,
   Mohammad 'Isháq's nephew
CHRISTOPHER TREGARD, District Magistrate of Ramnagar
KHÁN BAHÁDUR MOHAMMAD ALTAF KHAN, a leader

of the followers of Government in the neighborhood of Anantpur and Gosaini

PHÚLMATI, a bania's wife

MATHURA DÁS, her husband, a bania, of Púrá Kalán, near Anantpur

JHAMMU NAT, a gypsy engaged in an intrigue with Phulmati. *The Second Witness* against Gopál

CHABELI PARSHÁD, a hillman, said to have sold peas to Jeháran. *The Third Witness*

HANUMAN SINGH, a hanger-on of the Anantpur family

PREM BADRI NÁTH, a Brahman of Shahabad, said to have brought Jeháran's ticket. *The Fourth Witness*

DOST MOHAMMAD, a bus driver of Shahabad, said to have taken Jeháran to Galtháná. *The Fifth Witness*

AHMADI JÁN, his wife

BABBAN SAHIB, Ahmadi Ján's former employer

The infant Ganges

The Temple of Kali

THE FOOTHILLS OR

The shop of Chabeli Parshad

A fictional map of that part of INDIA where PYARI, Flame of the Forest, lived and where occurred the events surrounding her mysterious death.

MALLAPUR

The Nats

The River Ganges

MALLAPUR

The hous of Ghu Hus

SULTANPUR

To Hardwar & Garhwál

STATE

The Mallapur

Here Pyári was born and lived until her marriage.

Sáhib Singh's house

GALTHANA

the bus which Dost Mohammad drove

R.R. Station

SHAHABAD

DABERA

SHAHABAD

DISTR

Jhammu went south to stay with a landlord troubled by wolves

Author's Note

•◇•

ALMOST every incident in this story of village life in Northern India is similar in skeleton to one that has actually happened, but the flesh and skin, the characters of the people concerned and their reasoning and motives, are wholly imaginary.

For the pronunciation of Indian names, it is enough to say that the vowels are pronounced as in Italian, except the short *a* which has the sound of *u* in the English word butter. For the first few times that a name occurs, I have marked the long vowels with an acute accent. Thus Pyárí is Pyahree, Rámnagar is Rahmnugger, and Anantpúr is Unnuntpoor. But as the words become familiar, I omit the accents.

CALL THE NEXT WITNESS

THE FOOTHILLS OF THE HIMALAYAS

RAMNAGAR

MALLAPUR
STATE

DISTRICT

MALLAPUR

GUSAINI
ANANTPUR

RAMNAGAR

GALTHANA

SHAHABAD

SHAHABAD
DISTRICT

District boundaries ....
Railways ....
Roads _____

Scale of miles

0   10   20
   5   15

Part One

FLAME OF THE FOREST

Her Marriage and Death

•✧•

ON the last day of her life, Pyárí sat at her spinning in the veranda before her bedroom. The house was a large one, straggling out in lopsided additions and annexes that had been built on at one time or another by ancestors, and her room was on the first floor, a kind of summer-house set by an afterthought on the roof of an older and larger building. The room itself was very small. There was just sufficient space for the two wide string cots where she and her husband slept, for a few tin trunks piled on top of each other, and for the oddments of gear lying untidily here and there—her husband's English gun and a box of cartridges, an old red skirt that must have belonged to one of the servants and which no one had moved for months, a brass pot, and a photograph of some young men at Agra University. To English ideas the room would have been small for a bathroom.

In front was the veranda where Pyárí now sat spinning. It was really another room, with three arches instead of a wall on one side. The arches had been shaped very crudely into the escalloped flounces which the Moghuls loved, and though it was light here compared with the bedroom, anyone outside on the roof would have seemed to himself to be peering into a dark cave. In front of the veranda was a stretch of roof, as big perhaps as the room and the veranda together, fenced with a low wall against which stood some old kerosene tins cut in half and filled with earth; a few herbs and spices were growing in the tins and some weedy marigolds. Out there, the sun was a bright intensity.

If you stood on the space before the veranda you saw below you a tumbled huddle of flat roofs and sloped thatch, the mud

3

huts of the laborers gathered together in the skinners' quarter, the sweepers' quarter, the potters' quarter, rising through the sunbaked brick of the better class of small cultivator, and a few new red houses of fire-baked brick built by shopkeepers, to the group of large houses at the top of the ridge where for generations had lived the little group of connected Rájput families who owned most of the land in the neighborhood. Thákurs they were called, the old title of the head of the Rájput family, the caste of kings and warriors and feudal nobles. It was a long time since any of the Anantpur Thákurs had done much fighting, but they were still given the respect due to rulers and soldiers. They were still the chief landowners and their houses still dominated the village.

Beyond the huddled roofs the level plain stretched for seventy miles. There were little squares of wheat and barley in the vivid blue-green of their first youth, squares of brown earth where the autumn crops had stood, sugar cane in its close-packed cluster of lances, and here and there bright fields of mustard rejoicing in the sun. Islands rose from the variegated cultivation, dark glossy groves of mangoes, and villages standing up on mud-colored beaches; but there was no rise in the ground until the details of the plain were lost in the blue mist of the foothills, from which soared suddenly the high snows whose gleaming summits seemed to hang in the air, a vision at once gracious and majestic. The blue from which they rose was only a darker shade of the blue they pierced with airy pinnacles, that were as delicate as breath on frosted glass, but as hard as diamond.

But in spite of the wide expanse before him, anyone who had stood on the roof in front of Pyari's room would have been in a world of his own. The village had probably been built originally on a slight natural rise in the plain, perhaps where the changing course of some primeval river had piled the debris of its spate, and the continued activity of man, building his foundations on the ruins of his parents, had in successive generations inevitably raised the level of the site by a few feet, as a coral insect raises a reef. Thus the village stood out above the plain, and this house stood at the highest point of the village, perhaps as much as thirty feet above the level of the cultivated fields; and it was one of the very few houses with two stories. The roof was a kind of eyrie, too high for observation from below, and this was one reason why Pyari loved it. She liked to stand there above the village, whether in the early morning when only the tops of the mango groves showed above the white mist, in the limpid clarity of the first sunlight, or in the evening when the blue smoke was smoothed in level lines against the orchards, or now, at midday, when the village was hushed in the blinding light, and the few that were not in the fields sat indoors, spinning or sewing or cooking or grinding the corn.

But today the roof did not seem to Pyari so pleasant a place as usual, for as her fingers followed the distaff her thoughts dwelt on her husband, and on all he had failed to be. She had always known the kind of husband she would like. Even as a child she had never had any doubt about what she wanted, and she had never hesitated to declare her wants. She was like her mother in that: a masterful woman, the old Thákuráni! No one who had not known her would have believed that a woman who hardly ever left her house and never showed her face to strangers could have dominated a community as completely as she dominated the village of Galthána, where Pyari was born. Sáhib Singh, her father, had always been her mother's slave. He was the chief landowner in the place, not, as here in Anantpur her husband was, one of a group each of whom owned parts of a dozen villages, but sole owner of the village in which he lived. His grandfather would have thought Pyari was making rather a poor match, but lately they had had to sell some of the land outside Galthána, while the Anantpur Thákurs had been buying. But in spite of his sales, Sáhib Singh was still supreme in Galthána, partly because he was the landlord, and partly because everyone liked him. He was a slow pottering old man, but kindly disposed and singularly free from ambition or the love of intrigue. By virtue of his lands he was chairman of the village pancháyat, the court which could try the smallest local offenses, but he did not use the position for his own ends, and he had no desire whatever to be a member of the district board, or to change anyone else's way of living. It was the Thákuráni who managed the estate and very largely the pancháyat as well.

Pyari was like her mother, but her younger sister, Bitiya, took after their father. She had the same dwambling gait and confused way of speech, and she had none of Pyari's fierce beauty, like a Rajput queen in the old stories, a fit bride for Indra, the antelope, the fire-god. Bitiya was as slow in her thoughts as in her speech, and she had always followed Pyari's lead so naturally that the elder sister fell into an easy and unconscious habit of despising her and leaving her out of account. But Bitiya was conscious of this if Pyari was not, and, one day, long after Pyari had forgotten some hasty saying she had never intended as a slight, but which had filled her little sister with bitter resentment, Bitiya said from her deep brooding: "You deserve to have a husband as ugly as a water buffalo!" She pictured him to herself, the dark hairy skin, the heavy mustache, curling up like the buffalo's horns, the sullen mouth and stupid eye. She laughed aloud. Pyari stared at her in amazement. "Yes, and as cruel as Ráwan," went on Bitiya, thinking how the demon king who carried away Ráma's bride would have tamed her fiery sister till her beauty was spoiled with crying. She laughed again.

"You little stupid," said Pyari, too much amused to be annoyed. "Of course, I shall have a husband as handsome as Krishna, and he'll always be kind. It's you that'll get the ugly husband, 'cause you're so ugly yourself."

Bitiya began to cry, and Pyari at once ran to comfort her, which she soon succeeded in doing, for they were fond of each other at intervals, in a sisterly way. But afterwards Pyari found it necessary to tell people, what she had always before imagined they must know, that her husband would be as handsome as Krishna, the god of youth and love and laughter and music, whose pipes brought with them beauty, like the breath of Dionysus. She used to dream of him, sometimes clear and pale of skin, sometimes flushed with youth and passion, with the proud Rajput features, the nose straight and the nostril delicately arched, the brow low and broad, with the full lips of the Greek, tall and straight of limb, swift of body and mind and scornful as herself of all who could not follow. That had been her dream, and she had never doubted that it would come true until it did.

The house at Galthana was a much less piecemeal affair than

that at Anantpur. It had all been built at one time to one plan. It was built of old bricks mellowed to a pleasant warmth; they were very small and flat, which gave the building a queer air of detail and intimacy. It looked as though much work had been spent on it and many lives lived inside it. It stood about a big central yard, and the high walls were blank on the outer sides. You entered from the village street by a gate big enough to take a fully loaded cart, through a kind of tunnel in the house itself, to the yard, which was generally in some disorder. There were always pigeons cooing and fluttering about the roofs, and a rich smell of sugar filled the air. The cane was pressed in the fields where it was cut, but the molasses was brought to the house before being sent into Sháhábád, the nearest big town. There was usually a cart and a yoke of oxen standing there.

Her childhood at Galthana had been a happy one. All had been happiness and trust. Her father was a good landlord of the old-fashioned kind, who looked after his tenants in their troubles, sickness or lawsuits or failures of crop, and for whom in return they felt an affectionate respect. Perhaps because there was no son, but also because Pyaran shared the old Thakurain's adventurous spirit, she was treated when she was small much more as a boy is usually treated, and was allowed a freedom rare for girl children. She loved to go with her father, and he loved to have her with him, so go she did.

She even went with him on shooting expeditions, not long ones, for Sahib Singh had neither the keenness nor the bodily vigor for a really tiring day, but excursions all the more pleasant to her for that. They went after quail in the cool of early morning in the spring-time, when the light was clear and gentle, in the light land near the river. The men walked up to their knees in the low crops of wheat and peas, mixed in one field in an inextricable tangle, starred with the white flowers of the peas, still fresh with dew, until the sun rose higher, the dew dried, and the light hardened, and they would turn into a sandy track between the fields, and make for home, everyone talking at the same time about what he had shot. They went after snipe at midday in the winter, when the air was dry and invigorating and the sun a pleasant warmth, Sahib Singh and his friends wading in the shallow mud and water, while Pyaran followed on the bank of the bog, watching the black and white magpie kingfisher hovering and fishing, and the long-legged water-fowl rising at each shot, crying and turning. Sometimes they went for longer days after hare and partridge, in the crops along the edge of cultivation, and in the sandy country by the river where nothing grew but clumps of tamarisk and little patches of coarse grass. They walked through the sea of crops or tamarisk, Pyaran following in a bullock-cart, the beaters whacking with their sticks at the tamarisk bushes, and shouting to put up the birds. When the sun was getting high, Sahib Singh would call a halt and would find in the cart food for all the beaters, bread and curried vegetable and a lump of solid brown molasses. He would give it out with a word and a joke for everyone.

"Here's something for Loki; he needs a good meal, his wife had twins last month; a man as strong as he is must keep up his strength. Where's Mannu got to? Always behindhand! Come along! . . ." and so on.

But it was not only on shooting expeditions that Pyaran was allowed to go with the old man. Sometimes she would go with him to a neighboring village where he had land, where he would sit and talk to the tenants and to the village record-keeper, and drink a glass of milk or sugar-cane juice with the village headman. Sometimes he would take her with him in the evening, when he went down to the fields to one of the many sugar-cane presses, to ask how the work was going on. The cane was brought in from the fields as it was cut, and there fed into a press worked by bullocks which squeezed out the juice. The juice was cooked on the spot, in flat iron pans, arranged over a mud-walled furnace. The pans were arranged like the steps in a staircase, the largest at the top, where the heat was less. As the juice cooked, a thick scum formed on top of it, and from time to time someone ladled this rich sugary scum into a smaller and hotter pan below, until in the smallest and hottest of all it was of the color and consistency of hot caramel toffee. The furnace was fed by the dried pulp of the sugar-cane; and in the cold evenings of January the mouth of the furnace was a cheerful glow of light, always surrounded by a circle of cultivators and workers at the press who met at the one really warm place in the village. The warm, treacly smell of cooking sugar added to the feeling of companionship; and often when her father was not coming down Pyaran would slip away by herself and creep quietly up to the circle round the furnace-mouth, to listen to the slow bubble of the hookahs and the tales and the talk.

But usually it was in the central courtyard of the old house that Pyaran met the tenants. They used it as a camping-place if any business brought them into Galthana for the night—dealings with the police, the hospital, or with their landlord. They brought in their bullock-carts, lighted fires and cooked their meals, and their chatter was always there, as much a part of the place as the house itself. There was always work going on here too, for the solid molasses made in the fields at the little presses and furnaces was brought into the house and there refined into sugar by a simple centrifugal machine. Three influences pervaded the courtyard—the smell of sugar, the shrill voice of the Thakurani Sahiba scolding and commanding, and the physical presence of Ram Kallan Singh, the big Thakur who acted as watch-dog, sergeant-at-arms, and rent-collector.

Pyari had been on one of the verandas of the court when her father had come in with a letter from the post office, a little further down the street, and told her that he had arranged her wedding. She was wildly excited and asked at once to see a photo of her bridegroom. The Thakurani scolded her father for the way he had broken the news, but she was too pleased to be cross for long. Her plans had come about as she had meant, and she was almost as excited as her daughter, whom she took away at once to see a photo. There were two, neither of them very good. One showed him in a crowd of other young men, when he was at the University at Agra, and all she could tell was that he was tall, like the Krishna of her dream. The other, taken by a professional photographer, showed him grinning self-consciously in his best clothes. Pyari studied them for hours, and decided that he could not possibly be like that.

It was not till she was married and had gone to his father's house at Anantpur that she came to know her husband Gopal Singh. At the very first, she had been a little disappointed; all

the details of her Rajput hero were there, but there was something lacking in the total effect. There was the broad low brow,
the arch of the nostril, the flashing white teeth, but there was a
weakness in the round chin, a lack of fire in the eye and of pride
in the carriage of his tall body that made her think he fell sadly
short of Krishna. But it was a feeling that did not last long. He
was the first lover she had known; except for her father and the
servants and the laborers, he was the first man. He stirred her
mind by talk of a world she had never even heard of, and soon
he stirred her body too. He was a skillful and an ardent lover,
and when in the first moments of delight she felt the smooth
roundness of his arm and the supple muscles of his back, she believed that she had found the god of whom she had dreamed.
She began to love him as she had always known she would love
her Krishna, with an adoration near to devotion.

His education was imperfect, for he had no real taste for
scholarship and had only been a short time at Agra, but it was
sufficient to make him turn sometimes from the conventional
images of oriental love poetry and seek for a comparison that
he could invest with his own meaning. He had imagination, and
one day when passion was spent, in a mood of tenderness for the
lovely bride that fate had sent him, it struck him as inappropriate
to compare this fierce bright beauty with the pale and fragile
lotus blossom. He told her so, and sought in his mind for a flower
more suitable. "Flame of the forest!" he cried joyfully. "That is
what you are like." Pyari was delighted. She really was more like
the flame of the forest than the lotus, and it was a flower she
dearly loved. Neither scarlet nor orange, it is the true color of
flame, not the sullen glowing ember but the living, leaping tongue
of fire, fit garment for the bride of Indra! She had always loved
to go with her father to see the jungle in April, bright with these
burning trees, laden with blossom without a leaf showing; and
she had loved to take the flower in her hand, to feel its glowing
velvet and admire the two butterfly wings and the rich tongue
between. She was enchanted with this name for herself, and demanded a flame-colored dress from Benares for her next present.
Gopal saw that he had pleased her and he took to calling her
Phuliya—little flower—in remembrance. He soon came to use the

name to appease her when she was in one of her moods of temper
—and she flew into such tempers!

They had no honeymoon in the Western fashion, but went
straight to Anantpur, and it was there, living in her father-in-
law's house, that she first knew the delight of being loved and
first fell in love with Gopal Singh. But if that happiness had not
been there to sustain her, she would have hated the first months
after her marriage. She had lived all her life in one house with
her own family, and she was suddenly transplanted to a new
world where all the values were changed. It was a rambling,
untidy house, built like her own at Galthana about a central
court, but without plan or order. There were odd little staircases
running up outside to the roof or to little sets of rooms built on
to the roof. All the roofs were of different levels. There were
odd little rooms tucked away in corners, where you would suddenly find people whispering who broke off at your approach;
what was worse, there were odd little doors going to other
houses, the houses of distant cousins and uncles, and there was
a continual coming and going by those doors of closed and secret
lips.

At Anantpur no one could have got a cart into the central
court. So many additions had been built to the original house
and so many new houses as the family budded and branched
that you could not even approach the house except by tortuous
passages between high brick walls. The court had grown smaller
with successive improvements, until now it was dark because
the sun only reached it at midday. The farming was done by
tenants, or at little temporary houses in the fields where servants
worked; and there was no honest smell of sugar and straw and
cattle, and no murmurous cooing and rustling of pigeons. It was
a house of whispers and intrigue.

Pyari's mother was a managing woman, and feared by all the
neighborhood, but she was affectionate and honest. She loved
Pyari, and if she scolded and flew into a temper, all was forgiven
in half an hour. Now instead of her mother she had two mothers-
in-law: Gopal Singh's mother was dead, and Kalyan Singh had
two later wives, both childless. One nagged and the other sulked.
But a Hindu girl seldom expects much kindness from her mother-

in-law, and Pyari could have borne this if she had felt more at home in the house. She could never understand the continual family and political intrigue.

Kalyan Singh was nominally the head of the family group of Thakurs who lived at Anantpur. There were perhaps a dozen families, cousins, second cousins and third cousins, and Kalyan not only represented the senior branch but was himself the oldest and wealthiest. But he had less influence than he should have had, because he stood for no fixed principle but the acquisition of money. He was not exactly a miser, but while he liked money and had got into the habit of hunting it, he had no direct interest in politics; and yet as things stood he was not strong enough to keep out of politics entirely. His cousin Nannhe Singh was gradually taking his place as leader of the clan, just because Nannhe Singh did take an interest in politics and knew exactly what he wanted.

Nannhe Singh was a hater. It was written in his face, which was neither a healthy brown nor the clear pale color that sometimes survives among high-caste Indians, but a livid yellow. It was a bitter face, but full of purpose, and the purpose was hatred. He had a sufficiency of enemies outside the family group, but they were not enough for him when ambition drove him to politics. He became a nationalist; he was bound to. It was the paying side in district politics, at least for a Hindu; it gave him something to hate; and it was based also on a genuine desire to see his country entirely in the hands of his countrymen. But although Nannhe Singh became a nationalist, he was no unconditional supporter of the Congress party, for the Congress party had uttered some ominous remarks about the tenure of land. He did not mind wearing cloth woven in India, because it was cheaper, and he was no Musulman to dress up in fine clothes; but he had no intention of giving up the rents he collected on hundreds of acres he never plowed. So he was a nationalist, with reservations, and he became a member of the district board; and except for Kalyan Singh and one other, the Anantpur Thakurs followed him.

While most of the landlords carefully made themselves friends with both the Government and the nationalists, and while Nannhe

Singh's little group of Thakurs were unreservedly for the nationalists, one man in Anantpur was unreservedly for the Government. This was Hukm Singh, a second cousin of Nannhe and Kalyan. He had originally less landed property than the others, and since he was extravagant and a bad manager, his financial affairs became extremely involved, and indeed he continued from year to year with an expenditure larger than his income, by a process that was mysterious to everyone who knew him. He had not much to lose either way, and with a gambler's instinct he had thrown himself into the part of the friend of Government. His enemies—among whom he counted all his relations—sneered that his visits to the District Magistrate and his attention to the Tehsildar and to the police were entirely obsequious time-serving; but it would have been equally true—or untrue—to say that Nannhe Singh's nationalism was wholly selfish. Hukm Singh found that an Englishman usually received him with courtesy and with rather more than the respect due to his family. For several among the District Officers he had known he formed a real affection; so that behind his conviction that it would pay in the end to be the friend of power lay a vein of personal loyalty. It was pleasant to be chairman of the village panchayat instead of Nannhe Singh or Kalyan Singh; it was pleasant to have a license for a revolver and to enjoy the consequence its possession gave him, though he knew the District Magistrate did not really believe his story that Nannhe Singh would have him murdered in his bed without it; and it was pleasant to be allowed a little extra time in which to pay his Land Revenue; but these things were not really anything to do with his pleasure in talking to an Englishman, his pride when an Englishman came to his house, or his firm belief that chaos and anarchy would result if the English were not there to govern.

Kalyan Singh could not make up his mind to throw in his lot with either Hukm Singh or Nannhe. He had no ambition and he did not want to offend the District Magistrate; on the other hand, there was a good deal in what Nannhe Singh said, and he certainly could not afford to quarrel with all the rest of the Anantpur group. So he went to visit the District Magistrate, but not very often; he voted for Nannhe Singh in the District Board election, and he subscribed as little as he decently could both to the King-Emperor's Loyal Fund for Training Village Midwives, and to Mahatma Gandhi's appeal for distilling salt (strictly against the law) from the sacred urine of the cow.

It was this indecision that Pyari found so difficult to understand; she had no idea what either side meant, but, if she had had to take part at all, she would have been vehemently on one side or the other. Kalyan Singh himself she liked; only this bonelessness, as it seemed to her, filled her with irritation. She began to argue with her husband, but they could not understand each other, and she gave it up. A more serious trouble came between them over Jehāran, Pyari's old nurse, who had come with her to live at Anantpur. Jehāran was a Bráhmaní, as one of the servants in a large house often is; for a Bráhman is the only Hindu who can cook food which every other Hindu can eat. She had been widowed before Pyari was born, and she had no children of her own. All her life since had been given to looking after the two children, cooking and sewing for them, slapping, scolding, and doctoring. A good deal of slapping and scolding there had been too, but the old Thakurani never let her go. She knew that behind Jeharan's bad temper was a genuine love, all the deeper because no one but the children had a place in it. For the rest of the world she had only bitterness and contempt; her master Sahib Singh had her tolerance and her mistress her respect; but she loved Bitiya, and Pyari she adored.

It was natural that when Pyari was sent into this strange new world she should take her old nurse to live with her, at any rate until she found herself more at home. In the house of any well-to-do Indian, but particularly of the semi-feudal landowner, there are any number of hangers-on. Some are actually called servants, and are paid a nominal wage of a few shillings twice a year, besides receiving clothes and food. Others merely attend at mealtimes and depart from time to time on mysterious errands. Others will perhaps come for a meal once a week, or will stay for a few days at a time. Some are tenants come to pay rent, others are purely parasitic; but all owe a kind of shadowy allegiance to the head of the house, and they are understood to be his men in time of any emergency, whether an election, the coercion of a tenant,

a big shooting party or a communal riot. Among these depend-
ants, Jeharan was unpopular from the first. She had a sharp
tongue, which she never hesitated to use, and she never lost a
chance of expressing her contempt for Ramnagar district, Anantpur and the household of Kalyan Singh.

"Out of my way, first cousin of a flying-fox!" she would say,
expressing the relationship with an exactitude only possible in
a language which has a word for every different kind of cousin,
aunt or uncle. And if the victim was rash enough to answer, she
would put her hands on her hips and set about him till he flew.

To Pyari, however, she was a great comfort. They could talk
for hours together, when Gopal Singh was away from home, of
Galthana, the people there, and their superiority, for although
Jeharan had never had a good word for man or beast about the
place while she was there, now they seemed almost divine. And
Jeharan at least was always ready to comfort Pyari and understand her, after one of the mothers-in-law had been more than
usually unkind. It was this that had led to the first big quarrel
about Jeharan.

There had been from the start a certain amount of nagging.

"There are too many people to be fed in this house!"

"Useless mouths! And particularly when they belong to sulky
bitches that do nothing but snarl and bite!"

And so on. But one day, over a difference that had nothing
to do with Jeharan, Pyari lost her temper. She felt it swelling up
inside her till she must burst; red patches danced before her
eyes; she could hardly breathe.

"Dirty old monkeys!" she suddenly screamed, "sitting here
all day and biting and scratching! Too old and ugly to have
children!"

Everything she could think of that would hurt she spat at them.
The room was like a box of wild cats advertised by jays. All three
screamed as loudly as they could. When they had finished all the
abuse they could think of, they simply screamed without words.
The elder mother-in-law slapped Pyari's face, and at that Pyari
ceased to be human: she was more than a match for the two
together; she bit and scratched and tore until they were rescued

by Kalyan and Gopal. Pyari was taken upstairs and padlocked into her bedroom, still hysterical with rage.

But quite soon Jeharan found her way upstairs, and from outside it was quite easy to remove the padlock without a key.

For the moment, Pyari was ready to kill either herself or her mothers-in-law. She had only to think of them for that dreadful feeling to swell again in her breast until she choked with fury. She really was ready to kill herself if it would make them sorry, and assert her own importance. If Gopal had come to see her while she was still in that mood of hysteria, and if he had spoken a word of blame or unkindness, she would have thrown herself from the roof. But it was Jeharan who came and who agreed with everything she said and made her talk about Galthana, and at last suggested she should write home and ask to come back. Jeharan knew perfectly well that the old Thakurani would be much too sensible to take any notice, but it would give Pyari something to do at once and something to think about till an answer came.

Pyari could not write much, but she could write all she wanted to say now: her little note was badly spelt and dirty and crumpled and rather damp, but it left no doubt of what she wanted at the moment.

Jeharan slipped away with it to the post-box, where there was a collection every third day. But by the worst of luck, the Kahár who was the chief house-servant had felt the rough side of her tongue that morning, and he saw her come down from the roof. He followed her till she left the house; and he ran into the men's sitting-room where Kalyan and Gopal were still wagging their heads over the unchanciness of women. Gopal was just in time to catch her at the post-box, but he had to run.

"What's that?" he asked, out of breath.

"A letter."

"Who to?"

"It's no business of yours. It's my letter!"

"You can't write."

"Yes I can. I've just learnt."

He snatched the letter from her and read it as he went back. From that hour there was always war about Jeharan. The whole household except Pyari united in saying that she was a spy and had no place at Anantpur. But unless Pyari agreed they could not send her back, because that would have meant a definite breach with old Thakur Sahib Singh at Galthana. This they feared, because there were no sons and Sahib Singh could dispose of the property between his two sons-in-law very much as he liked. They combined then in trying to force Pyari herself to send Jeharan back.

In spite of the quarrel about Jeharan, Pyari continued to be in love with her husband. But gradually she began to find him out. The first fault she found with him was physical laziness, a thing she hated and could not understand. She would have given all that was dearest to her to go about the fields as she had done when she was a child, but though Gopal enjoyed both riding and shooting when he went, he was never eager to go out, and for hours together he would sit idle, or lie yawning on his bed. Then she would flare up at him like fire in the forest, and he would turn sulky until something she said hurt his pride, and he would lose his temper as quickly as she did; the same mastering passion would boil up in his veins, and she had to be very quick to avoid being hurt. For with him she had never blazed in fury as complete as she had known against the old women. She enjoyed taunting him, and she always contrived to keep near the door; by the time he had followed her downstairs his passion had disappeared in sulkiness.

His lack of character she realized more slowly than his laziness, but gradually she came to see that behind a superficial cleverness and imagination there was nothing solid except self-love. He was weak in quite a different way from her father, who was naturally kind-hearted and wanted to be friends with people, and who, being mentally slow, never realized he was being driven into a silly act till it was too late. And there were some things her father could never be made to do, because he would at once know them to be wrong or cruel. But Gopal was quick of mind; he would see at once where he was being taken, and along some roads you would never drive him, because his own interest and pleasure would suffer if he went. If he did anything silly, it was pure laziness that led him to it. And he was like a child with sweets;

he could never say no to pleasure. His laziness was such that he had never controlled himself or directed his own life, but had been blown where his immediate wants had led him.

As Pyari gradually saw through him, her love for him changed, but it continued. She no longer thought of him as Krishna; that was a childishness at which she smiled. But while of much of his character she thought fondly as a mother proudly recounts the naughtiness of her child, there was something in his utter selfishness and lack of moral standards that fascinated her and rather frightened her. He had, too, imagination and sudden spurts of originality, tempered by the laziness that prevented him from executing his ideas. And his body still held her; she never lost a little thrill of excitement at the sight of his tall figure; the turn of his head and his smile still seemed to her the comeliest in the world.

But though she loved him, Gopal could hardly be said to love Pyari. His was a nature that could be swayed by desire or passion, and to a very limited extent by affection, but the two were never fused into love. He had accepted without objection his father's decision that he should marry, since it never occurred to him to give up the amusements with which he had satisfied himself before. And he had been delighted when fate sent him a bride of such beauty. She pleased him so much that for a long time he was faithful to her, merely because he saw no prospect of an amusement more enticing. With the satisfaction of his desire, there grew in him a kind of affection, but it was little more than the affection of association, the kind of feeling a dog knows for the servant who brings his dinner. More than this it was difficult for him to feel, mainly because his nature was too shallow, but partly because he and Pyari had not chosen each other, and no consideration of whether they had any thoughts or feelings in common had entered the choice. She found a love for him because of his good looks and because he was Ferdinand to her Miranda. He was all she knew. But he had known many others, and it was only her body that drew him.

They had been married nearly a year when something happened to change everything. As is the custom, she went home to her family to stay for a month, taking with her Jeharan: and

Gopal Singh came to take her away. It was at first a friendly family party, with no hint of trouble. The Thakurani had heard the story of Jeharan, and the quarrel about the letter, but she realized that there must always be some feeling between a daughter and mother-in-law, and particularly so when the mother-in-law is a childless second wife. She knew the difficulty of the first year of marriage added to the difficulty of absorption in a new family, and in her wisdom she decided to forget all she had been told. She was kind to Gopal, and showed him all she valued most, as an affectionate mother might be expected to do with a son-in-law of whom she thoroughly approved.

Bitiya was married now, but as she had married a younger son and Sahib Singh was getting too old and too kindly to go round collecting rents, Bitiya and her husband Bhola Nath Singh had come to live with her parents in the house at Galthana. Bhola Nath collected the rents, and Bitiya was supposed to help her mother, but she was never allowed to do very much. Pyari envied them this, but she did her best not to show it and told them how much better everything was managed at Anantpur. But she told her mother the truth.

When Gopal came Bitiya remembered the water buffalo and began to giggle, which annoyed him and nearly earned Bitiya a slapping from her sister, who knew what she was thinking about. Gopal, however, was on his best behavior and at such times he could be charming. On the second day of the visit he surprised everyone by suggesting quite casually that Sahib Singh should come with him on a pilgrimage to Hardwár. Pyari was more surprised than anyone, for she had heard nothing of this, and she knew better than anyone that Gopal Singh had no interest in paying his respects to Mother Ganges. She supposed, though, that he wanted an excuse for a journey and perhaps planned to meet some old companions at Hardwar, but she could not imagine why he should take Sahib Singh.

The old man was delighted. He thought it would be a pleasant change and a holiday. He was proud that this handsome young son-in-law wanted him and at the same time he would be doing his duty and washing away his sins.

"When shall we start?" he asked excitedly, like a child.

"As soon as you like," Gopal told him.

Pyari was pleased because it gave her longer at Galthana. They were to come back there after the pilgrimage and then Gopal would take her away. Two days later they got into a bus and drove to the headquarters of the district, the city of Shahabad, to catch the train for Hardwar.

The station was crowded, as stations in India always are. This is because no one but an Englishman leaves till the last minute so important a matter as catching a train, and the ordinary person prefers to come two or three hours before the train is due. The trains are always quite full, and thus there is at least a trainload of people waiting on every platform.

Sahib Singh looked at them with pleasure. He loved the adventure of a train journey as much as the simplest peasant did. Most of the people who sat there waiting were cultivators. The men wore clothes of heavy but very coarse white cotton cloth, of about the consistency of meal sacks. They wore a loin-cloth of finer cotton, a kind of shirt, a pair of unlaced slippers curving up like a canoe at the toe and the heel, a turban, and a large sheet which they wound over their shoulders, like a shepherd's plaid, but as big as the sheet of a double bed. Most of them squatted on the ground, muffled to the eyes, but a few lay stretched on the platform sound asleep, wound from head to foot in their sheets so that they looked like corpses. A month earlier in the year, when it was really cold at night, every villager would have brought his quilt and would have sat muffled to the eyes in that.

The women wore gay colors. Of the peasants, the most part had a kind of bodice, or waistcoat buttoning down the front, and a very full skirt which made them a sufficient garment without underclothes. When it is spread out on the ground to dry, this skirt is so full that it makes a circle seven feet across, with a small hole in the middle, and even then the hem will not lie flat. In movement it is beautiful, frothing like the crest of a wave above the ankle to reveal the curve of the heavy silver anklet and the bare foot. The favorite color was a dark red with a broad black border at the bottom, but apple-green and canary-yellow shone there too, since everyone had put on her best to come to the city.

The richer women wore the sári, most graceful and becoming of garments, which winds round the whole body and over the head. All but the Musulman women wore as much jewelry as they could, heavy anklets and bracelets of debased silver, nose-pendants and necklets and long pendants from the ear: Musulman women of all but the lowest class moved like sheeted ghosts in the burqa, a kind of walking white tent, with a cowl for head-piece and netted eye-holes.

But the delight of the station lay in its variety. There were sweetmeat sellers whose wares looked as greasy and sordid as themselves, boys languidly trying to sell clay dolls or walking sticks, men raucously trying to sell nuts, or calling in a long wail: "Hot tea!" "Ho-o-ot te-e-e-ea! Musulman te-e-e-ea!"; while a rival bawled as loudly: "Hindu te-e-e-ea!" There was a band on its way to a wedding, the men worn out with having played continuously for three days and nights at their last engagement. They lay fast asleep on the platform, each man with his head pillowed on his precious instrument. Fakirs, their bare bodies smeared with ashes to disguise a chubbiness never seen among the villagers who fed them, eyed their next dupes with arrogance. There were coils of false hair on their heads, smears of paint on their faces, and their looks were lustful and beastly. Priests were there in long saffron robes telling their peach-stone rosaries, their shaven faces blind to this world; banias reckoning the day's gains; a group of swaggering young soldiers on their way back from leave; three or four clerks talking English, and a Pathan moneylender by himself, his wild face framed in his long black locks, glistening with oil.

Scraps of conversation drift up:

"Our pleader was a good one; he asked a great many questions. . . ."

"I shall have a new pleader next time, the Deputy Sahib was very angry with this one. . . ."

"He is only a very ordinary man, a bania, and his father had a shop in the village. You cannot expect the Sahib to be impressed with a man like that. . . ."

"I gave the Court Reader twenty annas. Everyone knows that is what a Court Reader always takes, but he said it was not enough. . . ."

"They were asking nine pice for a brass pot only *so* big. . . ."

"I know he will never pay me, but his land is mortgaged and he will have to sell me the land. It is good land and will take Coimbatore cane. I shall put in tenants and . . ."

And this in English, of which Sahib Singh could not understand a word and Gopal only a little.

"Yess, yess; if he pass, well and good; but until and unless he pass what for he put on airs?"

There was a gargantuan clanging and whistling; the rails gleamed in long silver lines; jeweled lights sparkled ruby-red and emerald-green.

Suddenly all was confusion; coolies rushed here and there among piles of luggage; hawkers redoubled their efforts; every bell in the station seemed to be ringing; far away the searchlight of the engine swung slowly round towards them, grew and grew and grew into intolerable intensity, while the thunder-muffled clank of its oncome swelled to a tremendous crescendo and died in a harsh grinding and hiss of escaping steam.

Sahib Singh and Gopal climbed into their train and were borne swiftly away to Hardwar.

Hardwar stands where the Ganges breaks out from the hills, and so it is doubly holy. For to the Hindu, the soil of Hindustan is only less sacred than its rivers, of which Mother Ganga, the Ganges, stands first; and the hills are sacred too, for they are the birthplace of the rivers, and the high snows are the homes of the gods. So Hardwar, which is the gateway of Hindustan, and the threshold of the hills, is the marriage-place of that remote wild holiness that dwells in peak and glacier and forest, and of the warm and comfortable godlings of the plains, who bless the plow and the firestone, the hearth and the bed, and give the water that means life.

It is by Hardwar that the Hindu starts upon the most arduous of his pilgrimages, to the many sources of the Ganges; and all the way his feet are set on sacred ground. For the hillman invests all his surroundings with some of the attributes of the gods. By an instinct that is surely older than any formulated religion a peak is often named for a goddess, while on the highest point of a day's march, on the summit of an isolated hill, or on any bold outpost thrown out as an eyrie above the gulf, stands a little shrine of stone, or a flutter of votive rags tied to a thorn bush. Inside the shrine is perhaps a wooden doll called by the name of a god of the Hindu pantheon, but the place was holy before the gods were named. For in the hills man is paradoxically struggling with nature, yet grateful for every favor wrung from the harshness that surrounds him, and always in the presence of a vastness he may love or fear but cannot hate. He is at strife with the power he worships, and he must give thanks for his life, for his food and for his rest. So when he comes to these high places he stands for a moment and awaits a blessing and he leaves his thanks for a sign.

Though it stands at the foot of the mountains, Hardwar does not belong altogether to the plains. The last outposts of the Himalayas are little pointed hills that guard the sacred place on either side. To the North is the great gash where the river splits the forest-clad foothills. They rise three thousand feet in a dark swoop of foliage and the summit breaks in a line of tawny cliffs. Behind is another range twice as high, of bare shoulders and pine-clad slopes, too far for any detail to be seen; and beyond are the high snows.

The streets of the holy town are steep and twisted; they are paved with cobbles like the by-ways of a country town in Yorkshire. They are full of people of every kind, for this is not only a place of pilgrimage but a trade outlet for the hill tracts of Tehri and Garhwál, and it is near the borders of the Punjáb. Where there is a shifting population of pilgrims it is easy for a criminal to hide himself, and Hardwar is a famous center for the traffic in women. "A bride from the East and a groom from the West" runs the proverb, but since the ordinary folk never arrange a marriage far afield, there is no legal means by which the surplus women of Oudh can go to the surplus men of the Punjáb. There are heavy penalties, but it does sometimes happen that a woman is kidnapped from the parts where she is an incubus and taken to the West where she has a market value. "I will sell you into the

Punjab" a father threatens his disobedient daughter. And if a woman is traveling unwillingly, what could be more convenient than to take her in purdah in a closed palanquin to wash away her sins at Hardwar, and there hand her over to one of the Punjábis of whom the place is full?

Sometimes, too, a hill-girl disappears and a rich man in the plains acquires a wife of rare beauty—once she is washed, for it is too cold to wash much in the hills. And nowhere could be more suitable than Hardwar for the transfer, for there is nowhere else where the hills and the plains jostle each other so closely, where meeting is so easy and where questions are so few.

Wickedness clings to the skirt of holiness, for what is holy becomes lost in superstition, and at once those arise who are eager to make a profit. There are charlatans among the priests, there are evil-eyed fakirs, and there is every kind of impostor among the hundreds of beggars. And it is because the place is holy and blessed by nature that it is also the home of pimps and panders, smugglers of the intoxicating hemp drugs, vendors of cocaine, cattle-thieves, kidnappers and gamblers. That was why Gopal had brought Sahib Singh to Hardwar; in an atmosphere so exciting and so strange to all the old man was used to in his home, he could most easily be brought to do Gopal's will.

It was still early when they left the station, and the snows were poised in a silver perfection more delicate than the mists of noon or the shell-pink of evening. There was a cold and stony light in the cobbled streets, some reflection of that bridal of stone and running water which is strange to the man of the plains, used only to dust and baked mud and stagnant ponds of water weed, and this clarity in the air helped to fill Sahib Singh with the feeling of holiday and adventure.

As they wound through the narrow bazaar Gopal had difficulty in getting the old man along. He wanted to stop at every shop and buy clay images of the gods, necklaces for his daughters, bottles of Ganges water, or tiny models of the temples; but it was not part of Gopal's game that any money should be wasted on rubbish of that kind and he earned the dislike of many eager shopkeepers by his firm hold on his father-in-law's elbow. They came at last to a narrow gate of stone into a paved courtyard, in the center of which rose a square pyramid of steps leading to the house where a black bull of polished basalt knelt in adoration before the god who became flesh in the bull's own form.

When they had done what is prescribed they went to the steps leading down to that pool of the Ganges which of all the holy river is most holy. This is the famous Har-Ki-Pairi, the steps of heaven, where the ashes of the most pious of the Hindus are returned to the gods. The wide shallow steps form an angle, against which the water flows, and a bridge crosses to a long pier built in mid-stream so that the pilgrims can bathe on both sides of the pool. The near bank is lined with many-storied palaces, where the Princes of India live when they come to wash away their sins, but the other bank, far away, is only a low line of sand and trees. Here in the pool great fish fight for the food the pilgrims throw them. When a man throws in bread, the water seems alive with dark lashing bodies, three or four feet long, while shadowy forms glide round the fighting tangle, silent and evil. Since the ashes of so many great ones are poured into the pool, there is sometimes to be found on the bottom the fused gold of a ring or a gem that was too hard for the fire, and there are men who stand all day waist-deep in water thoughtfully feeling with their toes among the fragments of calcined bone and the heavier ash, for a find that might mean a pension for life.

Standing on the pier in mid-stream, you are at the very heart of Hardwar. Stone is married to running water, emitting a freshness that is as much scent as sight, and from the wide expanse of glittering river, the sky itself seems to take an added light. There is light everywhere; it is a bath of light, which seems in its liquid diffusion to penetrate and soak through matter, so that even the under side of the bridge is patterned with shifting silver. When the sun is hidden in cloud there is a peculiar cold brightness like the brightness that fills a room after a fall of snow, and at all times there is a feeling of space, of limitless extension in every direction, that disregards both the buildings and the towering hills.

When they had bathed and fed the fishes, which delighted and fascinated Sahib Singh, they went to the dharm-shála where they were to spend the night. A dharm-shála is something between an hotel, an almshouse and a monastery. It is built as an act of charity by a rich man who is afraid his account with God is written in red like an overdraft in a pass-book; and the manager or warden is to some extent a cleric; there is a faint smack of sanctity about him. Unless they are destitute, visitors are given only accommodation; they buy their own food and cook it themselves, and if they are men of means they are expected to contribute something to the upkeep of the building. The dharmshála Gopal chose was built about a large square court in the form of a narrow two-storied cloister, but the cloister was divided into cubicles or stalls, one behind each arch. The rooms on the lower floor were about ten feet square, with one open wall giving to the yard. Above, they were not so deep because a passage ran along the front to give access to them. A building that might have been pleasant to the eye, though simple, was spoilt by the grass mats and screens which had been hung in front of many of the arches by pilgrims who had brought wives and children. By the pillar between every arch was a little blackened hearth, for two bricks will make a fireplace in India, and from most of them rose a wisp of blue smoke. The air was full of the sharp scent of wood smoke and burning cow-dung, and the warm rich scent of cattle, for many of the guests were villagers from near by who had come in the ox-drawn carts which take their families to fairs and weddings, their grain to the threshing-floor and their sugar cane to the press.

There were many others besides villagers from the neighborhood. Tall Játs from Delhi and Agra and the Punjáb; sly little Mahrattas in turbans strange to Northern eyes; sleek Mewári banias come to atone for a life of profit and loss—but not much loss; respectable Bengalis with slippers, spectacles and umbrellas; and hillmen of many kinds—Garhwális, crinkled about the eyes from gazing at the snows, Kumáonis, and Dogras clad in shapeless coats and trousers made from home-spun woolen blanket, and here and there the boyish Mongolian face of a Nepáli or the slant eyes and red cheeks of Tibetans, with long hair like a medieval page, and a wealth of strange gear—brass-bound instruments for mixing tea and butter, hooped cradles and copper-studded guitars set with turquoise.

Gopal Singh did not waste very much time over settling down for the night. He had not come here to spend his time in a dharm-shála. When the old man had eaten and had taken a handful of cardamom-seeds and some pán, Gopal suggested that they should go out and see the life of the city. It was dark now, and the shops in the bazaar were even more enticing than they had been by day. There were smoking paraffin flares, guttering over the goods spread out to catch the eye, and often the craftsman him-self sat at his work behind the goods. There was a whole street of silver workers, hammering with delicate tools over tiny fur-naces of baked clay; sweetmeat sellers behind pyramids of sticky gold, and piles of almond balls delicately browned and dusted with meal; shops clamorous with brass from Benares and Mora-dabad, and shops where sárís of cloth-of-gold were spread by the side of kingly purple, dark as blood; silver, palest blue, and apple green; scarlet, black, and flame-color. The cloth-merchants spread out the bales, but Gopal did not stop to buy a flame-colored dress for Pyari. He hurried on through the murky garish streets, but with as much consideration for Sahib Singh as he could manage. He did not pluck at his sleeve so impatiently now, for he wanted him to be happy and complaisant.

At last they reached their destination. It was a kind of bar, which aimed at a richer class of clientele than the ordinary grog shop; but though it was licensed, the two Thakurs were admitted only after a good deal of whispered conversation, for gambling was against the law, though drinking was not. Gambling is not a vice of the Hindu upper classes unless they have learnt it from Europeans; and any of Sahib Singh's friends would have scorned to play the games with dice on which grooms will throw away a month's pay or hill coolies the earnings of a season. There were unshaded electric lights, and the walls, distempered an ugly blue-green, were decorated with advertisements for cigarettes and whisky and tinseled pictures of Hindu gods with blue faces in red and yellow clothes. Hanuman's tail curved proudly over his monkey-mask, and Krishna piped to his milkmaids, but no one took any notice. Four or five young men in neat white cotton jodhpurs and coats cut in the English style were smoking ciga-rettes and playing a card game on which they betted heavily, with a great deal of shouting and peals of screaming falsetto laughter; and several more of the same type were watching and drinking.

Sahib Singh had never been in such a place in his life before, and to his simple mind it was a scene of the wildest dissipation. But Gopal had calculated well; all the novelties of the day had upset his moral balance, and he was ready for new experiences. He tried to pretend he took it all as a matter of course.

This was so grand a place and so much in the European style that there were chairs, and, what was more, you could buy whisky as well as the country spirit which is made from sugar, a kind of rum without much body, but very heady and exciting. Sahib Singh hardly ever touched liquor, though of course he knew the country spirit, and he had never tasted whisky. Gopal wisely avoided whisky and gave him a glass of the rum. He brought him to the table where play was going on and introduced him to someone he knew. He was most considerate and polite. He explained the game and after a little he made a small bet himself. He went on betting, in very small amounts that would not shock the old man too much; he kept talking about the game, but as he talked and as the rum went down, he contrived to suggest in a way that would have been irritating if it had not been so deferential, that of course a simple old country-man would never dream of betting. Sahib Singh became more and more intrigued, until at last he was really eager to bet, but he was too shy to suggest it himself.

After a few minutes:

"Care to share this bet with me? Oh, no, of course, you wouldn't."

The old man's face fell. Gopal won. Sahib Singh was bitterly disappointed.

"Well, why not? Share this with me?"

Of course he did, and he was so immersed in the game that he never noticed when his glass was filled. It was filled more than once, and when at last Gopal Singh took him away he was in just the condition his son-in-law desired. Gopal had had no intention of fleecing him in the gambling-den; he had only meant to lead him on till he was too much interested in other things, in the loud laughter and the shouting and the fellowship, to notice how drunk he was getting.

And he was not dead drunk; Gopal was too wise for that. He was extremely cheerful; he was ready to find the most ordinary things uproariously funny, and he was convinced that everyone was as full of good will as he was himself. What nonsense old people talked about these educated young men! They were charming, friendly, full of courtesy for an old man who was ready to share their amusements, excellent fellows all of them. And what an excellent fellow he was himself! Not many men of his age could spend the evening like that and enter into all the fun that was going. Old Kalyán Singh could never have done it; he wasn't man enough and it was really quite surprising that he should have begotten such a pleasant young dog as Gopal.

To all this self-flattery Gopal added as much, and then with a little thrill of excitement he introduced the crucial question of his brother-in-law, Bitiya's husband.

"That Bhola Nath Singh," he said. "*He's* not a cheerful man. He couldn't have made all those young fellows laugh like you did."

No, no, of course not. Sahib Singh laughed loud at the idea. Bhola Nath Singh was so small and prim! Not a fine roystering fellow who could spend the night drinking and gambling!

"And I don't think the tenants like him as much as they like you."

Of course they didn't.

"They have absolutely no respect for him. Now you, you frighten them."

Yes, he did, it was true; it was only his wife who said he was too soft with them. He was really a tiger!

"I expect he knows they don't respect him. I expect he's afraid you'll find him out. He's sure to be frightened of you."

Of course he was!

"I'm sometimes a little afraid—I'm not sure if I ought to mention it. . . ."

"Of course, come on! Out with it!"

"Well, I'm sometimes afraid he might play a trick on you and get you to do something that would tie you to leaving the land to him. You see he would never think for a moment of your good name and your family's and it *would* be rather a come-down if Galthana, that's been in your family so long, went from a man like you, with a fine presence, who's been so much the leader of the neighborhood, to a man like Bhola Nath Singh— so small and melancholy!"

It would, it would. Sahib Singh had never really thought of it before. "And I might easily be tricked," he said, "for I'm a generous, confiding man. I've always been trustful and loving and it's a shame I should be wronged in my old age." He began to cry.

This was splendid.

"It's all right, Thakur Sahib. Cheer up. Don't cry. I've thought of a way of saving you from this trickster."

"No, no, no. I can't be saved, I can't, I can't."

"But listen, Thakur Sahib; do listen. I'm sure if you try you can think of a way; you're so clever. Remember how you made those young men laugh this evening—people who've been to universities and been all over India. You're not going to be tricked by a fellow like Bhola Náth. He couldn't have made them laugh!"

"No, he couldn't, could he?" He sat up, suddenly pleased. "What shall I do?"

"Well, Pyari would look after the land well. She's a fine girl— everyone admires her. She always gets her way. Just like you she is!"

Yes, yes, there was something in that.

"Then don't you think you should leave it to Pyari now—in my name of course—and be safe from Bhola Nath? And of course Pyari would always see that Bitiya was properly looked after."

"Yes, yes, well perhaps. We'll see. We'll see later." The old man was getting sleepy.

"But why not do it now? To be quite safe?"

"Can't do it now. Can't do it now. Nothing to write with. And the Tehsildar isn't here."

"We don't want the Tehsildar. And look, here's an agreement I've drawn up all ready. There's just a little provision in it about an allowance for Pyari at once—just to show you're doing it because you love her and you're not afraid of Bhola Nath. There, you've only to sign there. Sit down. Here's a desk."

They had got to the dharm-shala now.

"Oh, all right, all right, but it's no good without the Tehsildar. No good. No good at all." Two minutes later he was asleep.

Sahib Singh had never been much of a hand at writing; even when he was sober his writing looked as though he were drunk, and it was not very different tonight.

Two young men whom Gopal had known at Agra had come from the gambling-den to witness the signature. Gopal asked them particularly to note that he had carefully explained the contents of the document and brought no compulsion to bear on the old man, who had discussed it rationally. They did note it and then they went away to bed.

Next morning Sahib Singh was bitterly ashamed. He felt very ill, of course, for he was quite unused to spirits, but far worse was his feeling of degradation. To a country-bred Indian of the highest castes, drunkenness is a shocking vice, the kind of behavior one only expects in sweepers, Christians, and hill coolies. "He drinks spirits," they will say of a man in final condemnation. And gambling too. Like a Musulman or a groom. It was disgusting. Nothing of the sort had ever happened to him before, and it never should again. He had been a decent god-fearing man all his days, and he would go back to his simple country life and never leave it. He felt all the dislike of which his nature was capable for Gopal Singh, partly because he knew he had been tricked and partly because Gopal was the only person from his other life who had seen him in that horrible condition. He showed his dislike by sulkiness; but towards evening when he felt a little better, he asked if he might see what he had signed.

Gopal showed him a copy, having wisely sent the original by registered post to Anantpur. Sahib Singh read it with a sinking heart. In the agreement he was made to say that he was feeling old, and being no longer able to enjoy the pleasures of life as he had in his youth, he had decided to provide for the happiness of his beloved daughter, while he could still watch her enjoyment. He was to give Pyari and Gopal three hundred rupees a month as an allowance for the rest of his life; and because of the especial trust and confidence he placed in his son-in-law they were to have all his land when he died. It was worse than he had feared, for three hundred rupees was half his income even in the best years, and in bad times, when rents would not come in but land revenue must go out, he would never be able to meet it and to keep up the house at Galthana.

All the pleasure had gone out of his visit. He went about with a leaden feeling in his belly and a sense of something dreadful to come. Yet though he could not enjoy the freshness of the hill air that blew down from the gap in the hills, nor the holiday atmosphere of the town, he could not bring himself to go home, because he was more frightened of what his wife would say than of anything he might be made to do. He would far rather pay the money quietly all his life than face the Thakurani's anger. Nor was Gopal very anxious for that meeting. He thought of going straight back to Anantpur, and sending a servant to fetch Pyari, but he knew that that would never do, because then they would never pay him anything and he would get no benefit from the precious document Kalyan Singh was keeping so carefully at home. He must make up his mind to face it, and so at last he did, and the two climbed into the train in sulky silence.

The old man knew it would be better to tell his wife before Gopal did, but though he tried once or twice he could never do it. He had always a kind of thickness and hesitation in his speech, and when he was nervous this became a stutter. As the Thakurani never stopped talking herself except when she was asleep, he never really had time to get under way, and so at last he gave up the attempt and left it to Gopal. Gopal also waited nervously, but when after a whole day had passed the storm failed to break he guessed the reason and decided he must speak himself. He chose a time when Sahib Singh and Pyari were both there, and said to the Thakurani, in a voice he meant to be casual, but which succeeded only in being noisy:

"The Thakur Sahib has been very kind. He has promised to give Pyari an allowance—and to leave her the land."

The last came out with a jerk.

The old lady sat up.

"How much?"

"Oh—well—well—three hundred rupees a month."

"Three hundred rupees a month! You must both be mad. As if I would take any notice of nonsense of that sort! Why, we should have nothing left to live on. Are you trying to swindle your parents in their old age? Promised indeed! A pretty sort of promise! What does he mean by making promises of that kind without consulting me? Promised indeed! I'll soon put an end to that."

She had hardly begun, but Gopal seized a moment's drawing of breath to say sulkily:

"It's a written agreement. Signed and witnessed and stamped. And sent to the Registrar to be registered."

The silence that followed was so astonishing that Sahib Singh thought his wife must be ill, and he was just going to risk his life by stepping forward to comfort her when she said:

"I have something to see to."

And before they knew what had happened she was out of the room, and they heard her in the courtyard calling for Rám Kallán Singh, her invariable associate, the big Rajput, who of all the hangers-on about the house was the most permanent and the most reliable. What she told Ram Kallan they did not know till later.

Sahib Singh vaguely followed her out, and left Pyari and Gopal Singh alone. Pyari turned on him with all the fury that Sahib Singh had expected from her mother.

"What have you been doing? What have you done to the old man? What wickedness have you been at?"

"I can't answer all those questions at once," he grumbled, sulkier and sulkier.

"Will you tell me what you have done to my father?"

"It was all for your sake, Pyari," he began.

"Don't tell me lies! Will you tell me the truth?"

She stamped with such exasperated rage and crouched so like a wild cat over its kill that he thought she would spring at him as she had done once before. She had scratched his face and torn off his turban and he had been afraid for his eyes. But he was not physically afraid of anything she might do; it was the flame in her spirit that daunted him when she was like this. He told her something so like the truth that she was easily able to guess what had really happened.

She flung herself on the ground and sobbed:

"That I should be married to a wicked man! Wicked and ungrateful! My poor old father!"

Gopal felt wronged and aggrieved and went upstairs to the bedroom. The moment he stepped into it Ram Kallan, who had been hiding in the shadows, snapped home the padlock on the outside.

"You'll stay there, my beauty, and you'll starve!" he said.

The Thakurani was indeed a notable woman. She had seen at once that her strongest card was possession of Gopal Singh's body, and she had gone straight to Rám Kallán with orders that Gopal was not to leave the house and was to be locked up as soon as possible, whether by guile or force. Ram Kallan grinned with delight. His usual occupation was to sit in the yard and order the carters about, but he sometimes went out with a large stick and two assistants to see that the rent came in a little quicker, or to convert someone to a more proper respect for the house of Sahib Singh. He hated work and he loved a row—as long as he was winning. And he was too clever to have much experience of a row when he was not. He adored the Thakurani Sahiba, who provided him with rows as a mistress provides a dog with walks and bones; and there had never been a wag in his tail for Gopal.

When she had made this arrangement the Thakurani looked for her husband.

To his great surprise she spoke to him quietly and with an affectionate contempt.

"Now, you silly old man, what have you been doing? Tell me all about it."

When she had heard it all, Ram Kallan came and made his report, and she at once sent him to Sháhábád to fetch her cousin who had been to England and was a barrister-at-law. Until he came no one went near Gopal and he had nothing to eat.

The barrister told them that the agreement could not have been registered, because both parties would have had to go before the Registrar and verify their signatures, which Sahib Singh had not done. This, he said, would tell against the document in court, because the only reason there could be for not registering it was that Sahib Singh did not want to, which would bear out his story. In short, he thought they would probably be successful in contesting the agreement, but it would cost money, and the Anantpur people had a longer purse. Everyone was agreed, however, that it must not go to court if it could possibly be avoided, for Sahib Singh's only answer would be the truth, which would involve admitting that he had been drunk and would disgrace him in the eyes of all decent Thakurs. That was the cunning of it. And Gopal had probably reckoned that sooner than contest the agreement in court they would be willing to enter into a new agreement, registered before a Registrar and therefore legally binding, for a smaller allowance. The barrister also felt bound to point out that Gopal Singh could bring a perfectly true criminal charge against them for locking him up.

"Oh, no, he couldn't," said the Thakurani with decision. "We should all swear black and blue it never happened and so would everyone else in Galthana. I would bring a thousand witnesses into court if it was necessary."

The barrister smiled, conceded the point, and went home with a basket of eggs and butter and vegetables.

The Thakurani decided that she would not be bluffed. They would not pay a penny, and Sahib Singh should at once make another will which should be properly registered and stamped. Meanwhile, Gopal was to have nothing to eat till he produced the document.

"But I haven't got it," he objected through the door. "My father has."

"You can easily write something that will make your father send it, and Ram Kallan shall take the message and bring it back. And the moment you write the message you shall have your food, but not be let out till it comes," the old lady explained.

"Well, I won't." He relapsed into sulkiness.

An Indian can do without food more easily than an Englishman and Gopal was not seriously inconvenienced till the second day. But Pyari was torn by divided loyalties. This was the only mistake the Thakurani made; she forgot that she herself did not

really belong to the Galthana household, or that if she did, by
the same logic Pyari belonged to Anantpur. It never occurred to
her that Pyari could be on any side but hers.

And indeed, all Pyari's reason was on her mother's side.
Galthana, as a place, as a house and as a family, she loved, while
she had as yet no feeling for Anantpur; though she often quarreled with her mother, she was fond of both her parents, and
she detested what Gopal had done. But she could not forget her
husband. All her life she had been taught that she would have a
husband she must worship, to whom she owed obedience as her
duty before all things, and added to that was her love for him
as a man. She would gladly have stabbed him when she heard
what he had done, but she would gladly stab herself for him
now that he was hungry and alone.

She ran up to his room the third night and opened the door,
brought him food and put their things together. They slipped
out of the village while it was still dark and stopped the first bus
that ran into Sháhábad.

After that, no one could pretend that their marriage was a
happy one. The Thakurani refused to acknowledge that the
agreement had ever been made. From time to time Kalyan Singh
wrote and said he would sue Sahib Singh in the Civil Courts if
the money was not paid, but his letters were never answered, and
he could not bring himself to go a stage further in the bluff and
put down the Court fees necessary to institute a suit. There was
no longer any show of friendly relations between the two families
and Pyari was not allowed to go home.

Things had never been very happy in the Anantpur household,
but now they were immeasurably worse. There was continual
nagging by the two mothers-in-law, sly hints when Kalyan Singh
was present, open taunts when he was away. Pyaran was told
that her family were dishonest and mean,—but the sneer was con-
veyed in conversation between the two so that Pyaran must put
herself in the wrong if she interrupted. They lost no chance of
laying at Pyaran's door anything they or their menfolk must
forego for want of money, and no chance of bringing home to
her any omission or carelessness of hers in the work about the
house.

"I can't think why Kalyan Singh is so patient. I shouldn't put up with it, would you? I should know what to do with people who didn't pay up. Just like lazy tenants. Waste the money they owe to other people on all kinds of things they can't afford. . . ."

"Well, I suppose we can't go to Agra for our cousin's wedding because those swindling folk at Galthana won't pay what they owe us . . ." and so on.

Very soon the servants noticed how things were, and they began to be insolent and disobliging to Pyaran. They were better when Kalyan Singh was there, but not very much. Kalyan himself was cold and distant to Pyaran, and his contemptuous politeness was almost worse than the nagging of his wives.

There was continual spying between the two households. The Anantpur people felt that they must know what was happening at Galthana, and whether there was any chance of a reconciliation and some kind of settlement by which they would get a share of the land when Sahib Singh died. So they sent emissaries to find out secretly how the land lay. Their reports were kept jealously from Pyaran, and there were always affairs going forward in the house about which she was being kept in the dark. As she came down one of the narrow high-stepped stairways she would find a little whispering group who would scatter quickly and furtively when they saw her. It seemed to her after a little that whenever she turned a corner, someone would stop in the middle of a sentence. Her anger at the insolence and meanness of it all turned slowly to a sullen sickness and despair. She did not see how her life could ever hold anything but misery.

To add to the tension in the household, Kalyan Singh became more and more irritated by his son's behavior. He had been angry with Gopal for causing a breach with Galthana by his short-sighted stratagem, about which Kalyan had known nothing beforehand, and he was increasingly irritated because the atmosphere at home sent Gopal afield, and that meant spending money. He felt rather obscurely, and quite inconsistently in view of his own manner to her, that it was up to Gopal to mend the breach, and that Pyaran was the only means by which Galthana could be approached; and he was annoyed with Gopal for not being on better terms with his wife. For things were not going well.

At first Gopal had been grateful to his wife for helping him when he was locked up, but his gratitude vanished quickly before the treatment she gave him. She was unhappy at the separation from her parents, and because she knew they would be grieved at her conduct. She was angry with herself for having taken Gopal's side against her judgment, and all this resentment, as well as her genuine dislike for what he had done, she poured out on Gopal. She mocked and rated, and he sulked, and then he would grow angry, when she always liked him best, and she would relent, and for one night they would be reconciled. Afterwards, it would all boil up again; she would feel that she had let him out of prison a second time and would be furious with herself for her weakness.

In the face of the steady rejection by her reason of any basis for liking or affection between them, the reception she gave him became less and less inviting. What little Gopal had felt beyond desire rapidly vanished; and for his satisfaction he began to look elsewhere. Pyari noticed a change. She did not definitely and consciously suspect him, but with increasing frequency the thought would flash through her mind: "Perhaps there are other women." It was always a stab of pain, but she would let the thought go, she would neither forbid it her mind nor sit in judgment on it, because she did not dare. To add to her shame, she was first told the truth by one of the maids about the house.

She had given her a shirt of Gopal's to take to the washerman.

"And tell him to be quick," she said, "for the Thakur Sahib will want it this evening. I'm not quite sure when he'll be in."

The maid looked at her in surprise.

"Oh, but he'll be late this evening," she said.

"What makes you say that?"

"Oh—well—he's over at Kaimuán," she giggled.

"What do you mean? Tell me at once."

"Ow, you're hurting me. All right, all right. I'll tell you. I thought you'd have known. Well, of course, everybody knows what he goes over to Kaimuan for. It's that little slut of Thakur Ajudhiya Singh's. She's a Kahári girl and works in the house. Dirty little bitch! But she's lucky. He gives her lovely presents."

She added rather sadly, "I don't know why he takes the trouble to go so far as Kaimuán."

Pyari could hardly breathe. But she remembered she was a Thakur's daughter.

"Oh, that gossip," she said, "I know all about that. And it isn't a word of it true. And you shall be slapped for repeating such things."

Slapped she was, again and again, across the face, till Pyari's arm ached and her fingers were sore. The girl ran away howling and Pyari found her way, she hardly knew how, to her room where she flung herself on the bed in a paroxysm of shame. She, Pyari, who was to have had a husband like Krishna, deserted for a Kahari maidservant. She, the daughter of Thakurs, with her beauty and her spirit, who had always been the leader, always loved and praised and petted. Flame of the Forest. Bride of Indra. Little Flower. A husband like Krishna. A servant.

She said nothing when she saw him. She was too proud to speak to him of that. She could not trust herself to speak of anything else. And she was too proud to confide in a servant and so learn more. She knew it was true. If she had tried to learn more she would have known there were more women than one. She went about the house in silence and she could not think of the future.

So it was that on the last day of her life, Pyari sat at her spinning in the veranda before her bedroom, and as her fingers followed the distaff her thoughts dwelt on her husband. She had no illusions about him now. She knew the desires he did not think of controlling, and the vanity that made any woman's flattery satisfying, the weakness of his slavery to himself, and the silliness that had led him to defeat his own ends by quarreling with her father. She had lost her family because of him, and now he had destroyed her pride and self-respect. And because she still felt that little hammer at her heart when she heard his laugh or his step, smelt his hair, or saw the anger flame up in his sullen face, because of that she hated and despised herself, and still more hated him. To leave her for a servant! He was worth something better than that, better than running after dirt of that kind. The girl ought to be whipped. But was he worth something better? She was a Thakur, and the daughter of Thakurs, and she was the flame of the forest; he wasn't worth her, he wasn't! And yet, when she heard him come, she knew how she would feel. She knew her heart would turn within her and her breath would come short. She was bitterly ashamed. And just then she heard his step on the stairs. She sat up, her eyes hardened, her mouth drew to a thin line.

He came in, and said, as casually as he could: "Will you please hem me these, Pyari?"

They were three kurtas of fine thin cotton. A kurta is a garment worn both by men and women, not unlike a shirt, but a woman's is cut differently. These were women's. Pyari broke her silence.

"These! But they are women's!"

"I know. That's no business of yours. I tell you to hem them."

"No business of mine? Is it no business of mine whom you sleep with? Isn't it enough that you should make your house a by-word so that the maids in your own house laugh at you—oh, and at me, too—but you must bring your whore's clothes here? And ask me to hem them. Is that work for me?"

"They're for my sister at Káonlá."

"Sister at Káonlá! Sister at Kaimuán. Sister of the dog that eats dung in the streets. Sister of the jackal. Eater of rat's filth. What have you come to? Thakur you are supposed to be, but you get drunk like a sewage man, you gamble like the skinners of carrion, and you take their leavings. Yes, the filth the dung-pickers drop is good enough for you. Any woman will do for Thakur Gopal Singh." And then she dropped her note; for there was only bitter pain to her, and she was blind to stab home every wound she could. "Are you sure, Thakur Gopal Singh, that your father was really a Thakur? Can it be that your mother stepped aside with a skinner of dead cows or an eater of jackals? Are these tastes in your blood?"

"Stop your evil tongue. Shut that filthy mouth. You'll do what I've told you, you'll hem these clothes."

"So I am to hem those clothes? Because your drab said you were afraid of your wife? She said you wouldn't dare to ask me, so you did, just to show her? Well, I'll show her you *are* afraid. Take back your filth!"

"Be quiet. I'm your husband. I order you to do them."

"I'd rather die," she said with intense low bitterness. "I'd rather you shot me. If you were a man, you would have shot me for the things I've said to you. I'd be quiet then. But I won't be quiet now. I'll tell you whenever I see you that I know you're a cur. I'll tell everyone I see what you are. A cur! An eater of filth! A picker of leavings!"

He strode across to her and slapped her face.

"Yes," she said, "that's more like a man. Hit me again if you like. But I'll never touch your filth. Do you think I'm like you and have no pride? Yes, hit me again. Why don't you shoot me? It's the only way you'll quiet me. But you wouldn't dare to shoot me—you're afraid of a gun because your father was an eater of carrion. I'd dare anything, because I really am the daughter of Thakurs. I wouldn't run away. I won't be afraid. Shoot me and show that you're a Thakur."

Half an hour later Pyari's dead body lay limply on a string cot. Kalyan Singh and Gopal stood over her in consultation.

"No one must know how she died," said Gopal.

"No, we must say she died of cholera."

"Pneumonia," said Gopal. "Cholera is infectious, and we should have sanitary inspectors here."

"Yes, pneumonia. She must be burned at once, tonight," went on Kalyan. "And she must be burned very thoroughly. It must be too late for a post-mortem, before anyone knows anything about it."

"Why did we burn her so quickly? That's what they'll ask. It must be cholera after all. We burned her at once because of the infection, and all her clothes with her. There must be no bloodstains. We'll have to take the risk of doctors coming. They'd never find anything, after all."

"No, doctors wouldn't find anything," said Kalyan. "No one in Galthana would tell them anything."

"Except Hukm Singh or his people—Where's Hukm Singh? I wonder if he knows anything about this?"

"He is in the village. I saw him yesterday," said Kalyan Singh.

"He'll tell the police if we burn her tonight. He knows she was alive yesterday. Why haven't I been friends with Hukm Singh and the police and the English?"

"Never mind that. Is it worth the risk of keeping her two days? Then there'd be nothing for him to tell the police."

"They might hear she was dead. That Constable Rúp Singh hears a lot. And then there'd be a post-mortem and an inquest. All we want to avoid. No, she must be burned tonight."

"Would it be any use your talking to Hukm Singh, father? Could we make him keep quiet? Or would that make things worse?"

"I don't know. I must think it over. I must ask our cousins."

"And what are we to do if the police do hear something? They will hear something sooner or later. That Sub-Inspector will be here asking questions. We'll have to give him money, father."

"I won't do that. I won't throw away money for nothing."

"Father, you must."

"Why, what could he do? She's burned. We say it was cholera. What can he do, except say we should have reported to him and had an inquest? He knows an inquest and post-mortem would disgrace us."

"But you know what the police are—and this Sub-Inspector's the worst of any. He'd say we'd murdered her."

"But he wouldn't get any evidence. Whatever he threatened, no one in Anantpur would say a word against us."

"Except Hukm Singh, or perhaps the Nats."

"They wouldn't. And if that Sub-Inspector asked for money from us, he'd ask for a lot. No, I won't pay him—I won't."

Gopal Singh decided to give up this point for the moment. But he persuaded his father to go and see Hukm Singh as well as Nannhe Singh and then he went about the business of the funeral pyre.

It was a lovely evening when they took Pyaran down to the river to burn her. The cattle were coming into the village from the day's grazing in the waste land by the water, and the air was full of the milky scent of their breath. About the height of the lowest branches of the trees the smoke lay in long blue lines, straight as a ruler. There was a stillness and sharpness in the air, as though a little breeze had for a moment blown from beyond the world and died away. In the west the clouds were smooth bands of saffron and amber, melting through palest primrose to a blue fainter than a hedge-sparrow's egg; and on the high snows to the north lay a bloom of shell-pink that faded as swiftly as life from the eyes of a dying bird. Light thickened, until there was no transparence in the water of the stream; it gleamed opaquely in smooth ripples beneath the breath of the evening. The sand-dunes stretched wide and illimitable into the gathering darkness; and there they burned Pyaran. At the last, the pyre fell in and there licked greedily at heaven a great tongue of fire with a swarm of sparks like bees.

So she went, the bride of Indra, wrapped in flame.

Part Two

THE WITNESS TO HER DEATH

Chapter One

The Search Begins

•◇•

IN the jurisdiction of Gosaini police station there were perhaps a hundred villages; and the staff consisted of a sub-inspector, a sergeant and eight constables. Each of the constables had a circle of about a dozen villages; and he was supposed to visit each from time to time and come back to the police station with every possible scrap of gossip and with information about every twist of local intrigue. His only agent on the spot was the village watchman, who in return for six shillings a month and a suit of clothes once a year undertook to report to the police station any crime that occurred and, if necessary, to oppose and arrest the criminals. Dacoity—armed robbery in gangs—never dies out entirely in India; it is sporadic, and moves from district to district following the weakness of the police. To a dacoit worth the name, the life of a village watchman does not cause a moment's hesitation; and there are probably nowhere in the world men who risk their lives by violence so readily for so small a reward and for so little honor as the Indian watchman.

Anantpur was one of the villages in the circle of Constable Rúp Singh, a man who combined a simple fidelity with a remarkable flair for ferreting out information. He had been chosen for this circle by the Sub-Inspector, who was himself a Musulmán, because the Constable was a Thákur, and therefore better placed than anyone of another caste for hearing the gossip in Anantpur, which was not only one of the largest villages under that police station, but, on account of the presence of the group of Thakur landlords, by far the most given to intrigue.

Pyari died at midday on February 6th. On the afternoon of
the same day, at about three o'clock, Rup Singh came to the
village on his usual round of inspection, and according to his
custom went first to the house of Hukm Singh the village headman and chairman of the village committee. Here he could rest
after his journey in the heat of the day, assured of a drink of
milk and a handful of cardamom-seeds or a meal at evening; and
while he rested he would usually hear more than he learnt in
the rest of the village put together. His was a peculiar position,
because while an Indian constable is relatively not much higher
in the social scale than his counterpart in England, and the
servants would thus talk to him without restraint, he was also at
home with the gentry of Anantpur because they belonged to
his caste.

Today, as he came up the narrow dirty path between the tall
homes of the Thakurs to Hukm Singh's house on the crest of
the ridge, next to Kalyan's, he saw one of the Kahar house-
servants standing on the platform which overlooked the lane. The
man ran quickly indoors, but, by the time Rup Singh arrived,
he had come back to make him welcome and to ask what refresh-
ment he would take. The Constable settled down watchfully,
but he saw nothing else that was unusual. He was puzzled, because his visit was a matter of course and there should have been
no need to warn anyone of his coming. He thought too that he
noticed something odd in the man's manner. Presently, Hukm
Singh came to see him, and apologized for not having come at
once. This again was unusual, for the Thakur was often out
when the Constable came, and there had never before been any
question of apology.

They began to talk. The Nats were back, a tribe of gypsies
who had no fixed home, but were more often in Kalyán Singh's
guava orchards to the north of Anantpur than anywhere else.
Rup Singh was not very interested in the Nats. Nannhe Singh
had said he was going to get Congress workers from Rámnagar
to make salt in Anatpur village; but he had been saying that for
the last year, and no one had ever come. For a long time now,
even the prospect of acquiring merit by going to prison had not
been enough to incite Congress workers to sit all day over a

hot brazier, only to produce in the end a handful of salt that was not worth a fiftieth of the fuel that had gone to make it. Some of the Chamárs, the skinners and laborers, in the next village were getting rather above themselves and had refused to take away a dead cow. They had even said the Thakurs should move it themselves, which was blasphemy against religion as well as against the social order; but they had seen reason in the end. The crops looked very promising. Rup Singh felt he was getting no further; he was sure there was something afoot, but it was not among the things Hukm Singh mentioned. He decided that he was in the wrong place to find what he wanted. He made his excuses and said he was going to the next village.

Rup Singh was in rather a difficulty. He wanted to see the watchman, but he did not know how to get him; usually, a servant of Hukm Singh's went and called him to the platform in front of the house, and the Constable talked to him there. This would obviously not do today, because he had a feeling that Hukm Singh wanted to conceal something, and if the watchman knew what it was, he was not very likely to give it away on Hukm Singh's doorstep. On the other hand, it would never do for a constable to go to the house of a watchman; all his influence in the village would vanish at once, for if a man does not respect himself, why should anyone else? The watchman must come to the Constable, but who was to fetch him, and to where? It had better not be any of the Thakurs; he suddenly thought of the Bráhmans.

There was only one family of Bráhmans in Anantpur, and they were very well-to-do. To be family priest to one rich Rájput house is lucrative enough, but Sheo Dat Parshád attended to the ceremonies at birth, betrothal, marriage and death in a dozen. He was much too dependent on Nannhe Singh and his group to give anything away to the police, but he would be delighted to send a servant for the watchman. Rup Singh went to his house at once.

Sheo Dat Parshád was just leaving the house on important family business. He was as usual blandly unconscious that anything ever happened which might interest the police, but he at once sent a servant for the watchman and begged Rup Singh to regard the house as his own. He would understand, of course, that the Brahman himself must go at once, or the propitious hour would pass. Rup Singh understood perfectly, but in the absence of its master he would prefer not to enter the house; he would wait outside under the sacred pipal tree. Sheo Dat Parshád told a servant to make the Constable comfortable, and left him his blessing and several pious thoughts.

Rup Singh was pleased; the pipal tree was perfectly respectable, and better than the Brahman's house, and he tried to persuade himself that Sheo Dat Parshad had been even more noncommittal than usual. The only thing he regretted was that everyone in the village would wonder why he had not seen the watchman at Hukm Singh's house, and the excuse he had made to the Brahman, that he had forgotten to call him, and didn't want to walk up the hill again, sounded feeble even to himself.

The watchman was not long in coming; his police duties were not supposed to take up all his time, and he had been at work in the fields, but quite close to the village. He repeated the information about the Nats, and added that Jukki Chamar had beaten his wife so badly that she had not got up for two days, and the other Chamars threatened to excommunicate him from caste privileges unless he behaved better in future. Loke Dhobi had lost a donkey, but it would probably come back soon and was not worth much anyhow, probably not as much as two shillings. But what about the Thakurs, Rup Singh asked. Had nothing of interest happened there? Oh, yes, the watchman had forgotten about that.

Rup Singh knew, of course, that Kalyán Singh had quarreled with the family of his son's wife, and he knew that for some months the son Gopál Singh had been behaving very badly and having affairs with several women in the neighborhood. But the watchman had heard a day or two ago that Gopál's wife had only just found this out, and had slapped the servant who told her unmercifully; and she had spoken neither to her husband nor to anyone else in the house for the last week.

This was getting warmer, Rup Singh felt. But he still didn't understand; this was nothing to do with the police, and he would only have noted it as a piece of information that might some day be useful, if it hadn't been for Hukm Singh's manner, and the servant's running indoors to warn him. There was really very little to go on, but he felt sure there was something in the air and it might be something big. He decided he would give up his story about not wanting to walk up the hill, and go to the heart of the thing. He told the watchman to wait under the pipal tree, and himself walked up the hill to the house of Kalyan Singh.

For most of the way, he was hidden from the house by high walls, but before the last sharp turn to the door the lane ran for about ten yards clear in view of anyone on the roof; and there was someone there who disappeared the moment the khaki shirt and scarlet turban of the policeman came round the corner. Rup Singh was delighted with himself for coming. He rounded the corner to find the gate shut, which was most unusual. He called to ask if he might come in; there was a whispered consultation and someone said:

"Please wait a moment."

There was a pause, and more whispering. At last, Thákur Kalyán Singh himself opened the door and stepped out. He did not suggest that Rup Singh should come in, but asked if he had come for any special purpose.

"Not at all, not at all," Rup Singh explained. He had only come up to the house to pay his respects to the Thakur Sahib and sit in the courtyard and gossip with the servants.

Kalyan thanked him for his courtesy.

"But not today," he explained. "We are always glad to see you, but not today because we have had a sad bereavement. My daughter-in-law—it was pneumonia—she went very suddenly— only taken ill yesterday. You will understand the house is very upset, and we are all most unhappy. Perhaps you'll come and take a meal here next time you're here, instead of always going to Hukm Singh's?"

Rup Singh understood perfectly and had no wish to intrude. He went back to the watchman.

So that was it. The daughter-in-law dead, after a violent quarrel a week before, and she had been angry with her husband all the week. Taken ill yesterday and died of pneumonia today; Rup Singh knew very little of pneumonia, but he thought it took longer than that. And why hadn't they sent for a doctor? They were rich folk. It sounded uncommonly like either murder or suicide.

He decided that the best he could do would be to pretend to leave the village and lie low in a mango-grove near by till evening, leaving the watchman to find out anything he could. He told the watchman what he suspected, and instructed him to go round to the laborers and the servants from the Thakur houses, and finally to the Nats, and to come with his gleanings to Rup Singh in the mango-grove soon after dark. Then he would go as quickly as he could to the police station at Gosaini. Very pleased with his day's work, he left the village by the most populous quarter.

It was about half an hour after sunset when the watchman reached him.

"They are burning her now," he said.

"Now!" said Rup Singh. "And she only died today. Then I was right. They are trying to hide something. Anything else?"

"I have found one Chamar who heard a shot at midday from Kalyan's house. But tomorrow he will say he heard nothing. All the rest have been told to keep quiet, and this man was left out by mistake."

Rup Singh was at once on the road to Gosaini.

It was very early next morning when the Sub-Inspector, Ghulám Husain, set out for Anantpur. He was a stuggy little man, with very small eyes set rather slanting in his square face, and a jaw like a pike. He filled his khaki tunic and Sam Browne belt very thoroughly, and looked quite as heavy a weight as his stuggy little brown mare was meant to carry. She usually walked, but when pressed would break into a wooden and angular canter, with her head carried very low and her jaw thrust as far as possible from the bridle-hand, of which she was justifiably afraid. Rup Singh came behind, sometimes running and sometimes walking. He reached Anantpur not long after Ghulam Husain.

The mist was still as high as a man's waist on the fields, and the trees and villages stood up from it like islands. Anantpur in particular swam like a wooded Pacific atoll, and as they approached revealed the details of which it was composed with the same shy charm as a small island to an approaching boat.

Ghulam Husain, however, was not a man to waste time on scenery, for his pike-like jaw told the truth about his character. A sub-inspector of the old school, not over-educated, he had the faults of the old police service without many of its virtues. He was extortionate, unjust and tyrannical; and the only good that could be said for him, if it was good, was that he had no great prejudice in favor of any religion, his own or another, and that criminals were sometimes too frightened of him to do what might put them in his power. But more often they were ready to gamble on not being found out.

When Ghulam Husain reached Anantpur he went straight to Kalyan Singh's house. He had sufficient knowledge for a bluff, and if his bluff came off and it was made worth his while to hush up the whole affair, he would not want any more mud to have been stirred up than was necessary.

Thakur Kalyan Singh appeared to be expecting him. He made him welcome with the greatest politeness and led him to his sitting-room. There was no one else there. They talked for some time about the crops and the weather, and then at last Ghulam Husain said:

"You must forgive me, Thakur Sahib, for troubling you on an official matter, but as you know I must do my duty. I am told your daughter-in-law died yesterday."

Kalyan admitted it, adding that he felt very sad in consequence and for this reason the Darogha Sahib must pardon the poverty of his hospitality.

Ghulam Husain expressed his sorrow and sympathy, and explained how much he regretted the intrusion on his host's grief; but, he went on, since the lady had died suddenly, the law unfortunately demanded an inquest and he suggested holding it at once. In India the officer in charge of a police station can conduct an inquest himself on the spot and, standing up, Ghulam Husain said:

"And now, please may I begin by seeing the body?"

"But we burned it. We burned it last night. She had—she died of cholera, and we thought it best to get rid of her body and all her clothes at once."

"Cholera?"

"Yes. Yes, it was cholera."

"Rup Singh!" The Sub-Inspector turned aside and verified in a whisper that Rup Singh had yesterday been told it was pneumonia.

"And we never thought," Kalyan went on, "that an inquest was necessary when she died of sickness."

"Did you make a report to the Sub-Assistant-Surgeon at Jangábád?"

"Not yet. We were just going to."

"Surely it is unusual, Thakur Sahib, for people of your caste and standing to burn their dead so quickly?"

"No, no, not unusual, Darogha Sahib; not when it is cholera. Oh, not unusual at all."

"Ah, you surprise me. Now, Thakur Sahib, may I see your son, please?"

"I'm afraid he's not here. He's on a visit to friends at Agra, he went two days ago."

This was a surprise. Up till this point the Sub-Inspector had imagined nothing worse than suicide, concealed because of the disgrace involved in post-mortem inspection of a woman's body, but as soon as he heard that Gopal Singh was missing he decided it was murder, and his little eyes glistened. He multiplied his price by three, and he began to talk in a blustering voice quite different from his previous silky tones.

"Now listen to me, Thakur Sahib. This won't do. Your daughter had quarreled with her husband. Everyone knows that, and everyone knows he had been behaving badly and running after other women. Yesterday she died suddenly; and I can produce a man who heard a gun fired in this house just about that time. You make no report to the police and none to the doctors. You tell Rup Singh she died of pneumonia and me she died of cholera. You say your son went to Agra two days ago when I know that he was here yesterday. That's just a few of my reasons for thinking it wasn't a natural death she died. I shan't tell you all I know, because I don't want you tampering with my witnesses. But that's enough to show you"—he dropped his voice—"that it's my duty to enter at the police station a charge of murder against your son."

"It wasn't murder," the old man muttered. He was silent for a long time, greed wrestling with fear. At last he said:

"Would anything convince you that your duty was different?"

Ghulam Husain looked at the ceiling with an air of satisfaction.

"I might be convinced," he said. "The gunshot might be forgotten, and the pneumonia. You might find your son hadn't needed to go to Agra after all."

"How much?" The old man's lips hardly moved.

"If you happened to go this afternoon to Gosaini and paid fifteen hundred rupees to a bania I would name . . ." began Ghulam Husain.

"Fifteen hundred!" The old man's whisper was almost a scream. "Fifteen hundred! You can get to hell out of here, for you won't get a penny." He had worked himself up with the greatest difficulty to giving five hundred, which would have been Ghulam's price for concealing suicide.

"It is your son's life," said the pike jaw.

"It's not. You'll get no evidence in Anantpur and you know it. Not a penny. Not a penny from me. Do you hear?"

Bargaining was impossible, for the policeman was now too hot on the scent to reduce his price, and the Thakur too frightened at the figure mentioned to give anything at all.

At last, Ghulam saw it was useless. He gave up the idea, and turned with vindictive eagerness to his official duties. He asked for Gopal Singh's gun and cartridges. Kalyan Singh hesitated, and at first would not say where they were. When pressed, he admitted they were in Nannhe Singh's house and took the Sub-Inspector there to recover them.

As he left:

"He'll hang," said Ghulam.

"He won't," said Kalyan Singh.

Ghulam Husain left the house in a thoroughly bad temper. He had seen a pretty windfall and had lost it; and while he now felt it essential to his prestige to work up a good case against Gopal Singh he was not at all sure how he could do it. He thought for a moment and then went to Hukm Singh's house. Here he had to be careful, for though he might be able to blast Hukm Singh's reputation with the Superintendent of Police, he thought it quite likely that Hukm Singh could blast his with the District Magistrate. So, evil though his mood was, he had to walk gingerly.

Hukm Singh also was in a very delicate position. His reputation, his good name in the eyes of his fellows, his influence and his power in the small world he knew, all depended in the end on the good will of the District Magistrate and the Superintendent of Police. Without them, he was alone in a sea of enemies and creditors; he might continue for a time if the Superintendent did not believe in him, but ultimately, what one thought, both would think. And he did genuinely want to help the police; he always had helped them and he enjoyed the possession of their confidence and their friendship. But in this case—it was not like any other. For whatever the truth of Pyari's death might be, he knew that there would be talk of murder, and however estranged one may be from one's relations, it is a terrible thing to put a rope round the neck of a cousin. Both Kalyan and Nannhe Singh had spoken to him, and had made it quite clear that if anything happened to Gopal by his doing, not only would his creditors close in on him like wolves on a dying deer, but his life would very likely come to an end in some curiously contrived accident.

Hukm Singh met the Sub-Inspector apprehensively; and the latter wasted no time.

"Hukm Singh," he said, "you've always been a friend to the police; but you wouldn't tell Rup Singh yesterday about this murder of Gopal Singh's."

"I hadn't heard even that she was dead when I saw Rup Singh. Is it a murder? I didn't know. They say . . ."

"They say it is something different every time you ask them. I know she was shot."

"Then this much I can tell you, Darogha Sahib. After Rup Singh had gone, when I heard she was dead, I remembered I had heard a shot in the house about midday. But I beseech you, Darogha Sahib, not to bring me into court against my own relations."

"I'll see. Now tell me; what do you think it was yourself? Murder?"

Hukm Singh looked at the sky; he looked at the floor. At last he said:

"I think it was suicide. But I don't know what happened."

"Who does know? Who can tell me what really happened?"

"No one who knows will tell you what really happened."

"I didn't ask who would tell me. I asked who could tell me if he chose."

Hukm Singh looked at the sky, he looked at the floor. He leaned forward and whispered:

"There is a Kahár who knows, Prem Ráj. He was in the house; he knows everything. And every evening, after sunset, he goes down to talk to the barber at the foot of the lane."

"That will do. Thank you. Are you sure that's all you can tell me?"

"I swear it is all I know for certain," said Hukm Singh.

Ghulam Husain gave some orders about the barber's house at the foot of that lane, and sent for the leader of the tribe of Nats. They were wandering gypsies, who made their living partly by hunting and partly by displays of their skill by the roadside. They were acrobats and trainers of performing animals, bears and monkeys. The women carried on a thriving by-employment as prostitutes, and though they were not primarily thieves, neither sex would be shy of snapping up a trifle, whether considered or not. There were perhaps a score in the little community who made Anantpur their headquarters and their beat ranged from Rámnagar city in the south-east to the Indian state of Mallápur on the north-west. They usually came back to Anantpur for a few days once in the month, and when they were there they camped on Kalyan Singh's land; so that although they were essentially masterless men, they might be considered to owe his house some slight debt of loyalty. On the other hand, they had no wish to fall foul of the police, for most of their activities were on the borders of the law.

Picturesque creatures they are, tall and well-devoloped, the men almost naked, the women in bright colors with necklaces of scarlet jungle-berries. The Nats carry themselves proudly, with a look of independence and the wild; and their shapely features and reddish skin give some color to the story they tell themselves of their origin. Long ago, they say, a Rajput princess was betrothed to a king she had never seen, and she set out to her wedding in his country with a great train of Thakur nobles and an escort of soldiers. The journey was a long one, and on the way she fell in love with the captain of her bodyguard. One day she sent for him and told him her love, and he confessed that he had long loved her. Whereupon the two went hand in hand to the nobles gathered together and told them how things stood. The nobles vowed they would follow them both wherever they went, and since they dared go neither back nor forward they became a homeless people, living on the country, as their descendants do today.

Jhammu, the leader of this particular community, was a man of character and enterprise, who had led them well. He had kept on good terms with the police, and with the larger landlords, for he had been useful to both. On this occasion he was in the camp and he soon came to the Sub-Inspector. What he knew he told quite frankly; he had heard gossip in the village that there had been murder or suicide, but which was the truth he did not know. He considered for a little.

"But," he went on, "if I hear of anything I will help you, and if you will tell me anything you want done, I will see if it can be arranged. You have left my people alone, and though we have used Kalyan Singh's land we have never had a drop of milk from him we have not paid for. And he has threatened us for taking his guavas, which we had never done, for we always respected his land."

There was nothing more to be got from Jhammu for the moment. Ghulam Husain turned to the Chamar who had heard a shot fired at midday. He sent a man down to the part of the village where the laborers and skinners lived, in their little houses of baked mud, but he came back soon with the news that the man had vanished. He had left his wife and child behind, and no one knew where he had gone; but gone he undoubtedly had, that very morning. He had left for the fields as usual but had not come back and he was nowhere to be found. Oddly enough someone else had disappeared from the village that morning, the woman who had laid out Pyari's body. No one could think what had happened to her.

Ghulam Husain sent for Sheo Dat Parshád. Certainly he knew Pyari had died and he had performed the last ceremonies, but he was no doctor to say what had caused her death. Her body had been covered when he saw it. He had heard nothing that had any bearing on the subject. Nor had the barber, who usually knows all the gossip, and is the priest of the poorer classes.

Ghulam Husain gave up the village. He left as he had come, with Rup Singh walking behind, both in uniform; he told everyone he was going and let everyone see that he was in a very bad temper. But he left behind two constables in plain clothes who had slipped quietly into Hukm Singh's house during the course of the afternoon. A little after dark these two slipped with equal quietness out of the house and down the lane to the barber's house. There sat Prem Ráj, the Kahár from Kalyan Singh's, with a little circle of his fellows, handing round the mouthpiece of the water-pipe. The pipe gurgled slowly and musically as the mouthpiece went from hand to hand, and the deep voices answered each other in monotonous murmurs. There was no lamp, but a fire on which from time to time someone threw a handful of the dried pulp of pressed sugar cane, and then the flame shot up and lighted the dark faces, and the encircling night grew darker. Suddenly there stepped from that encircling night two big men who seized Prem Raj.

"The Darogha wants you," one of them said, and before anyone else really knew what had happened they were on their way to Gosaini. The Kahars who were left at the barber's were for a few minutes too surprised to act; then one of them ran up the hill to Kalyan Singh's house. But before he could get inside another minute or two were wasted, and then the Thakur could not be found. By the time he was found, and his household collected, the constables and Prem Raj were a mile away and the idea of a rescue had to be dropped.

Now, of course, the Sub-Inspector had no right whatever to carry off Prem Raj like this, and this was perhaps the reason why he asked solicitously whether his captive had eaten. Prem Raj explained that he had not, since he usually ate last thing at night after the Thakurs had finished. Ghulam Husain explained kindly that he had had a meal prepared by Hindus with all the necessary precautions, and he sent it to Prem Raj by the hands of another Kahar. Prem Raj was pleasantly surprised, and still more so when it arrived and he found it was richly spiced and salted, not plain village food at all. Half-way through the meal he suddenly remembered a story he had once heard that poisoners always gave their victims food that was heavy with spice to conceal the taste of the poison. This frightened him, and he waited a long time, but as nothing happened he forgot his fright and went on with the meal.

Now Indians seldom mingle eating with drinking as Europeans do; they eat first and when they have made an end of eating, drink deep and clean their teeth. And they drink frequently when they are not eating, every two hours or so if they can. So it was not till he had finished that Prem Raj looked round for water.

There was none. When he asked for water he was told he should have some when he was ready to tell all he knew about Pyari's death. He said he knew nothing and for a short time he was left alone. His mouth was on fire, and the knowledge that he would not get water made what might at first have been only an inconvenience a positive torture. His tongue would hardly pass from side to side of his mouth. He thought of water drawn cold from the well and poured through the hands into the mouth; he thought of water lapped up straight from a stream; he thought of water in every form he had ever seen; but it did not yet occur to him to tell.

Ghulam Husain felt it was unfair that such a case should have been sprung on him in the winter. The spiced food and the absence of water is a summer torture. The subject is left alone all night and next morning he stands without any clothes on against a wall with a south face, and he tells all he knows before evening. That is all; it is beautifully simple and it leaves no marks. Whatever the victim says afterwards, he has no proof because there are no witnesses, not even the evidence of his maltreated body. But in the winter, it is a slow process, and Ghulam Husain was in a hurry. He had got to get evidence, and if necessary he was ready to make it. But he first must know what had happened, for there was all the difference in the world, in a big case like this, between inventing a story and manufacturing evidence to prove a story you knew was true. It would be very silly to invent the whole thing; there was sure to be something unforeseen that would trip you up. And on the other hand, the true story might lead to a perfectly genuine witness.

Prem Raj would never say anything to the judge, but if he would tell the true story in the police station someone else could certainly be found who would tell it in Court. That was where the need for hurry lay; it would never do to have a witness coming out with a circumstantial story a fortnight after the event.

No, Ghulam Husain decided at last, thirst alone would be too slow. It must be helped. He gave the order to make a cock of Prem Raj.

Being made a cock has affinities with being trussed for cockfighting, as the deceitful Stalky trussed the tigers attracted by the bleating of the kid. The difference is that it is not the wrists but the head that is lashed between the knees. There are two methods. The first, which is slower but safer, is to pass behind the neck and under the knees a broad strip of webbing—not rope, which would mark. The webbing is then passed over the knees, under the chin and drawn tight, so that the head cannot be moved. This is not very painful at first, but becomes uncomfortable with the passage of hours. By the second, and more drastic method, the subject is secured in the same position, but by means of the lobes of his ears, which are usually already pierced for rings. This has, of course, the disadvantage that a determined and obstinate prisoner will sometimes jerk himself free by tearing the lobes of his ears, to which he will afterwards point as evidence of the way he has been treated. Ghulam Husain chose the first method. They made Prem Raj a cock and left him for the night.

When they brought him to Ghulam Husain next day he could not stand, and his tongue was so swollen that he could not speak clearly. But he was able to make it clear that he knew nothing about Pyari. They took him into the sun and laid him flat on the ground on his face, with his hands stretched out before him. This was a method Ghulam was reluctant to use, because it indubitably left marks, though it was not easy to say with certainty what had caused them. He felt, however, that time was running short and he must take the risk. They brought out a string cot, and placed two of the legs on the backs of Prem Raj's hands, stretched on the hard mud ground. Two men sat on the cot. After a little, another man was added. The weight was increased gradually for half an hour. Then he was released from the cot and made a cock once more. The muscles that had been stretched all night had stiffened, so that this was extremely uncomfortable. Then they brought him back to the cot.

About half-past ten in the morning Prem Raj began to speak.

Chapter Two

The First Witness Appears

•◇•

ON the evening of February 9th, three days after the death of Pyáran, Mohammad Isháq, Inspector of the group of police stations which included Gosaini, was talking at ease in the space in front of his house in Rámnagar with his nephew Salámatullah, who was a Sub-Inspector in charge of one of the police stations in the city. Mohammad Isháq's house was on the edge of the city standing on one of the big main roads that ran out in five directions like the spokes of a wheel, just where the spoke left the hub. There was a stand for motor-buses only a hundred yards away, and as buses in India never run to a program, but wait till they are full before they start, there were usually crowds of people standing, talking, spitting, eating, buying and quarreling before the house. On the other side of the road was a bright blue petrol pump, a new concrete office, and several large tin advertisements for motor tires. Except for the office, the houses were old, built of thin flat bricks, and, in spite of the efforts of the Municipal Board to make at least the main thoroughfares respectable, there was something mean and squalid about them all, chiefly due to no one's ever putting anything tidily away, as is the habit in more blessed lands. There were old clothes and bits of rag and newspaper and string cots and dogs and hens and, above all, goats in the street, and the traffic—hampered at best because the road was not really wide enough for traffic simultaneously in two stages of evolution, motors and bullock-carts— was often completely blocked by the arrogant progress and insolent pauses of a sacred bull.

Mohammad Isháq's house had one great advantage. Before the road was widened, a subsidiary lane must have turned off here at an angle, so that the house was set askew with the others in its line, and there was left before it a triangular space, certainly not very large, nor particularly beautiful, but at least a place where one could sit in the evening, to discuss the day's doings at ease and to see life and movement, hear laughter and loud cries; taste the savor of breath and dust, smoke, petrol and food. Mohammad Ishaq liked it, and it was incidentally an excellent place for discussing intimate affairs, since it was raised a little above the road and the noise was too great for eavesdropping.

It was here that he used to talk over his cases with his nephew, each benefiting by the different constitution of the other's mind. For while Mohammad Isháq was of the old school, poorly educated by academic standards, but wide in experience and endowed with the crisp native shrewdness that seems seldom to accompany book-learning, his nephew Salámatullah had been at Aligarh Muslim University and was clearly destined for the Criminal Investigation Department and perhaps ultimately to be a Superintendent of Police. The reading of one helped the experience of the other, and nephew and uncle were very good friends. They were both honest, at least in the sense in which the term is understood in India, where no one's pay is commensurate with his powers and responsibilities, and where, by old tradition, an honest judge is one who takes presents from both sides and gives an impartial decision.

Mohammad Ishaq was telling Salamatullah about what was already called the Anantpur murder case, although no one was yet absolutely sure that it was murder. Pyari had died on February 6th at midday. Rup Singh had reported the death at Gosaini late that evening and Ghulam had gone to the village on the morning of the 7th. He had entered a case of murder on the 7th and sent word to his Inspector first thing on the morning of the 8th. The Inspector had sent back a message that he would meet him at Anantpur a little after noon on the 8th, giving Ghulam Husain only just time to conclude his examination of Prem Raj. Mohammad Ishaq had gone straight to Anantpur because it was more accessible than Gosaini, being close to the main railway line and the main road from Ramnagar, which ran side by side, and while in the village he had been able to confirm the Sub-Inspector's story of the blank obstinacy of everyone there.

Salamatullah listened to the story with no very keen interest.

"It sounds like an ordinary zenána murder," he said. "You never get any evidence."

"It's not quite ordinary," his uncle answered, slowly.

"Well, what have you got? The woman dies, which they admit. They say first that she died of pneumonia, then that it was cholera. But you've only police evidence for that. They'll swear they always said cholera, and Rup Singh's word by itself isn't worth taking to Court." It is an axiom in Indian courts that the police are never to be believed. "Then, beyond that, you've got nothing but Hukm Singh's hearing a gun at midday—and it doesn't sound as though he'd stick to that in Court—this extraordinary haste to burn her, and Gopal Singh disappearing."

"Two other disappearances," said Ishaq, "the woman who laid her out, and the Chamar who heard the shot."

"But that doesn't help you. All these disappearances and their burning her that evening are causes for suspicion, and they're weaknesses in the defense, but they're not proof. Get your case, and then, if they can't produce this woman and Gopal, it will tell against them. But you can't think of taking a case to Court on defense weaknesses."

Ishaq smiled.

"I had thought of that, nephew," he said. "But there are just one or two things about it all I don't understand. First of all, Ghulam Husain. You know what I think of him; he's corrupt and a thorough scoundrel, but there's no denying he's experienced and he isn't a fool. Now he heard of the case on the night of the 6th, spent the 7th looking into it himself, and only sent for me first thing on the 8th. Now if it weren't Ghulam I shouldn't grumble at that, he might want to make sure it wasn't a mare's nest before troubling me. But as it is Ghulam—" He paused.

"You think he went first to see if they'd give him anything to hush it up. I suppose Kalyan Singh was too much of a miser."

"I think that sounds rather likely. You see, the really important point is when he entered the case in the police station diary. He's put it down as the morning of the 7th, and the other entries for that day come later—the usual routine things, you know. But it looks to me rather as though all the entries for the 7th had been written at the same time—late in the evening, when he came back from Anantpur with empty pockets. He must have told the Sergeant to keep all the entries for the date on a separate paper, and copied them in after the entry about Anantpur."

"Yes, of course, if he'd made the entry in the evening it would be obvious he'd held his hand to see what he could get. Wouldn't it have been simpler to leave a blank after the entries on the 6th, and include this case then if he wanted to?"

"Perhaps he'd already signed the entries for the 6th when the Constable came in. And he'd have to delay his entries for the 7th anyhow, because he'd have to enter up that he'd left the station for Anantpur."

"Of course. Still this doesn't get you any further. It's proof of nothing."

"No, but it's interesting because of two things. If it's true Ghulam went to see what he could get—and you'll agree that is more than likely—"

"I should say there was no doubt."

"Then if it's true, *and* there's no evidence, Ghulam ought to be sick as a dog."

"Isn't he?"

"He isn't. He's like—he's like a boy with his first mistress. Pleased with himself as hell, and trying not to show it."

"Yes, that's certainly interesting."

"He never suggested that the case would fail because there's no evidence, which on the face of it is what looked likely, as you said. He said he'd go on working and let me have daily reports. And another thing, Hukm Singh—you know Hukm Singh?"

"I know about him. He lives at Anantpur and has always helped us."

"Hukm Singh's like a cat on hot bricks. He won't look anyone in the face. He doesn't want to let us down, and yet he daren't go against Nannhe Singh and Kalyan in anything as big as this. He only said one thing that was interesting. I'd been talking the case over with him. I said we'd get no evidence from Anantpur. He looked at me out of the corner of his eye and said, "No, but wait and see what comes out from the other side!"

"What did he mean?"

"He wouldn't explain and seemed sorry he'd spoken; I got nothing else out of him, and I'm not sure what he meant, but I think that by the other side he meant the girl's family. She came from Sháhábád district, and if any evidence does appear from Sháhábád, well—I shan't be surprised, but I'd be interested to know how Hukm Singh knew in advance."

"Yes, very. It *is* interesting, uncle. You'll tell me what happens, won't you?"

"Of course I will. And now let's hear what you've been doing."

Sálámatullah had a good deal to say. He had come up against something he didn't like, he was finding it a little too big for him, and he was kicking. When he had first come to take charge of one of the four city police stations he had noticed that cocaine was being used much more commonly than in Agra, where he had been second officer in a city station. In all Indian cities cocaine can be bought; there are pán-shops where, if you ask for pán at a certain exorbitant price, cocaine is slipped into the lime that goes between the big leaves; and most of the prostitutes will throw in cocaine with their other wares for an extra rupee or two. Salamatullah had learnt in Agra to know the nervous manner and discolored teeth of the addict; but what surprised him in Ramnagar was the number of these people. It was not difficult to find the market price of illicit cocaine, and it was interesting to notice that it was not much more than half what it had been in Agra. At once Salamatullah decided that here was his chance of coming to notice. He knew cocaine could never be kept down altogether, and it was never much good pulling in the retailers, but clearly in Ramnagar there was a big organization, and if he could get further back, at some of the people who received large quantities and distributed it to the little boys at the corners of the road and the plump ladies of delight, he would have done something that would bring promotion. But at once he had found himself in difficulties. He meant it to be his own coup, and accordingly kept most of what he knew or guessed to himself, but he had mentioned the subject to the Kotwál, the Deputy Superintendent of Police in charge of the city. The response had been chilling, a total lack of interest and a crushing reference to the inexperience of youth. He knew more now, and was sure that that particular eye was one the Kotwal would keep carefully shut for a long time. There was not much doubt now in his mind about the main lines of the organization. He was pretty sure that the cocaine came from abroad to the Indian State of Mallapur, and was delivered from the State into British India at the house of one of the leading gentry of Ramnagar, a gentleman of a fine old Rohilla family. Their land had been a little circumscribed of late, and perhaps they laid less stress on their Pathán ancestry and had less scorn for the native Sheikhs, but they still seemed to have money and were recognized as one of the three families who by right of birth and influence were the first among the Musulmans of Ramnagar.

The cocaine went to the house of Khán Bahádur Fazal Dád Khán Sáhib, and passed from him to six main agents who distributed it to the little retailers. Salamatullah knew the names of each of them, but that was not enough. The Khán Bahádur Sáhib was a powerful politician and a man of great influence, not one against whom a junior police officer could lightly bring serious charges. He would have to prove his charge by finding the cocaine actually in the Khan Bahadur's house. This would anyhow not be easy, for he did not know how it arrived, and it was never there more than a few hours, but the task was made impossibly more difficult by the hostility of the Kotwál and the fact that the Khan Bahadur Sahib's house lay outside Salamatullah's direct jurisdiction. There could be no doubt that the Kotwál had an understanding with the Khan Bahadur, and, in the face of that understanding and the old man's power, the young Sub-Inspector could not hope to touch the main receiving agent.

He could give up the struggle entirely and signify tactfully to the Kotwal his readiness to come in on the deal; or he could give up for the time being, collect his information, and wait for the days of a new Kotwal; or he could do what was possible to lay by the heels the principal agents, or at any rate the two who belonged to his own circle. The first of these was rank surrender to the principle of feathering his own nest, and he was not yet sufficiently disheartened for that; the second was a policy that did not appeal to his youth and he adopted therefore the third.

That too was not easy. He might know his man, and pass him every day in the street, but he was powerless unless he could say: This man has the stuff about his person. It is a common device of the police, when they know a cocaine-smuggler and want to arrest him, to plant the stuff in his pocket and convict him by suborned witnesses; but Salamatullah dared not risk this when the Kotwal was against him. He knew that he would be found out and exposed to his Superintendent, and if not broken at once his reputation for honesty would be gone. He had for the present to content himself with taking some of the bigger distributors, but he knew what he was missing, and he was angry.

It was about three of these distributors he was talking now to his uncle.

"Those three between them sold more than anyone else in my circle," he said. "They dealt direct with Husaini [one of the six] and they made their plans together. Bashir planned for the three of them."

"He was the eldest. I watched and waited till I knew their routine exactly. A day would come when Bashir went to see Husaini. When he came back, he would send for Ahmad and Ma'Shuq, if they weren't in the house already, and that evening they would go out, the three of them, Ma'Shuq to the prostitutes, Ahmad to the pan-sellers, and Bashir to people he used to find waiting here and there at street corners—often they sold matches and cigarettes. I couldn't take them all in one night, because I couldn't trust anyone else. I had to be there myself. So I took Ma'Shuq first; caught him with the stuff on him just going into the street of the harlots. He ran, of course, and threw the cocaine away, but I saw him throw it and picked it up, while a constable caught him. It made no difference; the other two went on just the same, though Ahmad was very sad."

"Why was Ahmad sad?"

"Ma'Shuq was the beloved of Ahmad, and Ahmad was the beloved of Bashir," replied Salamatullah. "Everyone knew it. The next time Bashir went to see Husaini I caught Ahmad, and Bashir was sad. Next time, I caught Bashir. It was very simple."

It was a simple story as Salamatullah told it, recounted in the most matter-of-fact way. He had no condemnation for their trade or their morals; and indeed the seller of cocaine regards the prohibition of the law as an unwarrantable invasion of private liberty. He never thinks of himself as responsible for those languid faces, nervous fingers, and tired wandering minds. Nor does the corner-boy of the big cities think it a sin to love, better than his wife, the friend in whose company he runs from the police, dodges from dark shadow to shadow and whispers a password at a shuttered window. His wife sits at home all day and sews: she understands nothing of the excitement of the city, the flaring lights, the thick greasy smells, the thrill of companionship and intrigue. It is natural to love a boy; he has always done it and so have his friends. Salamatullah did not think of this, nor did he think of the three he had arrested as persons. He felt no sense of pity when the features of Ma'Shuq, the youngest of the three, a boy of seventeen, handsome and almost beautiful in repose, showed when he spoke or smiled the twist of evil that life had laid on them. There was no sorrow in his heart when he saw the pale lifeless face of Ahmad, soft of flesh, the slave at once of his own and another's lust, nor the sturdiness of Bashir turned to sullen obstinacy and his cleverness to cunning. They were things to his hand, steps on his way. He had got them, and his only regret was that he had not got anyone bigger.

"No doubt about conviction, I suppose?" asked his uncle.

"I don't see how there can be. I did everything I should—witnesses searched me and each other—search-list signed on the spot, and all. Good witnesses, too—none of your professionals."

"You're pleased then?" asked Ishaq.

"How can I be pleased when things are as they are? The Kotwal will tell the Superintendent I did it—and shake his head —and say he wishes I were as honest as I'm energetic—and I'll be written down as a faker. I know how it'll be. I shan't get any credit."

"You've thought of talking to the S.P. [Superintendent of Police] yourself, of course."

"Of course. But you know him. Loyalty's his only word. It doesn't matter how stupid or lazy or corrupt a man is, he won't listen to a word against him from his own subordinates."

"Well," said the Inspector, "there are worse things than that in an S.P.—worse by a long way. Wait till you've been under a Hindu."

"Aren't I now? And next door to a bania, too, that Kotwal!" He spat.

"I mean a Hindu S.P. That really is hell. But I didn't mean you should go to the S.P. and blurt out the whole story of Fazal Dad Khan being in partnership with the Kotwal—just a hint or two that there may be two sides to a question. He's fair, you know."

"He'd think I was sly and disloyal. No, I'll keep quiet and hope he'll realize the Kotwal isn't all gold."

"I think perhaps you're right. What about the District Magistrate?"

Salamat looked up with less despondency.

"He's better. He's young too and wants to do things. Sorry, uncle." The older man was laughing at him. "But even he'll ask if I've talked to my Sub-Divisional Officer."

"You'll have to, of course. He's honest, though he is a Kayasth." [1]

"Uncle, how can I go to a Kayasth and call him sir, and be given a hard chair condescendingly as a kindness?"

"I know it's hard. It's bad enough with any Hindu; we were their masters once, and still are at anything but examinations, and it's hard to forget it. And it's worse still when it's a bania or a Kayasth. His father was a sniveling little clerk you wouldn't have bothered to kick, and the son is in the I.C.S. and we must call him sir and treat him as though he were English. But, Salamat, we must do it. This is the best Government we can hope for. The English are better than the Hindus."

"Why should it be either?" asked Salamatullah with a dark flash of eyes and teeth.

"The English have force and the Hindus cunning, and we can't compete with either at their own game. That's the answer, and you know it."

"Yes, I know it really, but it makes me sick," was the sullen answer.

"You'll have to go and see him, I'm afraid. And he's better

[1] The Hindu caste of clerks and writers.

than an old Kayasth—he's too young to be really cunning at intrigue."

"He won't take long to learn. How I hate them! Stinking of cow-dung, creeping and stinking—there's nothing they love but their fat bellies and their money and their scratching mangy monkeys and cow-dung." He spat again and rose to go. "I'll see his highness tomorrow, and then go on to the District Magistrate."

"Perhaps I'll see you there," said Ishaq, and they said good night.

Next morning Ishaq went to see the District Magistrate. Christopher Tregard was young for so important a charge as Ramnagar, but a sudden sickness had called away on four months' leave the officer who on the files at headquarters was referred to as the permanent incumbent, and Christopher, being on the spot as Joint Magistrate, had stepped into his shoes.

There are two schools of administrators in the Northern Provinces: one delights in rulings of the Board of Revenue and never leaves the desk except to reach for a more distant work of reference. The men of this school write excellent reports, but their name liveth not, for few in the district they rule have spoken to them, and those few do not love them. But there are still examples of the other kind of administrator, the man who does not put the letter of the law above the ends of justice, who rides among the villages and has shot snipe or partridges with half the landlords in the district. He does not write such long reports and he seldom quotes rulings of the Board of Revenue; but he spends many months in camp, and in the evening when he strolls out with a gun he meets people who never penetrate to the office where the works of reference are stacked. He knows what his people are thinking; and when they learn to know him, too, they will give him an admiration and even affection that will only slowly die. Hatred, too, he will earn, and very probably the distrust of Government.

It was in this school that Christopher Tregard had been brought up and just now he was very happy in his work and in his play. But by the time Ishaq reached him he was a little tired. He had seen twelve visitors that morning. First had come one of the lesser Musulman gentry, one who never failed to call on the District Magistrate, a hand-washing adherent of present power, one who had indeed earned the contemptuous name the Congress party threw at his kind, a "Government dog" who scrambled after crumbs with such obvious greed that it hardly seemed worth while to throw them. Christopher soon got rid of him. Next a Hindu priest of the old school, with that stamp on his face that gentle birth and the priesthood seem to set on a few faces in all ages and in all civilized creeds, a restraint, a certainty and a gentleness that conceals an inner strength. This old man came once a month or so to see his District Magistrate, spotlessly clean in lawn so white it seemed impossible he could have come along the dusty road from his temple. He did not want anything, but paid his penny to Caesar because it was his duty and because he usually liked Caesar personally. Much though Christopher enjoyed meeting the old man, he had to send him away long before he had finished talking about his temple and his disciple and the excellence of bygone Commissioners and Magistrates.

Next came Rái Bahádur Kunwar Mangat Lál, chairman of the District Board, large and fat and ruminative, blinking his sleepy eyes. He was a man of wealth and owned a great deal of land, and a man of considerable cunning, for he walked along an extremely narrow and slippery path without ever quite falling off on one side or the other. To his official title of Rai Bahadur he had himself added a title which he intended for his son, Kunwar, or son of a Rájá. But everyone knew that he was really only a Kurmi, a caste of cultivators, and he had reached his present wealth by the savings and scrapings of four generations of his ancestors. But though the Thakurs and Musulmans laughed at his dark face and pudgy features, they had to respect him. Each man voted for himself first, and for Mangat Lal second, the wild men of the Congress and the Nationalist landowners under Nannhe Singh, the banias, the peasants, and even the "Government dogs," the prehensile tongued. He came to pay his respects with no particular object, purely to preserve good relations and to discuss in a friendly way various questions of administration, schools and roads and sanitation, with the reservation that nothing he might say should prejudice his future action.

He left ponderously and was succeeded by Sáyyad Mubárik Áli, with his pale handsome face and fine head of white hair, an advocate with a still rising practice and political ambitions, who could not quite make up his mind whether the very small group of Nationalist Musulmans, or the much larger group who stood first for Islám, was really the party of the future. Then an old Musulmán landlord from the district, who still maintained feudal state among his tenants and staunchly supported the Government because he was too old-fashioned to change from the ways of his father and grandfather, and another Rái Bahádur, the richest bania in the city, a man of vast wealth and enormous girth, for whom a special chair had to be brought because the big office armchairs were too narrow for his hips. He wanted a forest contract, he wanted to be a Rájá and he wanted to be on good terms with all the officials of the district for so long as his usual thirty or forty suits for debt and arrears of rent were before the Courts. Then came an Anglo-Indian in tears, whose wife had gone astray, a Musulman gentleman from the city who was working hard for the title of Khan Sahib, a hard-faced Brahman landowner who lived in the city and had driven his tenants so hard that he dared not set foot in his villages, he too in tears because Christopher had begun to persecute him until he mended his ways. The first step had been a canceled gun-license, and he got under the table to clutch the august Sahib by the feet before Christopher had divined his purpose. He was removed, still weeping. A lady like a walking ghost in a burqa, whose husband had died and whose relations were trying to rob her of her share of the property; and an old villager who cultivated a large piece of land which he had been trying for years to get registered in his own name; he had met Christopher out riding one morning and the registry had been effected in a week. He had not come to ask for anything but only to say that he and his children and his children's children would pray always for his Honor's long life and prosperity.

Last came Khán Bahádur Mohammad Altáf Khán, a man of character and enterprise. "I will never have my son educated to read English," he said once to Christopher, "because I have noticed that the more a man reads, the more of a coward he becomes." Courage indeed was the first quality he admired and possessed. He had very little land, and only the name of his Rohilla forefathers; he still kept up some shadowy communication with cousins on the North-West Frontier, and although his family had been six generations in India he spoke of "Indians" with contempt, as a feeble folk with whom he had no part. Like many of the Musulman landowners he believed that he was much better off under the British than he could be under any national Government, but unlike the rest he had had the courage to back his fancy whole-heartedly, and he had committed himself so deeply that he could never go back. He was the one leading man in the district on whom the district authorities knew they could always rely for help. Yet apart from the fact that they would not have dared, no one would have felt inclined to call the Khan Bahadur a "Government dog," for his personality gave a character of its own to all his doings.

One exploit of his in particular would always be remembered. His home was at Gosaini, the police station for Anantpur, and early in the Congress revival of civil disobedience, in 1931, he had announced that no Congress speakers would be permitted to hold meetings in Gosaini. The Congress committee in Ramnagar responded by sending a dozen of their workers with flags and badges and Gandhi caps to spread disobedience. They held no meeting, and went back with neither flags, caps nor badges, but with backs of varying soreness. The committee sent some more, who came back sorer still. If they were to keep any prestige at all in that part of the district the Congress must now make a special effort, and they did. They broadcast the announcement of a monster meeting in Gosaini, and raised an army to march there from Ramnagar, consisting of a nucleus of workers from the city and several hundreds of the tenants of Nannhe Singh and his kind. They were armed with the six-foot bamboo quarter-staff of the northern peasant, which will crack a man's skull at a blow.

When the Khan Bahadur heard of this he made his preparations without consulting anyone. All his friends must send in their tenants, armed with quarter-staffs, and meanwhile he persuaded every leading Hindu in Gosaini to sign a statement that he did not want a Congress meeting in the little town because it would almost certainly lead to a breach of the peace. Then, secure in the knowledge of his man, he went to see the District Magistrate. Had the magistrate been one of those who delight in rulings of the Board of Revenue, all the Khan Bahadur's plans would have been forbidden in pious horror, the meeting would have been held, and for the next two years affrays, arrests and assaults would have been continuous. But the Khan Bahadur came to an old friend who had as much courage as himself and he was given this advice:

"Make your own arrangements; tell me nothing about it; don't kill anyone, and I'll back you up afterwards."

He could rely on that, and he went back to Gosaini in content. Ghulam Husain was warned to keep his constables inside the police station with their eyes shut and wool in their ears. On every road was placed a picket to explain that the meeting had been canceled and to prevent an influx of peasants with nothing to do, while the Khan Bahadur led out his main army to meet the Congress army from the south. His men were drawn up in two battalions, Hindus in front, Musulmans behind, since he proposed to keep communal bitterness from the struggle by holding his Musulmans in reserve and using them only if his first line was defeated. Early in the morning the two armies met, and the Khan Bahadur explained that he would not permit a meeting in Gosaini. Everyone sat down on the ground while the leaders parleyed. They parleyed all day and nothing happened, because both were too obstinate to budge. Towards evening the Khan Bahadur again took the opinion of the leading Hindus of Gosaini and recorded it in writing. He persuaded them to say that they were afraid that with the darkness the Congress army would slink into the town by twos and threes and a riot would result. He told the enemy leaders of this and said that if they were not gone in five minutes he would disperse them. They did not go. He dispersed them, by one magnificent charge; his reserves never came into play and the Congress fled, leaving fifty wounded on the field.

When zealous members of the Legislative Council tabled a long string of questions, beginning with "Is it a fact . . ." and

"Is the Government aware . . ." they were told that Government had no official information, but that as no assaults had been reported at police stations there seemed every reason for believing that the stories were grossly exaggerated.

There were no more assaults, arrests and affrays in that part of the district, and not even a whisper of meetings to preach civil disobedience.

When the Khan Bahadur came to see Christopher on this particular morning, February 10th, it was principally to talk about the Anantpur murder. He had been talking to Kalyan Singh, and he said that he himself thought it was suicide. They had tried to conceal the death because, if they had not, there would have been a post-mortem examination, and for them it was infamy that a man and a stranger should examine the body of their dead, particularly a woman.

Christopher listened with interest, and, though he had not yet formed an opinion of his own, he pointed out one or two oddities in the case. He had shot snipe with both Hukm Singh and Gopal, and indeed had handled and admired the fine English gun with which the crime must have been committed. To him, at first sight, the chief difficulties in the suicide theory were psychological; shooting seemed a most unlikely method for an Indian woman to choose, particularly with a shot-gun, and serious though the disgrace of a post-mortem on a Thakur woman appeared to be in all Indian eyes, he was not yet quite sure that it was serious enough to warrant the risk that her family had taken in concealing the woman's death.

"But, lord," said the Khan Bahadur, "they never thought that murder would be mentioned."

"Then why did Gopal Singh hide? And for that matter why is he still hiding?"

"Feeder of the Poor, he was suddenly frightened. He is a weak and silly young man."

"His hiding is one of the chief things against him. And if it is really suicide, you can tell Kalyan he'd do well to reappear."

"I have told him. But he won't believe me. If your honor would tell him—may I bring him to see you?"

"Who, Kalyan? Yes, by all means do. I'd like to tell him that. When can you bring him, Khan Bahadur?"

"He is outside now."

"Well, I see the Inspector, Mohammad Ishaq, is outside. Do you mind waiting while I see him and then bringing in Kalyan?"

"Of course, Sahib."

Mohammad Ishaq told Christopher most of what he had said to his nephew. He said nothing about bribery, but he repeated Hukm Singh's mysterious remark, and said he found the Sub-Inspector's apparent confidence rather difficult to explain. He was filled with admiration when Christopher, having asked if Ghulam had been right in not reporting at once, began to make inquiries about the entries in the diary.

"It is the first thing," he said to his nephew afterwards, "that would strike an old hand like me; but for a young man, and an Englishman, it is remarkable."

While they were still talking the telephone bell rang.

"Yes, Tregard," the Inspector heard. "Oh, we were just talking about it. From Sháhábád, have you? Yes, yes, what was the name? JEHÁRAN? Good, I've got it now. Reported only this morning—they've been quick, haven't they? Four days ago, the 6th? Yes, Nannhe Singh's house. Yes, yes. Well, it's very interesting, isn't it? We must talk it over soon. The Inspector's here now; I'll tell him. Yes, thanks for letting me know so quickly."

"Well, Inspector," he went on, "it's funny we should have been talking about that case just when the S.P. rang up; and what he has to tell me is very interesting indeed, particularly after what you've just told me, 'Wait and see what comes out from the other side' Hukm Singh said, did he? Well, it's come."

The Inspector leaned forward eagerly.

"Yes, early this morning a woman called Jeharan turned up at Galthána police station. She said she was the old nurse of—what's the name of the girl who died?"

"Pyaran, or Pyari she was usually called, sir."

"Yes, Pyaran's old nurse. She went to live at Anantpur when the girl married, and she was in the room when the shot was fired. There was a quarrel about some other woman, and then Gopal lost his temper and finally shot her. Gopal and Kalyan took this woman, Jeharan, across to Nannhe Singh's house and kept her locked up there the rest of that day, the 6th, all the 7th and all the 8th. Yesterday morning, the 9th, she escaped, went to the railway and walked along the line all the way to Ramnagar. She took train to Shahabad, got out to Galthana first thing this morning, the 10th, and made a report at the police station at once. The station officer realized it was important, let headquarters know and they've just rung up the S.P."

The Inspector smiled.

"Yes, sir, it is very interesting."

"What do you think?"

"It's too early to say, of course, but I should like to talk to that woman. I should like to ask her some questions."

"So should I. Well, we must wait till we see her actual report. Thank you, Inspector. Come and see me if anything else turns up."

The Khan Bahadur came back with Kalyan Singh.

"Sit down, Thakur Sahib. I wanted to talk to you, but it's only fair to tell you first that some new evidence has turned up." He reflected that the police would be annoyed with him for telling Kalyan Singh; but, after all, he thought, they want a conviction, I want the truth. And you must tell a man all there is against him. Nor can he get at this woman, who is safe at Shahabad. No, I'll tell him. And he told Kalyan Singh the story he had just heard.

"Lord, Cherisher of the Poor, it's a lie. Entirely a lie. She did come to Anantpur when the girl first came, but she went back after six months. She has not been inside the house for a year."

Very prompt, thought Christopher. He'd no time to think of that; but of course, if her story were true, he'd have known this was coming and had time to get that ready.

"Well, Thakur Sahib, naturally I'm not prepared to say if that story is true or not. You know best. But this I can say, that the only evidence against your son is that story, your extraordinary behavior after the death and your son's absence."

"Sahib, Presence, I was a foolish old man. There was a quarrel, she shot herself, and sooner than let her be examined by the doctors, we said it was sickness. That was all, I swear it."

"Well, Thakur Sahib, if that's true, I'll advise you as a friend, that the best thing you can do is to produce your son and let him give his own account of what he did. But, remember, that's only if what you've told me is true, and if he's prepared to tell the truth himself. The more truth he can tell, the better for him. But if it was really murder—which no one knows but you—well, I give you no advice. It's your own affair, but we'll find him sooner or later."

"Presence, it was suicide."

"All right; if that's true, you know my advice. Good-bye."

"Good-bye, Khan Bahadur."

He was left alone. He was still thinking about the case when Salamatullah was announced. He was, of course, in uniform and saluted with a large allowance of boot-clicking and leg-slapping.

He told Christopher of his arrest of the three cocaine-peddlers without either varnish or concealment. Christopher was interested in cocaine; he knew that until public opinion in the towns took a part he was fighting uphill, but the thought of the vacant gaze and nervous fingers of the addict always filled him with anger against those who made their profit from the trade. When Salamatullah had finished the straightforward part of his story, he entered on what was very much more difficult. He spoke vaguely of obstacles in his way, and the jealousy of people to whom he never gave a name, but his meaning was sufficiently clear to Christopher, who already had ideas of his own on the subject. The Sub-Inspector explained that he knew all that was necessary about the organization of the trade in the city, though it was another matter to make arrests, but that he was still puzzled about the way the dope came into Ramnagar from Mallapur; Christopher listened appreciatively, but without letting him approach too closely the infamies of the Kotwal, and sent him away encouraged and assured that he would be supported. Himself, Christopher decided he must have a talk with the Superintendent about the Kotwal, but must keep it very close that Salamatullah had lately been to see him.

Left alone Christopher ascertained that for the moment there were no more visitors, and decided to rest and smoke a cigarette for twenty minutes. First, his mind ran idly on the Anantpur case, and he wondered if any more evidence would appear. Of course, Hukm Singh's remark could be explained equally well whether the woman Jeharan's story was true, or whether someone had sent news from Anantpur to Galthana, and told the Galthana family to produce evidence from their end since none would be forthcoming from Anantpur. If Jeheran had really been locked up and escaped, everyone in the village would know about it and would be expecting to hear of her again. If, on the other hand, she hadn't, but the police were wanting a witness, it was quite on the cards that they had found out what had happened by some means they could not use in Court, and had sent the story on to Galthana. But there was nothing to do about that for the time being. His mind slipped away to the coming polo tournament. His own team were a scratch lot, coming up against a junior team of British cavalry subalterns in the first round. The Hussars would be better mounted, of course, and probably knew each other's play better, but they were very young, and would be sure to get rattled and start missing the ball once they were losing. Man for man, and with equal ponies, his own team were better, but they'd only played together once. It was a long handicap, that. And it was heartbreaking work, playing against more expensive ponies.

For himself, of course, the pleasure of the match would really depend on Sweet Janet. If she played as she had done yesterday, it would be joy whether they lost or won; and you could always rely on her to give her best, if she was sound; but it wasn't so very long since that splint on the near fore had stopped hurting her, and she might crumple again in a hard game. But if she kept sound— His eye brightened as he remembered how she would check when a scurry of ponies had gone over a missed ball, how she would check on her hocks and nip round, and be in full gallop back for the ball before the others had pulled up. Her delight in getting away in front was almost as great as his own, and her gallop was so steady it seemed impossible to miss off her back. Nothing on the ground would be as handy as she, nor so quick off the mark, nor so responsive to her rider; she seemed part of yourself between your legs. In a galloping game with long accurate hitting, of course, she hadn't the pace to get there first nor the weight to keep anyone else off, but the gallantry of her, when she went like a little cannonball of muscle and spirit into a bigger pony's shoulder! Ah, she was a darling, as much a darling as the Janet she was named for.

His second pony, Corvette, was a good reliable sort, always working hard, and as quick round as most. A shade faster than Sweet Janet perhaps, and a little heavier, but she hadn't the quickness in getting under way, nor that extra touch of sympathy that gave him such absolute confidence on the little bay. You had only to think what you wanted to do and Janet would do it, but on Corvette there was always a corner of your mind that must remember her as well as the game and the ball. It was worse still with the big English chestnut Gunboat. Half your mind had to be kept for riding him, and hitting the ball was much harder than on the others. But when he was at his best it certainly was a joy to be on a pony as fast and as heavy and bold as anything on the field; the sort of game Janet liked he hated, and after a few minutes of twisting and turning and missing he would get excited and have no idea in his head but hard galloping. Christopher wondered for a few minutes whether it wouldn't be a good thing even now to change Gunboat's bit, but decided at last that it was too risky just before a tournament; he'd have to experiment a little when it was all over. If Janet was lame and Gunboat got excited, it wouldn't be much fun, and if he had to fall back on poor old Sergeant, the old Waler, it would be misery. But it would be all right; Sweet Janet would keep sound! He thought with joy of the tattoo of hoofs on the hard Indian ground, the rattle of hooked sticks and the smack of the ball, the smell of sweat and horses and leather, and the little ache in the back when you slipped off your horse after the last chukker. His breath came a little shorter and his heart beat a little faster, as he saw the bright colors of the vests, the white breeches and helmets, the light of the sun like liquid silver and gold on moving quarters and shoulders, bay and chestnut and black, flashing like oiled silk. He saw the ball glance from a hoof ahead, felt Sweet Janet turn like an eel and race for it, heard the smack as he hit it beneath her neck, felt for an instant the silk of her skin and the harshness of her hogged mane against his cheek, as she turned again, saw his second shot for the goal. For a moment in anticipation he almost captured the utter abandon of a hard game, when nothing else matters but victory or defeat, when men fling their ponies against each other and ride for each ball as though it were their last moment on earth. Then he remembered that his files were waiting, laughed, and went to his desk.

Chapter Three

The Second Witness Appears

•✧•

ON the morning of February 11th, the fifth day after the death of Pyaran, Thakur Kalyan Singh came to Christopher Tregard with his son Gopal Singh, who wished to give himself up to justice and to make a statement. With them came the Khan Bahadur Sahib, Mohammad Altaf Khan, a genial figure who wanted to help both parties and knew that his local influence would benefit by his presence.

Christopher asked Gopal if he was quite sure he wanted to make a statement.

"I warn you," he said, "that if what you're going to tell me isn't the truth, you'd much better not say it. In that case, keep quiet. But if you can tell me a true story, by all means let me hear it."

But Gopal insisted that it was true, and he was determined to tell it, and so Christopher heard him and recorded his story sentence by sentence.

At noon on February 6th, he said, he had come to his wife, who was sitting upstairs outside their bedroom. He had brought her some kurtas of his own which he wanted her to hem. She had flown into a temper and asked if she were expected to be always working for him. Couldn't one of the maids do it? There had been a quarrel, he admitted it, a very bitter quarrel. His wife had been very hot-tempered for some time before this. She had accused him of taking an interest in other women. Women were always jealous, and just lately she had got these ideas into her head. At last, he must admit he had lost his temper too.

She had said:

"Why don't you kill me? If you are really a Thakur, why don't you shoot me instead of letting me say what I like to you?"

At that he had been furious, and had stepped up to her and slapped her face as hard as he could. This made her cry, but she did not stop abusing him, and he left the room quickly as the only way to save himself from doing more. He had gone out of the house, into the lane between Kalyan Singh's and Nannhe Singh's. He had stood there for a minute or two, thinking what to do next. Then he had gone up to Nannhe Singh's house. He had barely stepped inside when he heard the report of a gun in Kalyan Singh's house, and came running back. He ran at once upstairs to his wife's room, and found her lying half on the bed, wounded in the front of the body and dying. Half an hour later she had died. That was all.

"Then it is quite untrue that you shot her?"

"Quite untrue." He hesitated a moment. "I could not have done such a thing, Presence, for I loved her far too much."

"And why did you burn her that evening and say it was cholera?"

"We did not want it to be known it was suicide. That was in itself a disgrace. It would be a double disgrace, and an offense in religion, if she were cut up and not given proper funeral rites. And it would be a third disgrace that a stranger, a foreigner, not even a Hindu, should see my wife's body naked, even in death."

"I see. You realize that by your own confession you have committed an offense in withholding this information."

"Yes, Presence, and we are sorry for it and ready to pay the penalty. We have been very foolish."

"More than foolish. But there are two more points I should like to know about. Remember, though, there is no need to answer me unless you want to, and don't answer unless you can tell me the truth. You do understand that?"

"Yes, Presence. I will tell you everything. It is serious now, and I understand how foolish I have been and I have come to put myself in your hands."

"All right. Now tell me why you put the gun and cartridges in Nannhe Singh's house, and why you ran away and hid yourself? Wait a minute. Are you sure you want to tell me?"

"Yes, Presence. Quite sure. When the Constable came in the afternoon, we didn't think much at the time; but afterwards, when we had burnt her, we remembered that, and we were frightened and took the gun across to Nannhe Singh's. It was very silly. We took it across late that night. Then next day, when the Sub-Inspector came, we were more frightened than ever. We knew he was coming—we saw him from the roof—so I hid, and my father said I had gone to Agra. It was very silly of us."

"Yes, it was very silly of you. But it was silly in either case," Christopher went on half to himself, "whether it was murder or suicide. However, where did you hide, when the police came for you again?"

Gopal smiled a timid smile. "I never left the house," he said, "though they were looking for me everywhere. We had a man on the roof to say when the police were coming, and as soon as we had news of that I jumped into a corn-bin. I stayed there as long as they were in the house."

"I see. Thank you. I think that's all."

Christopher gave Mohammad Ishaq a copy of the statement and talked it over with him, while Ghulam Husain waited outside.

"Now we have two stories," he said, "Gopal Singh's and this woman Jeharan's. Both are consistent in themselves. Both fit the facts as far as we know them. Of course, we haven't really heard Jeharan's yet, but as far as we can see, there's no reason why we should believe her bare word any more than Gopal's. What do you think?"

"It's not quite enough for a conviction. As far as it goes at present. Is it?" suggested the Inspector.

Christopher agreed with him.

"Not quite enough yet," he said. "But if anything should turn up to show Gopal's lying, we'd have him."

The Inspector went outside to Ghulam Husain, who was waiting for him.

Next day, February 12th, the sixth day after the death of Pyari, there arrived a messenger for Mohammad Ishaq at his house in Ramnagar. He was from Ghulam Husain, the Sub-Inspector at Gosaini, and brought a note saying that some most important evidence in the Anantpur case had been found. Would the Inspector come out and interview the witness?

Mohammad Ishaq set off at once. The day begins early in

India, where everyone, except Englishmen, burglars, dacoits and city bullies, goes to bed as soon as it is dark, to save money on oil for his lamp. It was barely seven o'clock when his bus started out on the Mallapur road. It was soon after eight when it stopped twenty miles away and put him down on the nearest point of the road to Anantpur. Road and railway ran parallel there, and the village lay perhaps half a mile from the road, beyond the railway. The Sub-Inspector was waiting by the side of the road with his witness, but he did not want to go into Anantpur village. He led the way to a big tree in the fields to the south of the road, near another village, and there his witness told his story.

His name, he said, was Jhammu Nat. He was the leader of a band of Nats, about twenty, whose range covered the country-side between Mallapur and Ramnagar. They seldom left this area, chiefly because they knew it well, and because all the land-lords were friendly. Most often they stayed at Anantpur in the guava-groves to the north of the village, which belonged to Kalyan Singh. On the evening of February 5th, the day before Pyari's death, they had come back to Anantpur, and next day, a little before noon, Jhammu had gone into the village to talk to the barber and hear the gossip. Coming from the north he had naturally taken the path that led between the houses of Kalyan Singh and Nannhe Singh. As he came up the slope he had heard a gun fired in one of the houses on his left, but he had thought nothing of it, and a minute later, just as he was reaching the crest of the slope, he had turned aside to make water and had squatted down in a corner where he was partly hidden in shadows. As he squatted there, he had heard a step and had looked up in case anyone should blunder into him; he had seen Gopal Singh step out into the lane with a gun in his hand, pause a moment as if in indecision, and then go on into Nannhe Singh's house. It had occurred to him that Gopal Singh had probably fired the shot he had just heard, but there was no reason why anyone should not shoot a pigeon from the roof of his house, and he had for-gotten the incident half an hour later. He left the village that evening. His band had stayed in the Anantpur groves during the week, but he himself had been reconnoitering in the southern villages. He had gone to see a landowner who wanted him to help in a plan for exterminating some wolves, which were supposed to live in a patch of rock and jungle near his village, and had taken several small children in the last few years. He had only come back to Anantpur about midday yesterday, February 11th, the fifth day after Pyari died, and as soon as he heard the rumors about her death he had remembered what he had seen and had hurried off to tell the police. He had found that the Sub-Inspector was at Ramnagar, and he had had to wait till the evening to tell his tale. The Sub-Inspector added that he had let the Inspector know immediately because, in the light of Gopal Singh's statement, this seemed to him to be of the greatest importance.

Mohammad Ishaq looked curiously at them both, Ghulam Husain and Jhammu. It was indeed an interesting story. He entirely agreed as to its importance. But he could not help noticing that it came in absolutely pat with Gopal Singh's statement. Yesterday Gopal had put forward a statement which seemed to explain the acknowledged facts just as well as Jeharan's, and immediately, that very evening, a witness had appeared whose story tied the knot neatly round Gopal's neck. For if this story were true, and Gopal had been in the house when the shot was fired, and had walked out with the gun in his hand, there could be no doubt. His own story was a lie; he had shot Pyari, or he had stood by and watched her shoot herself.

Jhammu said he had been waiting with his evidence at the police station while the Sub-Inspector was in Ramnagar. It was probably true that he had been waiting at the police station, but the Inspector thought it most probable that he had been waiting without his evidence. That was to be composed when Ghulam came back and told him what Gopal had said. No use trying to verify that; but he must try to verify that the Nat had been to stay with the landlord who was troubled by wolves. There was not much doubt what the result would be though; a Nat would have traveled all night to tell the landlord what to say, and he and all his tenants would swear Jhammu had been there from the 6th to the 11th. And it would be no use asking anyone else in those parts; they could only say they hadn't seen him, which would prove nothing. It would be more helpful to find someone who had seen Jhammu in Anantpur. But there again—the Inspector shook his head. The villagers of Anantpur had been questioned so often now that they had relapsed into sulky silence. Nothing would get them to talk about anything, for the Thakurs had threatened them with persecution if they said anything that would incriminate Gopal, and no doubt Ghulam had now threatened them with persecution if they said anything that would disprove Jhammu's story. It would be a direct contest between police and feudal influence, and it seemed to him that the negative would win; they would go sullen and stupid, and say nothing that would get them into trouble with either side. And it might even be true that Jhammu had been away from Anantpur, lying low somewhere for the last few days.

Mohammad Ishaq looked at them both again, the Nat completely impassive, as though he had done his duty and had no thought whatever for the consequences, the Sub-Inspector looking fixedly at the ground, his pike-like jaw firmly set, but his fingers just a little anxious now and then. The Inspector continued to say nothing and to think.

The story itself. Would the Court believe it? Himself, he was always suspicious from the start of stories which involved a man stepping aside to make water; it came so often in evidence.

"I got up in the night and went out into the fields to make water, and I happened to see . . ."

It was a recognized gambit, and even the questions in cross examination were always the same to that particular statement.

"Was it a full moon?"

"What direction was he walking in?"

And so on. Mohammad Ishaq had been listening all his life to that kind of thing. And in this case it struck him as a little odd that a man coming into the village from the open country should wait till he was in a narrow lane for the purpose; but no one could say that he might not. No, on the whole, Mohammad Ishaq had seldom been more sure that a story was a lie; but it might go down in Court, and indeed he could see no reason why it should not. He resolved to make a few inquiries of his own near Anantpur, without mentioning them to Ghulam; and from headquarters he would send someone to test the story about the wolves; but nothing would come of it.

Aloud he said:

"Well, that's pretty conclusive. I'll arrange for a magistrate to record that statement tomorrow."

Back in Ramnagar, the Inspector wrote out a report for the Superintendent of Police.

He made a copy for the District Magistrate, but it so happened that the next day was a Sunday, and the report was not read by either the policeman or the magistrate till evening. When he had finished his report, the Inspector lay down on his bed and wondered how it was that Ghulam Husain had been able to induce this vital witness to give evidence against a leading landowner. Probably Ghulam knew something discreditable about him; but that was always inclined to cut both ways. If that discreditable something could be brought out by the other side in Court, his evidence would be damned. And they would be sure to find something, for one could be confident that the private affairs of such a man as Jhammu Nat would not bear looking into.

As a matter of fact, Jhammu's private affairs were already, quite independently, moving to a crisis.

Chapter Four

The Private Affairs of the Second Witness

·◇·

A FEW weeks before that morning when Pyari sat for the last time at her spinning, a woman whose fate was to touch hers, though they had never met, sat at her house door. She too was spinning and thinking of her husband. Her thoughts were as different from Pyari's as their upbringing had been and their houses. Phúlmati was a bania's daughter and she had been brought up all her life to know that she would be a bania's wife. It would be her duty to obey him and to worship him, and he would be her god upon earth. He had come, and the thought of him made her sick.

In her girl's dreams there had been none of the nobility of Pyari's. Her husband was to be no god but entirely a man of robust flesh and blood; she was made for love and she had always known it. She had always known that at all their arts she could beat the dancing girls, she with her pale skin, golden as wheat, silky soft, her swaying walk and her body that curved softly as though beneath an invisible caress. She wanted a man who would always be a lover, a master worthy of such a mistress. Very early in her life she had lain awake at night and thought of these things and longed for them, till her bed seemed on fire.

And they had married her at thirteen to an old man of forty. She thought of him with disgust, fat and greasy, with drooping gray mustache, and a great belly like a goatskin waterbag. He thought of nothing but money, and when he had grown so fat that he could no longer satisfy even himself—her he had never satisfied—he denied her even the outlet of pretty clothes and jewelry. Fat and ugly, shaven of head, gray of skin and yellow of eye and tooth—oh, he was unspeakably foul! And this she was supposed to worship. All day she must sit at home, cook for him and sew for him, and at night—she sickened at the thought of how he would come to her, putting on an assured and greasy affection that was worse than his daylong neglect.

She looked with distaste at everything she saw, because everything reminded her of that hateful presence. The brass pans of the household, with which she would have delighted to cook for a lover, the distaff and the needle—she hated them all. She hated the little brick house and the platform in front of it where in the evening her husband sat and talked to his relations—he had no friends—about the money he had made during the day, while the slow hooka bubbled and she looked after her pots by the fire. Even the fields before the house she hated, all that she saw stretching before her every day of her wearisome life.

The bania's house was a recent investment, built outside the village away from his shop, of fire-baked brick, which would resist the assaults of burglars very much better than the sun-baked mud of the villagers' huts. It was not very large, being only three or four small rooms with a veranda and a raised platform in front. It faced south, to the road and far away, the Ganges, its back to the village of Anantpur a mile away in the north-west and to the high snows in the distance. On the left was the village of Púrá Kalán, where her husband Mathura Dás had his shop, and to the right was a sugar-cane press where work was already beginning. As they finished cutting the cane with the heavy knives, that were almost axes, it was brought in by bullock carts to the press. Two bullocks were harnessed to a beam, which they slowly tugged round and round, treading in the narrow circular path beaten by their own innumerable revolutions. A man sat on the end of the beam, occasionally keeping them in motion by a poke with his stick, or a light hand on their tails, which he never needed actually to twist. In the center of the circle the beam was attached to the press, like a small steel mangle on its side; a boy fed the cane to it, three sticks at a time, but each about two feet ahead of the next, and there came out a steady stream of juice which ran into an underground receiver, and a steady ribbon of crushed pulp. All round the earth was strewn a yard deep with the pulp of the cane; it lay in the sun to dry, and would eventually provide fuel for the boiling process which turned the thin greenish juice to sticky brown molasses.

The air was always full of the pleasant scent of brown sugar, the murmurs of conversation and the creak of the beam.

Phulmati looked at the cane-press with distaste. All she would have liked if she had loved her husband, the household affairs, and the little house itself, and the road fifty yards away where the lorries roared by, was tasteless and insipid. There was only one pleasure in her life and of that she was afraid, for it was a disgrace to all she had been taught all her life; and ecstasy though it was in the moment of abandon, she could not see any happy end to it. It had first happened in spite of herself. She had never planned it, nor even thought of it until it happened. She had been sitting one day as she was now sitting, on the veranda in front of the house, for there were no other houses very close, and only the richest and highest caste Hindus observe Purdah with the strictness of Musulmans; suddenly a voice spoke softly by her side, a pleasantly caressing voice, and a tall man stood there, naked except for his loin-cloth, his lean muscles glistening in the sun, his teeth bright, and the hair lank on his shoulders, half hiding the necklace of scarlet jungle-berries. Before she knew he was there, he had slipped on to the veranda behind a pillar so that no casual passer could see him, and he had begun to talk. At first she had been too astonished to speak or even to understand him. Jhammu Nat had come silently, like a wild thing of the jungle. Then slowly she began to understand, as he told her how he had seen her go to draw water at the well and how the grace of her walk and a momentary glimpse of her face had bewitched him. Then he had watched and waited, and at last had seen his chance. None had seen him come. He spoke on, of her flower-like skin and her beauty, and the charm she had laid on him; for more than all he had hoped, he found the reality of what he had guessed.

He spoke on, and she listened in a mist of pleasure, without thought or fear; suddenly he stooped and kissed her arm, and when he rose, he said:

"Come inside!"

She followed like a sleep-walker, and before he left she knew the height of pleasure she had longed for all her life, the ecstasy of utter release. She turned to water when he spoke, and he could do with her what he willed.

But mad with desire for him though she always was, when he was away she was also frightened. She was denying at once her society and her race and her religion, for she could not forget that it was evil to sin against her husband with a man of her own caste, but doubly so with a Nat, an outcast from society, a wandering man of strange gods and a strange gypsy tongue. He was in everything the antithesis of her husband, straight and strong and lean, sudden and unaccountable in his ways, swift of body and thought. His skin was like silk upon steel, and she loved every inch of him, the rippling muscles of his back, the set of his loins, the iron strength of his thighs, the breadth of his shoulders.

Thinking of him now, on that morning before Pyari died, her belly moved within her; she closed her eyes with the intensity of her desire, and almost swooned with longing for him; for that moment she would not have heard if anyone had spoken to her; nothing but violence or the presence of her lover could have brought her back to herself. But no one came; nothing happened, and slowly, slowly she came back, as a fish glimmers slowly up from deep waters, first a something indiscernible, then a growing pallor, a gleam of light, and it is there.

She sighed and turned again to her spinning, and then to her surprise her husband came out.

"I'm going to the shop," he said. "I shall go through his accounts this morning. He won't expect me till the afternoon. I shall catch him out."

"How long will you be?" she asked.

"Two or three hours," he answered, and waddled off.

She watched him till he was hidden by a house, then ran quickly indoors and up by a ladder on to the roof. There was a pipal tree which, long before the house was built, had stood above a tiny platform with three red stones on it, and in the old days there had been a red flag on a tall pole to show the tree was holy. Since the house had been built, close to the tree for the sake of shade, the villagers had gradually let the little shrine fall into neglect, and one day the flag had blown down on to the roof of Mathura Das's house. No one had bothered to put it up again, and it still lay there, except when Phulmati chose. Today she fastened it in its old place as well as she could, slipped down, and went on with her work, her heart beating.

It was all the odds in the world he would not come, she knew, yet there was a chance; he might perhaps be out in the country that side of Anantpur and see her signal in time. She tried to keep her eyes on her work, and not to gaze and gaze for his coming, but at every sound she looked up, a whisper as a piece of old newspaper blew by in an eddy of dust, a sudden flutter among the crows about the horse-droppings ten yards away, the calf that trotted suddenly by towards the village. Slowly her excitement died in despair; he would not come; it was no use; and then suddenly he was by her side in his quick silent way, like a panther arriving on its kill.

She stood up.

"I thought you would never come," she breathed.

He smiled, and his fingers closed on hers, firm and tender in a caress; he led her into the house.

Mathura Das had waddled round the corner of the house nearly an hour before his wife melted into her lover's arms, and he had really meant to be gone for two or three hours. He spent a great deal of his time thinking of ways in which his shopkeeper might possibly cheat him, and devising means by which he could counter them. Last night he had suddenly thought of a most ingenious device for cheating himself, which depended on his following rigidly his usual habit of leaving his servant to himself all the forenoon and visiting the shop only in the early morning and the evening. Immediately, he convinced himself that this was actually happening, and was all impatience to put it right. If he had found what he expected it certainly would have taken him two or three hours to put things right, but he found nothing of the kind. Less than an hour was enough to show him that his servant was less ingenious than himself, and so he left his shop and waddled back to his wife.

As he reached the house he took off his shoes and stepped on to the platform. His bare feet made no sound on the baked mud, and there was nothing a listener could have heard but his heavy breathing. Heavy though this was, it did not disturb the lovers, deep in a timeless abyss. The old bania looked round for his wife; idling, he thought grimly. She was not at her cooking and her distaff was lying unused. He took a step towards the bedroom door and stopped.

The door was shut. Now that door had no fastening or handle or latch on the outside; it could only be fastened from the inside by a chain and staple, and unless it was fastened it would not stay shut. It was so hung that it always swung open, and Mathura Das knew that it was never fastened unless there was very good reason; and he could think of no good reason why his wife should fasten the door at this time of day. He listened at the door. Nothing. He looked carefully round the veranda. Nothing.

Mathura Das thought carefully for a minute or two. Then he went round to the back of the house, where there was a tiny window to the bedroom, about a foot square. Very quietly and slowly he approached it; but before he could see into the room he paused. Suppose—suppose—his wife was betraying him and there was someone with her there. His head would be very clear against the window. They would see him—and the man was sure to be some young lusty fellow, desperate and headstrong. As like as not, he would be violent; and Mathura Das was not used to violence. He did not want to be murdered. No, that was a fool's way.

He went round to the front of the house, as softly as he was able. He went back to that closed door and listened again. Yes, this time he could hear something. He could hear his wife's voice, some question she murmured languidly, vaguely. There was an answer, deeper, quieter, so quiet that not even the tone gave any indication of the meaning. But for Mathura Das it was enough. It was a man's voice. That was all he wanted to know. He went quietly out of the house and paused for a moment on the platform to consider what he should do.

A man to whom the thought of violence was a possibility would have felt very differently from Mathura Das. Almost any-one of the land-owning or cultivating classes would have felt hot anger surge up unmasterably in his throat, would have been driven to some ungoverned act. But for a bania it was different; for generation on generation his forbears had thought of gain and loss, of counting and entering and calculating, nothing else. They had never worked in the fields or marched to war, they had never seen the sea; they had never eaten meat or seen the violent death even of a hare. And there was no alien blood in the strain; on both sides, rupees, annas and pice ran in his veins. No sound but the chink of small change had ever called him to action.

This deep influence of heredity, the long preparation of centuries, lay on him so heavily that the shock of a moment could not change it. There is a proverb, "Even in falling, a bania's child will pick up a pice," and now when Mathura Das was falling, he turned to money as the weapon he would use, as instinctively as a man of fighting blood would have turned to force. And, as in all his use of money, he must first consider the problem in all its aspects, he must estimate the profit and loss. He was moved, not by mastering anger, but by a dull resentment, a feeling that he had been wronged and robbed, hurt in his deepest part, his sense of property.

First, he must find out who it was. There were only two ways out of the house, to the north and south, and from a patch of sugar cane to the west he could see both; but that was very near the sugar-cane press, and the men working there might see him hiding and laugh at him. Besides, when his enemy came out, he would turn away from the sugar-cane press, and it might be hard to recognize him from his back. If he stayed inside the house —no, it would be almost impossible to hide, and if he were caught, he might be murdered. And the man might leave by the back door to the north. To the east of the house lay the village, and between the village and the house there was no cane; the only cover was a field of cotton and pulse, whose tall stalks were planted in rows a yard apart. The leaves did not start growing till two or three feet above the ground, so that a man crouching down in the middle could see all round him, though he would be invisible to a passer-by unless he stood up.

Mathura Das would have preferred sugar cane, because it was thicker and safer, and the pulse was rather a long way from the house, but it seemed that he had no alternative. He waddled slowly to his hiding-place keeping a watchful eye over his shoulder.

He did not have to wait very long. Inside, the Nat gently slipped away from the hands that would have held him, and with a last caress looked down at that wealth of pale beauty sighing on the bed. She lay still, her eyes closed, drawing her breath deep and slow, and a tear ran down her face, but whether for happiness that had been or for sorrow at parting, he did not know. He opened a few· inches the door to the bedroom which faced north, and was at once outside in the young wheat that came within a few feet of the house.

Even at that distance he was unmistakable to the old man crouched in the field of pulse. The tall naked figure and the scarlet jungle-berries marked a Nat, and no one else. It was a second blow, almost as heavy as the first. An outcast, a gypsy. His wife sleeping with a man whose touch was pollution. He was unclean himself, and his wife must be destroyed like an infected rag, she and her lover together.

Even the pain of this double loss of property and position disappeared the next moment in fright, for the tall figure of the gypsy began to move towards the very patch of pulse in which he was sitting. The bania counted himself as good as dead if he were found, for there could then be no doubt that he knew of his wife's infidelity, and the lovers would strike first at him to save themselves. And he did not believe he could escape the notice of a jungle man in any cover so scanty. Gray and shaking with fear, the old man squatted on the ground, paralyzed, incapable of conscious speech or thought.

"Rám, Rám, Sita, Rám," he muttered, "Ram, Ram, Sita, Ram," calling again and again on the divine lovers who prevailed over Ráwan.

To the gypsy, however, the use of cover was instinctive, and he was not looking for spies. He was keeping the house between himself and the sugar-cane press, and he did not mean to go through the pulse, which would hardly have helped him. He skirted it, and went on towards the village, where he had affairs to which he could attend openly, using the pulse again as a screen between himself and the men at the press. The village was at this time of day practically deserted.

So Mathura Das escaped, and he knew now not only the caste but the name of his enemy, for he had seen at close quarters a man he had long known by sight. He did not at once go back to his house. In the first place, it took him some time to get over his fear; he was shaking and gray for another ten minutes, and he did not want to explain to his wife; and, in the second place, he had a great deal to think about.

Jhammu Nat, the leader of the band who used to camp at Anantpur. Jhammu Nat. He had indeed been lucky, for such a man would not have paused a moment to take the life of a bania. He was probably a dacoit and had murdered scores. Mathura Das trembled again. Then he pulled himself together and began to think as hard as he could. Jhammu Nat. What was there about him? He was on very good terms with the police, which was very unusual for a wandering gypsy. In fact, he never seemed to have been in trouble with them at all. That must mean he gave the Sub-Inspector a regular income. There could be no other explanation. But where did he get the money from? Hunting hares and catching mud-turtles, doing tricks with poles and bears and monkeys by the roadside where the buses stopped; that was all his means of livelihood as far as anyone could see. He might get a living that way, but he couldn't get money, and money he would need, to pay the police. And he always had money to spend; it was well known that he had money and would spend it, and he would buy expensive Government spirit from the grog-shop and ornaments for his women. Where did that money come from? And why should he pay the police? If he did nothing more than he seemed to do, they could only bother him, they couldn't do anything very serious. Wouldn't it be worth putting up with irritation, and dodging the police when need be, rather than paying them good money, unless there was something bigger behind? Say he was really a big dacoit. Say he used to go off into Mallapur, the Indian State, or perhaps the next district, hold up people on the roadside, or surround an isolated house and loot it; and then slip back again to Ramnagar? Then it would pay him to give the police something, ostensibly so that they wouldn't pry into his carelessness about other people's hens and goats and little lapses of that kind, so that his movements wouldn't be carefully watched and he could get away with his bigger schemes. Or perhaps he was running cocaine. Yes, it must be something like that.

Mathura Das went back to his house. He would have to be natural to his wife, or they would guess he knew and would kill him. But he would not touch her. He would have to eat food she had cooked, though, and he would have to tell the Brahmans that when it was all over, and it would cost a great deal to be made clean again. He sighed. But it was all so bad it couldn't be much worse, and even the thought of what it would cost did not really hurt him very much. He must think how it was to be done. Bribery. He might get one of Jhammu's followers to tell him. They wouldn't talk though. Not even money would move them. All these gypsies would stick together. No, he must get someone to ferret it out for him, to follow and watch and talk.

But who could it be? Another Nat would never tell; a man who wasn't a Nat would never find out. An ordinary villager could never go with them in their wanderings about the country. It was most difficult. Suddenly, a thought came to him. He savored it, elaborated it, tried it again; yes, that would do, if he wasn't betrayed. He would go to Kallu, in the next village, a sweeper, lowest and dirtiest of the village castes—the removers of night-soil, the sewage-workers, who will eat anything, on whom even a Nat looks down. Kallu was known for miles around as a bad character. "Kallu Badmash," he was called, as one spoke of Jhukki Dhobi, the washerman, or Ram Parshad, Bania. An occasional small burglary was the worst he ever did, and though he was never caught the police pulled him in from time to time when the list of crimes against his name was getting too big, and he would go to prison for a year because everyone knew he was a burglar, though no one could prove it. Then he would come out for two years or so, and back he would go. Yes, Kallu it should be. Kallu should go to Jhammu and say that he was getting very unpopular in his village, and he would like a change; he would like to give his reputation a rest and come with the Nats for a short time as their servant in return for his food.

It was a good idea, for Kallu would do anything for money, and the Nats would be so flattered at the idea of having a servant that they would never refuse. The only danger was that Kallu might tell the Nats he was being paid by Mathura Das; but he would not do that if he were paid enough, and in small installments. And unless they caught him spying they would have no reason for pressing him to tell. It was possible, of course, that Kallu might not find anything out, for he was not very clever; but even an account of Jhammu's movements would give Mathura Das an idea of what he was looking for. Once he had it—ah, then he would squeeze! And he would never let go. If he could get him a long sentence—failing hanging—he would be ready for him again when he came out. And he should never know who was the enemy who had destroyed him.

Yes, he would go to Kallu. That afternoon he set out, thinking it would be safe to leave the shop alone after his surprise visit that morning. The difficulty would be to get in touch with Kallu without setting the village talking, for if once it were known that they had met, there would be an end of the whole affair. He could not go to Kallu; but he could go to the bania in Kallu's village and ask him to send for Kallu. That was the way to do it. It would excite no remark, because Kallu was sure to owe the bania something, and once he was in the house it could all be arranged.

Arranged it was, and two days later Kallu was in the Nat's camp. At least, Mathura Das was told he had gone there to make his suggestion, and he did not come back, so it was to be presumed he had been accepted and was staying with them. Mathura Das waited. He was used to waiting.

It was a few weeks later, on the night of February 11th, the fifth day after the death of Pyari, and the day before Jhammu was to give his evidence to the Inspector, that Kallu came under cover of darkness to Mathura Das's house. The bania took him away into the fields, fifty yards from the house and a long way from either sugar cane or pulse. There Kallu told what he knew, and he was paid what he had earned.

Mathura Das's eye brightened. He knew what he had wanted to know. This was not luck, but the result of careful thought, patient waiting, and the outlay of gold. But next day in the afternoon he had a stroke of luck.

Chapter Five

Exit the Second Witness

• ✧ •

FEBRUARY the 12th, the sixth day after Pyaran's death, and the next day after Mathura Das had found out how the Nat earned his money, and a Sunday, although Mohammad Ishaq would not be allowed to treat it as a day of rest. Christopher Tregard was getting up at four in the morning to go pig-sticking.

Horrid, getting up in the dark, he thought. Wish I'd gone to bed early instead of dining with the gunners. One or two gins too many? Well, perhaps, but after all, he wouldn't be young for long, and it had been fun; and a few miles in the car would soon put him right. Thank God the meet was fairly close, only about twenty miles up the Mallapur road; and then—where was it?—oh, yes, Sultanpur, about seven miles off the road on village tracks. You turned off the road at Puran Kalan, quite close to Anantpur, where they'd had the murder, if it was a murder.

Khaki shirt, breeches, sweaters next; still too cold to paddle about in a shirt; very different, this, from the regular season in May, when the sweat runs off your elbows even at four in the morning with the effort of pulling on a shirt! Boots; that's better.. Feeling a little more human now I'm dressed. Nice clumping noise boots make on the floor. Once I've swallowed my scrambled eggs and tea—tea, that's the stuff—I shall get rid of this feeling like a yawn at the pit of the stomach. Odd, but getting up in the dark always makes you feel like that.

He finished his breakfast, lighted a pipe, and felt better still. Twenty-five minutes to five. Damn Charles for being late. I might have had another five minutes in bed. Hare-brained young ass at present, Charles, but a nice lad. Really rather stupid to trust yourself to that awful old car of his, but it generally arrived.

"Charles, you're late. Morning, Peter."

"Oh, no, not late. Not really late."

"Yes, you are, seven whole minutes."

"Well, that's in time for me, seven minutes late."

"I might have been in bed for those seven minutes, and they'd have made a difference of about a year to my life. You'll be sorry for that some day, Charles. All right, all aboard. Don't need anyone to push, do you? Well, don't talk to me, anyone, I'm going to sleep."

"You're not," said Charles. "You've got to tell me the way."

"Twentieth milestone on the Mallapur road. Don't speak to me again till then."

"I don't know the Mallapur road."

"Then you damn well ought to."

The old Ford rattled gallantly along over a road pitted with holes. Long lines of trees on either side and the lights made an arch of velvety green foliage that fled away before them in the dark, like the proscenium of an old-fashioned pantomime. A ribbon of silver in the east, a widening clarity; tiny clouds, small and naked as new-born babies, startling puffs of frozen steam, caught the light on their lower edges. The sky above put on color, turned slowly through the dark velvet of night in the west, and the delicate steel blue of the meridian, soft as a pigeon's breast, to the brightness and freshness of the east. Palest primrose against the dark purple of earth and trees, a growing line of light melted through misty silver to egg-shell blue; then rose-pink flushed the baby clouds, and suddenly he was there, springing from the plain as he springs from the sea, strong and full of life for the day, the golden sun in molten glory.

They turned aside at Puran Kalan and for a mile ran on a narrow road of earth which consisted of three deep ruts, one made by each wheel of the bullock-cart and one by the bullocks walking in the middle. As the wheels of the car were as wide apart as those of the bullock-cart's, they ran very comfortably along the ruts until they became too deep, when the axles caught on the earth between the ruts and the car stuck. To prevent this, they had from time to time to make detours over open plowland. Fortunately, there were no hedges, and the low banks between the fields could usually be negotiated; the Ford was used to this kind of journey and one almost expected it to change feet on top of the banks like an Irish hunter. Irrigation channels were the worst obstacle, but obstinacy, recklessness and gross misuse of metal triumphed, and they reached a village where they horrified the cattle tied by the side of the road and excited the children for the rest of the day. For the next stretch the road was much wider and the ruts not so deep, and where there was any grass to bind the soil it was possible to drive in something like comfort. The difficulty here, though, was sand, and where sand lay thick even the Ford had to go down to bottom gear. From the second village onwards, they found a road of the first type, narrow and deep, but with the added embarrassment of high hedges of briars which tore at the hood of the car and made it impossible to turn aside when the ruts were too deep. There was nothing to do but to get out and dig—if Charles had remembered to bring the spade.

It was a journey that would have surprised an English motorist, but to these young men it was a commonplace, and by six they were at the meet. This was held in a big grove of mangoes, where the horses had spent the night. First horses were saddled and ready, and there was nothing to do but to choose a spear from the cluster leaned up against a tree, and mount.

By a quarter past six they were on the line. Sixty coolies were drawn out over three hundred yards of country, with a red flag at either end to show the direction and to help to keep them straight, for his neighbors were often invisible in the thick grass to a coolie in the line. There were eight spears out that morning and Christopher found himself in the right-hand heat with Charles and Peter, the two gunner subalterns who had brought him out, and their captain, a wily and experienced hunter, on his famous chestnut, an old Waler of undiminished courage and surpassing handiness. With the four spears on the left, and any pig put up by the left of the line, they were not concerned.

The country was thick grass, in places higher than a mounted man's head, but as a rule up to his horse's belly. Here and there were patches of cultivation and here and there patches of ground too sandy even for grass, where nothing grew but the feathery tamarisk. It was not going to be easy country to ride, unless they could get their pig out into the open ground away to the right.

For half an hour they moved slowly forward without incident, the lead-weighted butt of the spear jogging on the toe, horses— except Charles's excitable country-bred—walking quietly behind the line. Suddenly there was a scurry underfoot, yells from the beaters, a flicker like a boat's wake in the grass; something had gone forward. Charles went forward too, lickety-split, his long-limbed country-bred flying tufts of grass as though they were jumps at Olympia.

"Squeaker," said the gunner Captain. "Too small. Don't go."

Ten minutes later Charles came back covered with lather.

"Squeaker," he said.

A sow went back through the line but they got a glimpse of her and this time stopped Charles before he got away. A little later the left-hand heat started a good hunt, but lost their pig in the end. When it was nearly eight there was a "Hrrmph! Hrrmph! Hrrmph!" in the grass and the coolies scattered, yelling. A big boar this time, there could be no doubt. The Captain and Charles were close behind the place where he had started, Peter and Christopher further away to the right. All four galloped, converging on the pig's wake. He was going fast, faster than the horses, and it was difficult to follow the ripple in the grass which was all of him that showed. He would probably have got away if he had gone straight on, but coming to a wide sandy river-bed that cut across his course half-right, he decided to avoid that hundred yards in the open and swung right. The Captain saw him turn, and his Australian followed, handy as a cat, so that both were racing parallel with the dry bed of the stream, horse and man thirty yards behind the pig. As he turned he yelled and waved, so that Peter and Christopher, further to the right and so closer to the new line, were able to join him in the classic V-formation, one a little behind on either side. Charles said afterwards he hadn't seen the signal, but everyone believed his real trouble was that he couldn't control his horse. Whatever the reason, he went straight on, and a ten-foot drop into loose sand at full gallop put him out of that hunt.

They had ridden about three hundred yards, and the pig's first burst of speed was beginning to slacken. He could no longer beat a horse in a straight run. He jinked again, sharp to his right, putting Christopher into the lead. The Captain pulled up a little to let Peter swing across his front to keep in place on Christopher's left, while he took the right. They were closing in now, and the pig was barely ten yards from Christopher, going through more open country, sandy, with patches of tamarisk. There was no ripple in the grass to show his track, but they could see him from time to time and knew he was a big one. He jinked again, sharp left, but Peter had room to turn and was left closer to him than Christopher had been. Now they were running parallel to the river-bed again, though further off than before, until a bend in its course brought them suddenly on top of it. This time the pig did not hesitate; he went straight down the bank and across the open. Christopher and the Captain, right and left and a little behind, saw Peter vanish and heard a yell. They had time to take the bank with some care, and saw Peter picking himself up, and his horse still struggling in the sand. They had lost a little, but were only twenty yards behind, and just here there was a hundred and fifty yards of open country. The Captain saw his chance, a tired pig and a clear run; he clapped in his heels and rode like stink. Christopher, too, rode all he knew, but he was not so well mounted, and it was the Captain who caught the boar a few yards from the opposite bank. He had not time to get level and drive in a killing spear to the shoulder. The best he could hope for was a spear in the ham, but he reasoned that this was an old pig, as ready to fight as to run, and that at the first prick of the spear he would turn and fight, before that ten-foot bank that might save him.

He came up in a storm of dust and sweat, low in his saddle with his spear-head down, and took his pig as he had meant to, as though it were a tent-peg. He had reasoned right; the old boar had run as far as he liked, and this time he swung not away from the horse, but towards him with a wicked grunt. It was lucky the Captain's spear had been a light one, for if it had stayed in it would have been dragged across his horse's forelegs. As it was, the chestnut jumped clean over the pig, and just managed to swing right to avoid the bank. The pig pulled up, turned on his hocks like a polo pony, and for a few seconds was actually chasing the Captain on the chestnut, who was riding parallel to the bank, trying to pull up and get back at him. Christopher joined the party at this stage, bent on getting a second spear, but keeping half an eye on the bank and another on the chestnut, for there was every danger of a bad mix-up. He managed to swing in behind the pig to ride parallel with the bank, but in doing it he failed to get in a good spear. He got the pig a glancing blow in the ribs, on the off-side, before he swung, but it was only a flesh wound.

By this time, the chestnut had turned. Christopher and the Captain were for a second riding straight towards each other, with the pig between them, each in a position to spear, but with the probability of a fall for one of them over the jinking pig. The Captain wisely swung off, leaving Christopher to deliver the first serious spear behind the shoulder. Blind with rage, the pig went straight on at the chestnut; the Captain managed to save his forelegs with his spear, but it was only a glancing cut on the pig's off-shoulder which turned him on to the horse's off-side, and he sprang up at the man, his tusks ripping his boot from ankle to knee.

By this time, Peter was mounted again and was coming up fast. The pig went straight at him. What exactly happened no one know; but it seemed that Peter's spear took him full in the chest and stuck. Horse and man were down again in a complicated tangle of legs and dust, and the pig carried the spear a few yards before it fell out.

It was here that the Captain showed genius. In twenty seconds the boar would have gone back and ripped to ribbons the horse and man on the ground, but with a lightning alliance of brain and muscle, the chestnut swept by them, and his rider drove in a second heavy spear as the boar was almost stationary in the act of turning.

It was the end. He uttered a last snort of defiance that changed to a groan, reared on his hind legs as though he were reaching up into the air for breath, a grand figure of courage and endurance, and collapsed. It was four minutes since they had found him, and less than a minute since the first spear.

Neither Charles nor his horse were hurt. Peter was shaken and bruised by his fall, and his horse's forelegs cut by the boar's tusks. The Captain's boot was cut almost in two, and there was a long scratch in his calf. None of them had breath to speak for a few minutes, and then they joined in praise of the boar and of their horses.

The right-hand heat killed once again that morning, and the left-hand once, but there was nothing else so exciting as the first boar. They hunted four pig which they lost. They stopped at twelve midday, after six hours in the saddle, and ate a large meal in the mango-grove.

There was really no more country to hunt, and after lunch the cars started one by one for home. Charles, Peter and Christopher were the last. They started from the grove at just about the time when Mohammad Ishaq got back to Ramnagar and began to write his report on the evidence of Jhammu Nat. At first they found that the last car had left a trail of dust hanging in the air, and it was not only unpleasant but difficult to drive on; accordingly they waited four or five minutes till the dust had settled. When the first cars were well out of sight and hearing, they moved on again, and they reached the first village without any misfortune. All the worst places in the road had already been smoothed by spades on the way out. But when they had passed the first village by about two furlongs, there was a long sigh and the Ford seemed to stumble. They stopped and got out.

"Front tire. Look, it's a clean cut," said Peter. "Bullock shoe in the sand, I expect."

"Yes, there's no doing anything with that. Charles, you are an ass to have tires like that," said Christopher.

"Never mind," said Charles. "I did remember to put the spare wheel in. It's in the back. It won't stay on its proper place. And there is a jack. I call it a rather remarkable instance of foresight and organization to have both a jack and a spare wheel on the same car. And you, Christopher, shall pay for mocking me by pumping it up. It'll be the first time for a long time you'll have done any honest work and I should like to see an important Government official pumping up a tire."

It seemed to take a good deal of pumping, but it was done at last. They packed up jacks and spanners, and Charles climbed back into his seat.

"Charles," said Christopher, "just get out and have a look at that tire, will you?"

It was half down again already.

"Peter," said Christopher, "you haven't done your duty by Charles. You haven't kicked him nearly enough."

"You couldn't," said Peter.

"Charles, you will carry that wheel to Puran Kalan and get it mended and bring it back. It's about five miles each way. You will leave Peter and me your cigarettes. You won't want to waste your breath smoking and we shall have a long time to wait."

"Oh, no. I'll sit at the wheel with the engine running. You'll pump the tire up as hard as it'll go, yell, and jump on the running board, and I'll go as far as I can. Then you jump out and do it again. You and Peter can take turns. I expect I shall get about a hundred yards each time."

"We'll adopt that plan with a slight modification. There'll be no taking turns. It will always be Charles that pumps. I'll drive, and Peter will apply persuasion if you seem to be tiring."

"Carried," said Peter.

They found that about a quarter of a mile was as far as the tire would take them. Charles pumped it up nineteen times, and they were all glad when they reached Puran Kalan and found someone who could mend the tube.

As they stood, hot, thirsty and tired, an ingratiating voice said: "Presence! Feeder of the Poor."

Christopher looked down. A particularly bania-like bania was rubbing his hands together, bowing and smiling, by his side.

"Come away," said Peter, "he has designs on your virtue."

Christopher said: "What is it, Lalaji?"

"Presence, will you honor me by resting at my house? Not here at my shop, but outside the village, where the air is clean and fresh. I have a house there, and you will come and drink some tea and take some rest. Only a little way, Sahib, less than a furlong. Please do me this honor."

Tea! They all brightened at the thought. Watery it would be, of course, with tea dust floating on the top, but at any rate liquid which it would be safe to drink.

"Thank you very much, Lalaji. We'd like to. What is your name, Lalaji?"

"Lala Mathura Das, Presence."

"Do you own any land?"

"No, Sahib, no land. I am a very poor man, Sahib. Only one little shop."

"I see. Well, it's very kind of you."

They reached the house, perhaps a hundred yards from where the dirty bazaar of the village lay on both sides of the main road. A woman was sitting in the veranda in front of the house, and as they approached she rose and went into the house, but, to Christopher's surprise, as she stepped into the door she paused for a moment, looking back over her shoulder, and let the sari fall to show her face.

"Odd," thought Christopher. "Pretty, too. She must be a bad lot."

Mathura Das found them chairs in the shade and went indoors to give orders about the tea. He came back almost at once, and came to Christopher with his hands joined as if in prayer.

"Sahib, Presence," he said, "another favor, will you do me another favor?"

"What is it?"

"Sahib, five minutes alone, to speak of a most important matter, please, Sahib, just five minutes. It is most important."

"Can't you tell me with these Sahibs here?"

"Presence, it is most important, most secret."

Peter said: "I told you he had designs on your honor."

Christopher laughed and went with him a little way from the house, to an open field with no cover near it.

"Jhammu Nat?" asked Christopher when he finished; "and to-night?"

"Yes, Sahib, tonight; he will come by the Rohilla Gate, between six and seven."

"And why do you tell me about it?"

"Presence, it was my duty to the kind Government."

"No doubt." Christopher remembered the pretty face and wondered.

"And what would you have done if I had not come to Puran Kalan this afternoon?"

"I was going to come to Ramnagar by the next bus and find you, Sahib. I was leaving my shop to do it."

"I see. Well, I doubt if you'd have found me. All right, Lalaji; thank you. I will see if your information is reliable."

"Presence, I swear by the skull of my father, it is as I was told it. If I have been tricked it is not my fault. But I believe it is true."

"All right. We'll see."

They walked back to the house, and when the tea was finished and their thanks paid, they went back to the village. The car was ready.

"Do you mind taking me to a police station, Charles?" Christopher said.

"Want to give yourself up for the way you treated me after lunch? I'll be charmed."

"No. Big stuff, Charles. The black hand. I may even commandeer your car to carry out an arrest."

Charles's eye brightened.

"Do," he said. "Commandeer it and smash it and pay me enormous compensation, will you? Three thousand rupees this car's worth. You're my witness, Peter, that I told him so before it was smashed."

"Thirty would be generous. But, seriously, Charles, I would be grateful if you'd help. We shan't have much time to spare, and there won't be a police lorry at the station I'm going to."

They had all three been up at four, had ridden six hours in the sun, and had a very tiring afternoon, but Charles, who was full of romance, was delighted at the idea of helping the police. They needed his car, for by the time that they got to the Rohilla Gate police station it was nearly six. Fortunately Salamatullah was at the station in plain clothes, and he was able to provide two constables, also in plain clothes, almost at once. The constables stood on the running board and Salamatullah sat behind with Peter.

The Rohilla Gate itself was a huge arch that bridged the road. The city walls of which it had formed a part were now almost entirely destroyed, and the gate was useless, and not particularly beautiful, but was maintained as a historical monument. Outside the gate there was a petrol pump and a place where lorries stood. Salamat found the proprietor of the pump and the man who took rent from the lorries for standing on his ground and took them with him as independent witnesses, while Charles backed in the Ford among the lorries, where its dilapidation was indistinguishable from theirs. The little group waited between the lorry stand and the gate, the three Englishmen, two Indian witnesses, and the Sub-Inspector drawn back a little from the road. The two constables sat right on the edge of the road on the opposite side, one opposite his officer, the other a hundred feet further from Ramnagar in case of a sudden retreat.

They waited nearly half an hour. Then the constable opposite stood up and began to adjust his turban, as a picturesque group of Nats came down the road, a tall man in front, naked except for his long hair, his loin-cloth and a necklet of scarlet berries. He was leading a big black bear that shuffled along in the dust, panting, his long tongue hanging out and his huge mop of hair shaking with every step.

Christopher stepped forward.

"Jhammu Nat?" he asked.

"Yes, Sahib."

"I am afraid we must search you. Please notice that these gentlemen search the police first to make sure they have nothing on them."

The owners of the petrol pump and the lorry-stand nervously patted Salamatullah and the two constables over the pockets and noted that they had nothing except a few rupees, some sealing-wax, a notebook, a pencil and some keys.

It was not very difficult to search Jhammu and Salamat was soon convinced there was nothing to be found on his person. He looked at Christopher.

"And now search the bear, please," said Christopher gently.

Jhammu was already protesting vigorously and calling everyone to witness his humiliation. At this he redoubled his protests and the constable began to find difficulty in keeping back the growing crowd. Salamatullah looked doubtfully at the bear.

"All right," said Christopher, "I'll help you."

He knew that an Indian who may be recklessly brave in other ways is often terrified of a dog, and a bear was obviously worse. He stepped up to the bear and Salamatullah with an effort came with him. Christopher cautiously buried his hands in the thick hair round the bear's neck.

"Hold the rope, will you, please, Charles?" he asked.

Just at that moment Jhammu shouted something in the Nat gibberish to his followers, and a command to the bear. The bear with a grunt reared up on its hind legs. Salamatullah and Christopher sprang back in horror, and the Nat dived among the legs of the crowd. Everyone was trying to get away from the bear, and the two constables, with Christopher and Salamat behind, were in a hopeless position. They were the rearguard of a panic-stricken crowd, and the more they pushed the worse things became. Jhammu, by his sudden action in going on hands and knees among the crowd's legs, had got ahead of the panic; they never stood a chance of catching him.

The only piece of good fortune was that the bear was incurably docile. It stood up as it had been taught, but it stood perfectly still and dropped again on all fours when it perceived that no one was urging it to do anything else. Charles had continued to hold manfully to the end of the rope, and when Christopher saw that the chase was useless, he called the witnesses again and resumed his search of the bear. There was nearly two pounds' weight of cocaine hidden in the long hair round the beast's neck.

When Salamat came back with his constables, confessing that they had lost the trail entirely and could find no one who had seen the Nat, he was cheered to find the cocaine. It was the biggest recovery of cocaine that had been made in the Northern Provinces for years; to find an ounce is usually thought a great stroke. But he was full of reproaches that he had not handcuffed Jhammu at once.

"You couldn't, with me here," Christopher told him with a smile. "We'd got nothing against him till we found the stuff. I shall tell the Superintendent the credit of the recovery was largely yours."

Salamat's face assumed a look of panic.

"But, sir, it was nothing to do with me."

"It was, indeed. If you hadn't told me about the missing link in the chain, how you were still looking for the way they brought in the stuff from Mallapur to Ramnagar, I should never have believed what the bania told me."

"But I ought not to have talked about it to you, sir, for I haven't told the S.P. I have spoken to the Kotwal, but no more."

"I see," said Christopher. "All right, I'll say nothing about it, if you'd rather I didn't."

"Much rather, sir, much rather."

"All right. I'll explain that I went straight to the nearest station and just had time to get you here without telling the Kotwal and the S.P. I'll explain that that was only due to the shortness of time."

"Thank you very much, sir."

"You'll take charge of the stuff in the usual way. Seal it in my presence, will you? And have it sent to the Chemical Examiner, as usual, in case we catch him and can bring him to trial."

"I will, sir. But we shall never see him again."

"I'm afraid not. Still, we'd better take the precaution. And by the way, let me know if the retail price goes up in Ramnagar, will you? I'd like to know if this is the main stream we've dammed."

"It must be. This is a very large quantity, sir. An unheard-of quantity."

"Yes, Jhammu must have been making a very good thing of it. I wonder why the bania was interested, and how he came to find out. I suppose we shall never know."

When the cocaine had been sealed up, Christopher went home, tired out, his mind running on whisky and soda.

There was a large envelope waiting for him, marked "Secret and Immediate." It contained Mohammad Ishaq's résumé of Jhammu's evidence about Gopal Singh.

Christopher whistled.

"Now did Ghulam Husain, the Sub-Inspector, know about the

cocaine, and use that to make Jhammu give that evidence? Or did Kalyan Singh find out about the evidence and get the bania to tell me about the cocaine? It's a puzzling life. Anyhow, that evidence is no use. It'll never come into Court."

He poured out a second whisky and soda, and began to read *The Irish R.M.*

Chapter Six

The Third Witness Appears

• ✧ •

IT was on February 13th, the seventh day after the death of Pyari, that the statement of the nurse Jeharan, who had seen her death, arrived in Ramnagar. Jeharan had first gone to the police station and made a bald report to a police-sergeant, whose general education had never gone very much further than reading and writing. It was the gist of this report that had been telephoned to the Superintendent of Police of Ramnagar, and up till now details of the story had been lacking. Now came a copy of a long statement made to a magistrate upon oath, prompted by intelligent questioning.

Christopher Tregard was most interested. On this statement the whole case would depend, for, now that Jhammu had vanished, without Jeharan there was really nothing against Gopal that could be taken to Court. He read it with the greatest care.

Jeharan said that after Pyari's marriage she had remained at Anantpur continuously, except that she was occasionally allowed to go back to Galthana for a short visit to Sahib Singh's family. She had been on such a visit early in January, and had come back to find that Gopal Singh was carrying on intrigues with other women even more shamelessly than before, and that his relations with Pyari were growing steadily worse and worse. Her account of the quarrel on February 6th was very similar to Gopal's, except that she said that the kurtas were not for himself, but for one of his mistresses. Pyari, she said, had been very angry, and they had both forgotten that Jeharan was in the room. The quarrel grew more and more bitter, and at last Pyari used these words:

"If you were a man, you would have shot me for the things I've said to you. Why don't you shoot me and show that you're a Thakur? I wouldn't run away because I really am the daughter of Thakurs. Show that you're your father's son, and shoot me."

Christopher laid down the paper in astonishment. The resem-

115

blance between this and Gopal's confession was so close that the actual words used must have been almost these, and yet, and yet— he was not yet ready to believe Jeharan had been there, but if she had not, how did she know so much? He remembered that Hukm Singh had warned them that "something would come from the other side." Well, it had come with a vengeance. He shook his head, and began to read again.

Infuriated by these taunts at his ancestry and his manhood, Gopal Singh had gone inside the bedroom and come out with his shot-gun, into which as he came he thrust a cartridge.

"That's right," Pyari had screamed. "If you're a man and a Thakur you'll shoot me." He had raised the gun and fired at her body at about three or four yards' range. She fell, and when they ran to pick her up they found three wounds, one in the stomach below the navel, one in the left breast and one in the left eye.

Again Christopher put down the paper. Three wounds, two feet apart, at about three or four yards' range! It was incredible with anything but a blunderbuss, and this was a beautiful gun by a famous English firm. He thought about this for some time but could get no further. It did not make sense either way, whichever story was true. He read on.

She lived for about half an hour, during which she only spoke once to ask for a drink. When Pyari died, Gopal Singh and Kalyan Singh took Jeharan by the arms and led her to Nannhe Singh's house, where she was shut up in a small room, padlocked. There she stayed for the whole of the next two days, February 7th and 8th. She was given food and water, but had no chance of escape until the morning of the 9th, when very early, before dawn, she asked if she might go out into the fields to relieve herself. For the first time she was allowed to go without a guard; they were getting careless. As soon as she found herself in the fields, she made for the railway. She knew where it lay, because she had often heard the trains at night from Anantpur. It was only a little way off, and when she reached it, she turned south-east along the line to Ramnagar. She did not try to find the road, partly because she had always come by train, and partly because she was afraid that when they missed her the Thakurs would look for her on the road.

All that day she walked along the line, eighteen miles, to Ramnagar station. She turned aside only once, to buy a handful of dried peas. They cost her two annas, and as she had started with ten annas she had only eight annas left when she reached Ramnagar. The peas she had bought from a man who sat on the bridge where the road crossed the river, about a hundred yards from the line, and about twelve miles from Ramnagar.

Arrived at Ramnagar, she had been overcome by the realization that her great effort had really brought her no nearer home. She had only eight annas, and it was sixty miles to Shahabad and ten more to Galthana. She sat on a bench and sobbed.

As she sat crying a man came up and spoke to her kindly, asking what was the matter. She said she had seen her mistress shot and had been locked up three days by the murderers; now she had escaped, and had walked all day, but she had no money to get home.

"Hush," he said. "Don't talk so loud. Where is your home?"

She told him, and he said he lived at Shahabad and knew Sahib Singh by reputation. He asked her caste, and when she told him she was a Brahmani he said that he was a Brahman, and he decided that he would help her. He told her not to speak to anyone else about what had happened, and said that he would take her to Shahabad, where she should spend the night with him and his wife; he would send her out to Galthana in a bus and trust Sahib Singh to pay him back.

All this he had done, and next morning he had seen her to the bus and told the driver who she was, and that Sahib Singh would pay him for taking her. She had reached Galthana at about eight in the morning, and as soon as she had told the Thakurani what had happened she had been sent off to the police station to make a report.

Christopher laid down the papers and thought again. There are three checks on her story, he thought, the man who sold her the peas, the Brahman at the station and the lorry-driver. The last two came from Shahabad; they had probably been made secure already by the Galthana party. The man with the peas

was more doubtful. There would be a race for him between
Ghulam Husain and the Anantpur Thakurs. But apart from the
checks—and one couldn't really rely much on them, in a case
where so much was involved as this, for they would all have
been got at—there were some queer things in the story itself.
Why lock her up for three days and then let her walk out by
herself? Still, that was possible; no degree of carelessness is ever
incredible. But it was a great feat, for a woman who'd lived all
her life shut up in the women's quarters to walk twenty miles,
all the way to the station, through the maze of shunting lines and
side-tracks and timber-yards as she came into the city. And very
odd that the first man she'd met at the station was her own caste,
and knew Sahib Singh. But the whole thing was odd.

Mohammad Ishaq, the Inspector of Police, came in to see him.
The police were already trying to get hold of the three men
who could check the story of Jeharan's escape. There would be
no difficulty about the two from Shahabad, no difficulty at all,
for Sahib Singh had been able to supply their names at once.
They were Prem Badri Nath and Dost Mohammed. It seemed
likely that they would come into Court, too, for it would be
difficult for the Anantpur people to bring much pressure to bear
on people from Sháhábád. The man on the bridge who sold grain
was more difficult. There had been such a man there at the time,
but he did not belong to the district, and he had only been there
for a few months. He was a hillman, and no one knew exactly
where he had come from nor where he had gone. They knew
his name, though, Chabeli Parshad, and they would find him in
time, but of course he might not remember Jeharan.

"I suppose that will depend on who finds him first," said
Christopher.

The Inspector permitted himself to smile.

"Perhaps," he said. "Only God knows."

The Inspector rose to go.

"I will let you have reports on all three witnesses as soon as I
can get them," he said.

Chapter Seven

The Private Affairs of the
Third Witness

·◇·

HIGH up on the hillside, a thousand feet above the little shop where he lived, Chabeli Parshad sighed and sat down to rest and to let his goats feed. He was on a southern slope, looking away from the snows of the main range, and he was just high enough to see over the next ridge to where through a distant gap the plains showed in a sea of blue mist, laced by the silver snake of the Ganges, winding on the first stage of its pilgrimage to the sea. The ridge before him sprawled in broken-limbed abandon for fifteen miles, running down from an eight thousand foot knob to the main valley away to the west. It was precipitous on the northern face, with cliffs of sheer rock between slopes two thousand feet long, where the pines grew so steeply with the ground that you could almost have stepped from their tops to the hillside. The wide valley below him wound away out of sight to the west, and beyond it the foothills rose again, in line upon scalloped line. Their contours were broken and uneven, with none of the smooth lines of English downland, but their irregularities repeated themselves in the five ranges that were visible, establishing a kind of rhythm, both by their form and by their gradation in color from the variegated green and gray of those in the foreground, where dark pines and lighter oaks alternated with terraced cultivation, sparse wheat and growing maize, to the blues and purples of the distance.

If human affairs had not intruded themselves, Chabeli Parshad would have been happy alone on the hillside. Another flock of goats was feeding in the corrie where the next stream took its course, and the boy who was looking after them was playing on a wooden pipe. Through the pleasant tinkle from the stream at his feet, the sound of the wind in the grass, and the occasional bleat and hiss of his goats, the essential stillness of the hills re-

mained unbroken, as it always does. But Chabeli Parshad was
unhappy because of his wife.

He was a Brahman, but a hill Brahman, and therefore exempt
from many of the rigid vetos that govern his caste in the plains.
No one sticks to one trade in the hills. The man who keeps a
shop will also graze a herd of goats and sheep and in his spare
time spin yarn from their wool and weave it into heavy blanket
stuff. He is cultivator as much as shopkeeper. The cultivator will
go away for six months to one of the big hill stations, where with
three others he will carry slim young women to dances, fat old
women to bridge parties, and fat old men to offices, and at the
end of the summer he will come home with the price of a bride
in a bag of silver rupees.

Chabeli Parshad, like any other hill Brahman, farmed his land,
plowed, and sometimes even ate meat. He was a man of peace,
but he was a man, not a specialized counting-machine as a plains
shopkeeper would be. The constant use of his legs on hillsides
five thousand feet up and down had somehow reduced his belief
in the importance of calculating interest.

Unfortunately his wife seldom left the house. If Chabeli
Parshad had made his wife go out and dig potatoes in his narrow
terraced fields, as was the custom among the hill folk, he might
have come at night to a quiet and happy home. But he did not;
she came from the borders of the plains, and stuck to the ways
of the plains; and he let her sit in the shop and count the change
while he went out on the hillside and talked to his goats. So the
small change with which she was concerned grew smaller and
smaller every year. It was a pity she had not married a real shopkeeper, who would have thought of nothing but gain. He looked
back over nearly thirty jangling years with her, of fuss and
bitterness, which he met by an opposition more and more passive.
Silence and flight were his weapons: he fled to draw reinforce-
ments for his silence from the reservoir of silence in the mountains.

He remembered the first quarrel about money. An Englishman
had climbed the ridge on his way to a fortnight of marching and
camping alone in the hills. When he reached the shop, he stopped
to talk, and to see what was for sale, and he remembered that he

had brought no cigarettes for the coolies who carried his baggage. He bought a dozen packets of the cheap little factory cigarettes that are replacing the old hand-made twists of leaf without paper. Chabeli charged him the price he would have asked from the coolies themselves. Janki, his wife, was furious.

"You could have charged him three or four times the price," she said, "and he would never have known. A few rupees are nothing to him."

She was perfectly right. The Englishman was surprised that his cigarettes were so cheap, and he would have paid double without question; but that made no difference to Chabeli who was honest, not in the Scots way, because of a profound reverence for money and a sense of its importance, but because of a deeper indifference. He did not want those few extra pennies because he did not need them.

Next it had been his turn to be angry. He had come back one day to find Janki using a new set of weights, and when he had put them in the scale against the old ones he had found they were lighter. He had rolled the new ones down the hill; and since then there had never been much pretense between them of anything but quiet aversion on his side and active irritation and aggression on hers.

As it went on, and as Chabeli took refuge more and more on the hillside with his fields or his goats, he turned more and more to religion. The dew of his birth was of the womb of the morning, and it was from the hills that his strength came; but he was not aware of this, for he had read only the books of his own mythology. He was not conscious of natural beauty as the educated European is today; he absorbed it without any conscious formulation of ideas, but he was not afraid to call its influence on him, God. He had no theology, and if anyone had asked him what he meant by God and what by the gods, the relation between the Lord Krishna and the Queen Kali, whom he worshiped at the temples, and the God in whom he believed on the mountains, for whose blessing he asked and whose presence was by his side, he would not have known what to answer.

But simple and unlearned as he was, the influence was there and it grew. It grew along the conventional Hindu lines; more and more he wearied of the world and desired only to leave it, to sit on the top of a hill where the wind was clean, and forest, stream, and cliff lay unrolled below him in long contorted ridges and wide branching valleys, to consider mortality and the end.

Two years ago the desire had become too much for him. Without a word to his wife he had left her with the shop and had set out on a pilgrimage to the temple of Kali, thirty miles away, on top of one of the highest peaks among the neighboring foothills. First, he must go down to the infant Ganges, then up again, up and up. He had left his home in the early morning when the light was still innocent, and first wound his way two thousand feet higher to cross to the north side of the ridge on which he lived. There were villages scattered here and there on the southern slope, wherever there was water and the pitch of the ground was gentle enough to let terraced soil nourish crops. While the light was still almost parallel with the ground, the hillside seemed like the skin of some great animal, wrinkled by the tiny terraces of the fields. Often they were not more than six or seven feet wide, a gently sloping shelf that followed the contour of the hill for a length of thirty or forty yards. Below the shelf, a drop of a man's height, built up of unshaped stones, another shelf, and another drop. Little runnels from a stream perhaps hundreds of yards away brought water to the tiny fields. The deep labor of many generations had gone to the growing of each ear of wheat or maize.

As he went up and the shadows shortened, the cultivation grew more and more sparse. Now came a belt of great broken rocks and boulders, where the Himalayan oak mixed with the pine and cedar in a corrie that was sheltered by a southern spur from the morning sun. Then out into an eastward facing cup, drenched with sun, where the heart sprang up to see the sudden blue of gentians against white rock, where milkwort and the scarlet potentilla of Nepal starred the grass, and the wind blew with a new freshness, the exciting tang that creeps into the air near the top of a pass.

He rested and paid his duty at the crossing of the ridge, by two tiny shrines, built like dolls' houses of unshaped stone on either side of the path; they contained little wooden images, like wooden spoons, on which had been roughly scotched nose, eyes and mouth; and on a bush overhead fluttered strips of colored rag. When at last he went on it was like plunging into another world. He left the pleasant alpine cup, rejoicing in the sun, to descend the north slope where the warmth had not yet come. This side of the ridge was far more precipitous, and wherever there was roothold it was thick with trees. Streams abounded, and the leafy soil, where it had collected between the stones, held the moisture that would have evaporated on the southern face. He left a sunny, dry and windswept country for an ice-cold forest, where water dripped from the mossy rocks and the boughs of the dark trees. He went straight down for two thousand feet, on a track of loose stones that was a water-course in the rains, glimpsing from time to time on his left through the trees a knife-edge of cliff that cut the sky for a sheer three thousand feet, or before him, the open sunlit valley for which he was making, and beyond it the foothills rising again to the jagged scimitar of the snows.

Now his way lay along the north side of the ridge for thirty miles, following roughly the seven thousand foot line, two thousand feet below the crest. He rested at midday in a lap of the hills, where the water from a spring had been led along a wooden spout so that it made a bright falling curve where a brass pot could conveniently be filled. It was very cold and sweet to the taste, and he ate a handful of parched barley. Cooked food he could not eat, for even a hill Brahman must eat his bread where it is cooked. On again for three hours, through ilex and cedar, pine, and a kind of elm, still on the north side of the ridge that towered above in cliffs of tree and rock, and sent out long knees above the valley. One of these knees ran out every three or four miles, and the end would rise to a little peak with a temple and a cluster of houses. Between the knobbly knee joint and the main ridge lay a saddle of rich soil brought down by the rains from the tree-clad slopes, and here grew potatoes and maize and wheat. It was autumn and the maize had been cut and the heads laid out on the roofs of the houses to ripen in the sun. There were patches of madder set out to dry as well, and when Chabeli's road came to a clearing he would look down through the dark trees at the next village, thrust out from the forest into the warm coloring of the evening sun, bright with the orange of the ripening maize and the deep crimson of the madder, instinct with life and happiness and maturity. Down, down he would plunge and up again by a long shoulder to the village that had seemed so close, but was really separated by miles of the little winding track.

At one of these villages he spent the night with a kindly wrinkled old hill man, who had not been on the south side of the ridge nor down to the valley for thirty years. He went on his way with a farewell present of harsh pears and little shelly walnuts, long before the sun had reached the village, for he comes late and goes soon from these hidden northern valleys. The path was moist with dew, and the morning freshness heavy with the sweet woodland scent of bruised leaves, wet dust and rotting wood. Down, where ferns grew in the spray of a torrent; up, over long slabs of glistening rock and moist gravel, and at last out into the sunshine where the fields were bright again before a wooden temple with wide concave eaves, where there were orchards of apple and cherry and walnut, and where the cows went out to pasture in meditative lines.

Here a festival was planning and the band who had come for the occasion were resting from their journey, drums of every size lying about them, and great trumpets six feet long, bound with silver and brass. Chabeli rested and talked, ate his food and told his business, drank deep of the crystal hill water, and went his way. Up again, up and up, a thousand feet to cross a shoulder that ran out to the south, and there across the valley, half the world away, and fifteen hundred feet below glowed the crimson and orange of the next village. Down, through leaf and wood and shade, past ponds where the cattle came to drink and the water was dappled with sunlight, through thick forest where the moss hung in scarves from the trees, and no one came but woodcutters and sometimes an Englishman to shoot bear or pheasants; out into golden warmth by the village and then again up, up, up, by the side of a tangled stream between narrow cliffs, where the path led over boulders as tall as an old man could reach, where he must pull himself up with his hands, up and up for two thousand feet, till he struggled out exhausted on a pleasant downlike saddle where the cows were lowing for their evening milking.

He was tired that evening, and his next march was a short one. It was mostly down hill, and the fourth day he went down steeply till the cactus took the place of pine and cedar, and he came out at last to the infant Ganges. He stayed three days paying his respects to the gods, but he found it hot, and it was with relief that he turned his face to the hills again, to the high temple of the goddess. He went up for two days on the same track by which he had come down; the third day he left the track and turned into a new part of the forest where the trees were of gigantic size. Now he must climb steadily, for the temple was at ten thousand feet; and the way zigzagged between cedars ten feet thick, pines like church steeples, and thick patches of the twisted Himalayan oak. It grew darker and more lonely as the path grew steeper, and Chabeli Parshad looked nervously behind him at every corner for fear of bears or panthers. The path had been built up with unshaped stones and the trunks of trees, for often it ran across a damp rock face or over a torrent bed full of boulders, where the water fell twenty feet in a foaming curve. Always there was the sound of streams and the sharp scent of moisture and rotten wood, and a pleasant chill on the face. It seemed incredible that the sun was still really shining somewhere behind him and above him.

At the last, the slope grew gentler, the trees thinner, and he came out on a bare ridge where the wind tore at his clothes and the bones of the hill showed in knife-edges of rock through the sparse grass. He turned east and followed the ridge, rising gently, till he came to the temple of Kali on the square summit. East and west the ridge fell away in a long line, north dropped the great forest-clad side up which he had come, and south was a bare sweep of two thousand feet, naked rock and close grass, too poor even for the hill goats, torn by wind and scorched by sun.

The temple was of wood, one square room with a low veranda running round four sides. Inside, the goddess of destruction, painted red, stood facing the entrance; her steed the tigress stood before her in adoration and outside the temple the image of her servant carried her trident. The hill top would have been a more impressive place of pilgrimage if the temple had not been there.

Chabeli Parshad stayed only a few hours. He sighed when he thought that he must go back to his wife, for the idea of leaving her altogether had not yet occurred to him as something that might actually happen. For a few days, yes, after thirty years of bondage, he had made up his mind to that; but that he might do more was a resolve which could only slowly harden.

It had been worse then ever when he got back. The memory of the clean wind and the taste of the hill springs, and the friendship he had found by the smoky wood fires at night stood in the way, in perpetual contrast with the nagging of the bitter woman he had married; and her bitterness was increased by his desertion. More and more he thought of going again, but he decided that this time he must go south to the plains. He would go for longer, for a month or two perhaps, and he must earn some money to send her while he was away. If he went anywhere in the hills she would hear where he was and come to fetch him back. No, he would go to the plains this time, and find a place where people passed from time to time, where he could sit under a tree and sell cigarettes and corn and matches, and make a few rupees to send to Janki. It was a plan that grew slowly in his mind for a year, and it had only been three months ago that he had gone.

Once more he had walked all the way. He had gone down through the squalid little town at the foot of the hills to Ramnagar district, and there where the road from Mallapur crossed a river he had sat under a tree and sold from time to time his cheap wares. He had not sold very much, but he had been able to send Janki a little from time to time, not because she would need it— for she had the shop and could get a neighbor to help with the goats, and the fields would not want much attention in the winter —but because he felt it would satisfy her pride a little to know he had not forgotten her entirely. And if he was sending her money she would be the less likely to look for him. He had enormously enjoyed the relief of solitude, release from the foreboding sense he always had at home of trouble coming, but he had not been as happy as on his first escape. The air in the plains seemed to him stale and over-used; it had passed through too many lungs before it came to him, and it was laden with dust. He did not like the water, which he found muddy and insipid, and it disagreed with him; not enough to distress him, but enough to cause him some unease. No, he thought, sitting up on the hillside above his house, no; it had not been a good place; next time he would go somewhere in the hills, far away, too far for his wife to follow. He would go on a pilgrimage to Badrináth, most arduous of Hindu pilgrimages. It would take three months at least. He realized suddenly and guiltily that he was already planning to go again, to go indeed every year. Well, why not? She was really much happier without him.

He stood up and moved slowly down the hill to his house. Someone was waiting to see him, a plainsman, it seemed, a big man, with a turban, who came to meet him and asked if he were Chabeli Parshad. His own name, he explained, was Ram Kallan. He came from Galthana, a village in Shahabad district. He came to his business very quickly.

Chabeli Parshad, he asked, had been in the plains that winter? Yes? And he had sold grain and peas and cigarettes on the road between Mallapur and Ramnagar, where the road crossed the river? Now came the important point. Could he remember a woman who had come to him one day, to be exact, on February 9th, and had bought two annas' worth of grain? She had come from the railway, and she had been very tired and frightened.

Chabeli Parshad thought for a little. He did not think he would remember anyone, because his mind was not really on what he sold; and unless the buyer stopped and talked to him some time he did not think he would notice him as a person, less still if it were a woman. Ram Kallan pressed him to try to remember; he suggested that he might be wise to remember; he showed him a photograph of a woman, a narrow face, with thin lips, the face of a hater, with something in it viperine and bitter. Chabeli Parshad thought she looked like his wife, but he shook his head. He did not remember that he had ever seen her before; but he could not say that he had not.

Ram Kallan looked at him for a minute or two, considering. Then he turned to Janki, who was standing listening.

"It might be of great advantage to your husband if he could remember," he said.

Ram Kallan looked at her and smiled.

"Twenty-five rupees now. His fare to Ramnagar—but we would recover that from the Court; one rupee for every day he was away from home; and a hundred rupees when his evidence was given."

"He will remember," said Janki with decision.

"I will leave the photograph and perhaps he will remember the face," he said. "Now I shall go to the village and come again tomorrow."

Chabeli Parshad looked at the photograph again.

"I shall not remember it," he said.

For the rest of the day and most of the night the battle raged. Chabeli Parshad did not want the money, and he believed that it would be a sin to give false evidence. He did not believe it would be a sin in the same way as a Christian would have done, for the idea of truth as a correspondence between what is said and what is seen is not so clear to Hinduism. "What is truth?" they say with jesting Pilate; and they persuade themselves that their story is true. To Chabeli the sin was a sin only for him, because the deceit would lead to an entanglement with all that he believed was evil. To do this would be to meddle with the world in its worst form. He was not a strong man, and if his wife had been trying to prevent his doing something he thought right, she might have won by the energy she put into the struggle. But she was trying to make him do something he knew to be wrong, and which furthermore he did not want to do, so that the powerful forces of inertia were on his side.

She threw all her reserves into this fight, partly because of natural greed, but still more because she felt it was a test of her dwindling influence. Twice he had left her, and gone away by himself; and though she did not mind his absence, and what little work he would have done in the winter she had persuaded a neighbor to do for less than the money he sent her, yet her pride had suffered. She had always despised him and had exaggerated her own strength, because in the small matters about which they usually quarreled he was not sufficiently interested to oppose her. She had forgotten the incident of the weights, and she had come to think of him as something she could always bend to her will; now, unaccountably, merely by disappearing, he had beaten her, and she must reassert her mastery.

But she had no weapons. Her arguments were meaningless to him, as his would have been to her if he had uttered them. She could not make his life at home less comfortable than it already was; and she was wrong in supposing that by her personality she had any grip on him whatever. He was entirely unmoved by the storm she loosed on him; he listened for a short time, and then began to move away. She ran after him, caught hold of his clothes and held him. He sat down and waited till she let go and moved on again. She held him again and struck at his face. He caught her wrists and held her quite still till she began to cry. Then he left her, stonily.

When the Thakur came back next day Chabeli Parshad was out of the house, on the hillside. Janki confessed that it was no use; she could not get her husband to Court, and she was afraid she never would. Ram Kallan listened attentively. When he was satisfied that Janki had done all she could he changed the subject. He asked a few questions about the weather and the crops, the ownership and rent of the house and land, and then he said he would come back in a few days, and disappeared.

It was two days later that a second stranger appeared at the little shop. He too was a Thakur from the plains, and like Ram Kallan he did not waste long in coming to the point. His name, he said, was Hanumán Singh, and he lived at Anantpur in the Ramnagar district. Then he asked the same questions as Ram Kallan, whether Chabeli Parshad had sold grain during the winter there near Ramnagar; but he went on, not to ask whether Chabeli remembered a woman, but whether anyone else had been asking him questions about a woman.

Janki turned to her husband.

"Go out and look after the goats," she said.

She expected him to obey at once, for he had never before shown any reluctance to leave the house. But he would not go: he did not trust her, and she was frustrated for the moment in her design of taking money to say nothing because she could not bring her husband to take money to say something.

Chabeli told the stranger about Ram Kallan Singh.

"But you do not remember the woman he asked you about?" asked Hanuman Singh eagerly.

"No, I do not remember her," the Brahman replied.

"But you might suddenly remember her," put in Janki.

"I shall not," he replied.

"Can you be certain that you never sold peas to her?"

"No, I cannot be certain one way or the other."

Even so, Hanuman Singh seemed pleased, he said good-bye and left the house, but he did not go very far. In the little belt of pines above the house he waited until he had seen Chabeli some distance from home; then he came back and talked to Janki. He rightly estimated that she was not in control of the situation; her husband had made up his mind without consulting her, and her help was not worth much. He did not offer much; but he did promise her fifty rupees for herself, to be paid the day the case ended, if her husband had not remembered Jeharan's face. It was not much, but it made a difference to Janki, for she felt now that in Chabeli's despite, and on his account, she was sure of something whatever he might do. When the stranger had arranged this, he went away.

A long time ago the old house and shop that Chabeli's father had built had been partly swept away by a torrent in a time of heavy storm. It had been rotten for a long time, and the storm had been the finishing touch. There had been no question that a new house must be built, and Chabeli needed some money to build it. He had never lent money himself, and he had no capital except the land. He borrowed to build his house, and mortgaged the completed result as security. Being an atrocious man of business he had never seriously thought of paying off the principal; the interest he regarded as a kind of rent, and he had paid it regularly for years.

A few days after Hanuman Singh had gone, Ram Kallan came back. He had bought the mortgage on the shop and he was going to foreclose unless Chabeli Parshad would be a little more reasonable. If he would remember Jeharan, the deed would be torn up.

"You did after all see the woman," he pointed out. "We know Jeharan's story is true, and so it is only a question of remembering what is in fact true. There is nothing wrong in it."

It was an argument that did not appeal to Chabeli. He told the Thakur to come again next day for an answer, and he slipped away from the importunities of his wife on to the hillside.

He had much to decide. He could not find the money himself. He looked down at the little farmstead where his father had lived and where he himself had spent the fifty years of his life. The house stood just below the main path up the mountain, a long room below, where the goods of his trade were stored, a shed to one side for the animals and three smaller room above, in which they lived.

Hateful though his wife had made it, that little building still stood for all he had known, haven against snow and wind, the scene of his childhood. More than his home he would regret the fields in which he had toiled, the noble sweep of the valley below, and the serrated purple of the ranges to the west.

If this had happened to him two years before he would have been lost; but now the door was open. If he went, leaving his wife to look after herself, what would her position be? If she sold everything they had, she could pay off the debt, and there would be something left. She could go to her brother if the worst came to the worst, but it would not. She had saved some money of her own from what they had made in the shop, he knew. And if Chabeli himself went, there would no longer be any reason for foreclosing. No, she would not be much worse off without him, for he knew his work had scarcely been worth his food. He could find the little food he needed as a religious beggar.

He stood up, and with a glance over his shoulder moved cautiously up the hill.

🪷

Chapter Eight

The Private Affairs of the Fourth Witness

•❖•

ON February 11th, the fifth day after the death of Pyari, Pandit Prem Badri Náth, a Bráhman of Sháhábád city, was journeying meditatively towards the village of Dabera to collect rents on behalf of the temple of Shiva. All the land in the village belonged to the temple, and since the Mahant or Abbot in charge was a just and kindly man, his agent was popular in the village, and, being better educated than anyone except the schoolmaster and the Government record-keeper, and far less inclined to intrigue than either of these two, he was often asked to execute small commissions and to give his advice in matters that would perhaps better have concerned a lawyer. He was thus in a position of peculiar responsibility, of which he was entirely unconscious, for his mind was a strange mixture of simplicity and cunning. His subtlety in connecting cause and effect or puzzling out a raveled skein of consequence would have far surpassed the capacity of most Englishmen; yet he never looked far enough ahead, or deep enough behind, to see the ultimate results or reasons for what he did, and though he had been trained to regard as sacred the temple money, and was entirely reliable so far as that was concerned, he was often involved in what to a European, and to the penal laws of India, would have seemed the worst kind of dishonesty.

Today, as he rode slowly to Dabera on a pony so small that his feet almost touched the ground on either side, he was considering a series of circumstances born of his own brain, which had begun quite simply but had grown to a complication that was appalling. When the benign Government first decided that India should have self-government, there were instituted in the more important villages pancháyats, small judicial committees of five or six leading inhabitants, who had power to try small cases, to fine a convicted culprit as much as ten rupees, or to settle disputes involving property worth less than fifty rupees. Such a Court had been started at Dabera, and although Prem Badri Nath, who was neither a resident nor a cultivator, could not be a member, he had been from the first a kind of unofficial secretary, recording the evidence of the witnesses and the decisions of the members, and telling the bearded old men where to put their thumb-impressions or their straggling unformed signatures, if they could sign their names.

But the panchayat had not been a success. There was a small group of Musulmáns in the village, small tenants, but the majority of the tenants, and all the larger holders, were Játs, a people allied to the Rájputs, or Thákurs, soldiers and farmers. There was also a large population of Chamárs, the caste who originally skinned dead cattle and worked in leather, but who have grown and grown until in every village they supply most of the landless agricultural laborers. The panchayat consisted therefore of one Musulmán, three Játs, and, by a great concession, after bitter opposition from the Játs, one Chamár, the unquestioned leader of that humble but numerous people. It had been hoped that this would provide a board of members sufficiently impartial to give the villagers confidence, but it had not. To do them justice, the members did their best as a rule, but their task was impossibly difficult, for side by side with the Government village panchayat existed the old unofficial caste panchayats. In these everyone had the greatest confidence, but they dealt exclusively with disputes within the caste. Thus whenever there was a quarrel between two Chamars they naturally preferred their own Chamar panchayat to one consisting mainly of Jats, while the Jats chose to keep their differences from the eyes of the Chamars whom they despised and the Musulmans whom they disliked. And if a quarrel arose between a Chamar and a Jat, the Chamar was not likely to choose a tribunal consisting of his hereditary masters, while the Jat preferred that the dispute should be settled by force, on the time-honored principle that a Jat was always right and a Chamar always wrong. So that very few cases ever came before the panchayat at Dabera.

Lately too there had been increasing trouble with the Chamars. One of them had some years before left the village for the city of Shahabad, where he had set up as a shoemaker. He had worked hard and saved money, and taken a hired assistant. Business continued to prosper until he had a factory with twenty workers, and enough money to buy up everyone in Dabera again and again, and he came back to the village and talked to the young men. He asked them why they worked for the Jats for a bag of corn and a suit of clothes, when they might go to the city and earn good money. Some he took away to his factory; some went to work on the roads or the railways; and those that stayed behind grew increasingly insolent. They wanted money, not the traditional wages they had always had, but as much as they might earn in the city; they drove their cattle to drink at places which had always been reserved for the cattle of the Jats; all but a few professional skinners began to refuse to touch carrion; they even talked of asking for admission to the temples or of drawing water for themselves from the same well as caste Hindus.

All this had helped to make the panchayat a failure, but nonetheless its members valued it and were proud of it. It set an official seal on their position as leaders of the village; and it was a possible weapon against the Chamars, even though it was not used. It had never actually happened that the members had set up a Jat to complain falsely against a Chamar and had convicted him, but it was the sort of thing that might happen, and the Chamars doubtless bore it in mind as much as the Jats. Besides, if the panchayat were dissolved, its members felt that they would suffer a blow to their prestige and influence, in the mere fact of its failure, quite apart from any value which it actually had or might have; and it was with a certain amount of concern that they heard that the District Magistrate himself was coming to inspect their work. He was in camp near by, and panchayats were his special pets. He believed that they were essential for the success of self-government, and most conscientiously he tried to make them work.

He found there had been no case of any kind tried by the Dabera panchayat for a year. He eyed the five members very sternly, the chairman, massive and magnificent with a round gray beard; the Musulman, older still, his beard long and white, straggling to his waist; a younger Jat with a reddish complexion, a handsome man with his mustache neatly trimmed; the third Jat, gray and brisk; and the Chamar, smaller, darker, squat of feature, sitting apart, but with a dignity of character and purpose that became his age and leadership. The District Magistrate lectured them for some time. If there were no cases, the village did not trust them.

"Sahib, Lord, this is a peaceful village and there are no quarrels," explained the chairman.

The others, except the Chamar, gravely nodded assent. That was it, there were no quarrels.

"If that is true, it is good. But it is strange that there should be no quarrels in such a village as this, a large village with many people, while at Sikohabad yonder, which is smaller, there should be many disputes, all justly settled by the panchayat."

He lectured them for a long time. If the village did not trust them, and that could be the only reason for there being no cases brought to them, their Court did no good and must be dissolved. But perhaps they were only lazy, and had not encouraged the villagers to bring them their troubles. He did not wish to be hard and would give them another chance. They should have six months and then he would come again; if they had still no work to show him, their Court would be dissolved.

He extricated himself from their offers of hospitality, and went. The members of the panchayat looked at each other. It would never do to have their Court dissolved. They would ask Prem Badri Nath for his advice; and next time the temple agent came to the village he found them gathered together, except for the Chamar. When he had heard their story:

"If the Sahib wants quarrels, he must have them," he said. "Let us invent some quarrels."

It was the obvious solution, and it did not occur to any of them that there was anything wrong in what they were doing. They were only trying to satisfy the Government by supplying what it needed; though of course they would take good care that no one knew the exact means by which they did it.

They sent for two Jats and explained to them what they must do. Subh Rám's cattle had strayed into Bhola Rám's field of sugar cane; Bhola Ram had seen it happen and had spoken to

Subh Ram and he had answered with threatening and abusive language. The Court fined Subh Ram two rupees and awarded the same amount to Bhola Ram in compensation for the damage to his field. Prem Badri Nath recorded the evidence and the judgment and affixed the thumb-impressions.

They sent for two of the more complaisant Chamars. Loki agreed that Jukki had tied up his bullock so that Loki could not get into his yard. Jukki's protest that he had no bullock was regarded as irrelevant and even frivolous, but the Court mercifully agreed to let him go with a warning on his promise never to do it again.

Next came two Musulmáns. Ahmad Khán was prepared to complain that Guláb Khán had come into his grove of mango trees, torn down several branches that would have borne good fruit, and fed them to his goats. Guláb Khán was fined two rupees and eight annas, which went to Ahmad Khán in compensation.

So it went on. Each case took most of the day, since it must first be thought out by Prem Badri Nath, and then carefully explained not only to the parties and the witnesses—and there were generally two or three witnesses on each side—but to the members of the Court. It took a good deal of ingenuity, for Prem Badri Nath had to invent first the complaint and its evidence, then the defense and the evidence for that, and then reasons why one side should be believed rather than the other. But it was very convincing when he had finished. Altogether, he manufactured twenty-five cases during the six months they had been given. The District Magistrate was delighted. He was satisfied that the Dabera panchayat was now working well and had the full confidence of the villagers, and he told the story for years as an example of the value of constant inspection, coupled with wise forbearance and a full explanation to the villagers of what was needed.

But he said he should come back again in another six months.

This was a little too much. In the first place, Prem Badri Nath had several other villages to attend to, and really had not time to maintain the high reputation of Dabera for the swift and just disposal of panchayat business. Again, his imagination was beginning to flag; there are only a limited number of small offenses involving nothing to which anyone would be ashamed to own, and it was becoming increasingly difficult to work in those artistic little touches of difference between one case and the next in which he had at first delighted. And there was the increasing risk of detection. Altogether it was hard to know what to do next. It was becoming impossible to continue, and yet if he gave up, the panchayat would be dissolved, the members would blame him and his influence in the village would be largely gone. It would be much less easy to get in the rents, and furthermore it would be extremely difficult to explain to the District Magistrate just why the confidence of the village had died so soon after its birth. He would almost certainly be found out, and then anything might happen.

He was still thinking about this when he reached Dabera. When he came to the house of the panchayat chairman he was met by a Kahar, who came out to meet him and to send him a little further on into the village itself. There the old Jat had a room and a mud platform away from his house, where he sat and talked to his friends, smoked his pipe of the evening, collected gossip and transacted business. Here Prem Badri Nath found a burly Thakur called Rám Kallán Singh, who had followed him from Sháhábád to the last village where he had called and had come on in advance to catch him at Dabera. Ram Kallan Singh asked to speak to him alone.

He had a curious story to tell. A Brahman, he said, a woman of Prem Badri Nath's own caste, had been traveling from a village in Ramnagar district to Shahabad, and it had come to the ears of Thakur Sahib Singh, the woman's master, that Prem Badri Nath had helped her on the way. Sahib Singh wished to reward him for his kindness.

"It is very good of Sahib Singh," murmured the Brahman, his eyes discreetly on the ground.

"You remember the woman, of course," went on Ram Kallan.

Prem Badri Nath thought for a moment. It seemed unlikely that Sahib Singh was really offering him something for nothing. No, they wanted him to do something, and whatever it was he had better be slow in responding, and they might put up their price.

"It is not always easy to remember details," he said evasively.

"But you could remember details if you tried?"

"I might." It sounded more and more as though he would be asked to give evidence in Court. "Perhaps it would be better if I knew what details interested you. Then I could see if I remembered them."

"Ah." Ram Kallan perceived that they were coming to business. He spoke at some length in a low voice. Prem Badri Nath nodded appreciatively. At last he said:

"I will see how much I remember."

"How soon will you know?"

"In a week, perhaps."

"No; sooner than that you must remember, or it will be too late."

"Then the day after tomorrow."

"Good, I shall come and see you in Shahabad."

It had occurred to Prem Badri Nath that there were always two sides to a question and it might be worth his while to consider the inducements to be offered by the other party before he finally struck his bargain. To Ram Kallan it had occurred that this was probably the Brahman's line of reasoning; after going back to Galthana that night, he returned to Dabera, where he spent a day in discreet questioning of his hosts, when opportunity offered, as to the life and habits of Prem Badri Nath.

Prem Badri Nath returned to Shahabad even more reflectively than he had gone. He was naturally a friendly and unambitious man, ready to help anyone he knew, and he was quite seriously anxious to help Sahib Singh, even though he saw a favorable opportunity of helping himself at the same time. For him the question of whether his evidence was right or not depended not on whether it was literally true but on whether Gopal had actually murdered his wife. If he had, any evidence which tended to convict him was good evidence; if he had not, any evidence which tended to acquit him was good. And of the basic fact, he had no direct proof; he had only heard one side of the story, and he was open to conviction. It might be wrong to make a statement which he knew to be true, if it was likely to give the Court a wrong impression.

That evening there was an anxious conclave at Galthana. Next day, Jeharan was to make her detailed statement to a magistrate; any contradictions between this and her final evidence in Court would be eagerly seized upon by the defense, so that there was a danger in saying too much. Equally there was a danger in saying too little; for omissions would be very welcome to the defense. "They left that out," they would say, "because they had not had time to manufacture the evidence for it." At the moment, the chief question was whether to include the name of Prem Badri Nath. If his name were included, and he then turned awkward and denied all knowledge of Jeharan, they would be lost. And by including his name, they would reveal it to the defense sooner or later. If, however, they referred to him vaguely as a Brahman of Shahabad, the defense would say—and the Court might easily agree—that his name had been omitted because he had not yet been instructed what to say. There was a bigger risk in naming him; but their counsel was inclined to take it, and Ram Kallan Singh supported him, being of the opinion that he could make Prem Badri Nath tell the right story—or at the worst ensure that he disappeared and blame the defense for making away with him. So it was decided at last that Prem Badri Nath should be named.

Jeharan's statement took a long time to record next day, since it was taken down word for word in the vernacular by a clerk, while the Magistrate kept his own notes in English. When it was finished the clerk contrived to slip away, for half an hour, leaving his assistant to read the crabbed Urdu and Hindi petitions to the Magistrate. During that half-hour he gave two very confidential interviews, one to an emissary of the Anantpur Thakurs and one to the clerk of the counsel for the Galthana family. It was the best day's work he had done in his life, and very nearly paid for the wedding of his second daughter.

An hour later Prem Badri Nath found a tall Thakur on the platform before his house. He pretended that he had not expected him, and made him welcome. The Thakur came from Anantpur in Ramnagar district, and it was surprising that he should have business with Prem Badri Nath, who had never been to Anantpur, though he often had business in Ramnagar. He asked to be allowed to give Prem Badri Nath a free holiday. All his expenses would be paid, and a handsome reward at the end, if he would disappear from Shahabad until such time as he was told he might return.

Prem Badri Nath shook his head. What about the temple? Who would collect the rents?

The tall Thakur would pay a reliable substitute.

Prem Badri Nath was not satisfied.

"My master would not be pleased," he said. "The man you will pay will not get the rent as well as I do. He will not know the people. He will not know who to threaten, and who to flatter. And he might not be honest."

"We will answer for the rent, that as much is collected as you collected last year."

"And then the police. The police will look for me. When I come back they will want to know where I have been, and why I went suddenly and did not say where I was going."

"You went on a pilgrimage. Suddenly the voice of God spoke to you, and said you must go to Badri Nath, the place for which you are named. There snow fell on you from a hill and hurt your knee and you had to rest till the bone was healed."

"They might inquire and find it was not true."

"Make it true; go to Badri Nath and hurt your knee."

"It is the wrong time of year to go to Badri Nath. It will be deep in snow."

"Then go somewhere else."

"It will be very inconvenient, and my wife will be most unhappy."

"The money will make her glad."

At last Prem Badri Nath said he would consider the matter and the tall Thakur promised to come again next day.

"In the afternoon," said the Brahman hastily. He did not want a disturbance between the two rival agents at his door.

Next morning Ram Kallan Singh appeared. Prem Badri Nath explained that it was really very important that he should leave Shahabad. His prospects would suffer if he did not, and with his daughter's marriage approaching he could not afford to neglect such considerations. Ram Kallan Singh agreed to a rather more considerable compensation than had at first been mentioned. Prem Badri Nath regretted that it was not sufficient. Ram Kallan was not prepared to give more. They parted, the Thakur explaining, with a rather perturbing look, that he would be back before long.

The tall Thakur from Anantpur came in the afternoon to find Prem Badri Nath in an indecisive and capricious mood. He was not sure; it was a great deal to give up. Perhaps, if the reward was slightly increased, he might agree; or if some were to be paid down at once? But the Thakur was quite firm:

"Nothing now but your expenses and the cost of the substitute. At the end—when we ask you to come back—that reward I will increase," he named a figure, "but not one pice more. And you must go tomorrow. I can give you no longer to make up your mind. And if you don't go—" he paused impressively—looked for a long time meaningly at the Brahman—and went on slowly— "you might perhaps wish you had gone. We shall look after you very carefully if you don't go."

Prem Badri Nath trembled. He promised to give a final answer next day. That evening Ram Kallan Singh came back using very different language. He no longer wasted time on politeness or circumlocution.

"First," he said, "I think you had better read this."

It was a complaint to the District Magistrate, setting forth all the circumstances of the tricks practiced on him by the Dabera panchayat. It purported to come from one of the Chamars who had been convicted. He said he had agreed to the deception without thought, being a simple and unlearned man who could neither read nor write, on the understanding that when he had been convicted and had paid his fine, it would be handed back to him, but the agreement had not been fulfilled. He had paid his fine, but had never seen it again. To prove the truth of his story he asked the Magistrate to examine the complainants and defendants in the panchayat cases independently and at once. They would not agree on any of the particulars of the story. They would not be able to remember what their evidence had been, or even what complaint they had brought. Jukki, whose bullock had offended Loki, had no bullock; Bhola Ram had no sugar cane and Subh Ram no cattle; Ahmad Khan would admit that his mangoes had never been injured; and so the tale ran on. The Chamar complained against the members of the panchayat for conspiracy to defraud, and against Prem Badri Nath as their instigator and abettor, the fountain of the whole offense. He also pointed out that if the District Magistrate chose he might prosecute them all for conspiring to give false information to a public servant.

The Brahman was overcome. The complaint was true, and truth rang in every line of it. If it were handed in, he was ruined; for even if he were not punished very severely by the Court, he would be dismissed by the temple and his reputation would be gone. No one would employ as a rent-collector a man who had been convicted of conspiracy to defraud. And the chances were that the Court would take a serious view; he had deceived the District Magistrate himself, and on his own pet subject, the cause nearest to his heart.

Prem Badri Nath began to weep.

"This need not be handed in," said Ram Kallan. "It will never be handed in if you agree to the terms I have offered you, which still hold good. But this is not dated. It will be dated and sent to the District Magistrate if your evidence is not satisfactory. Is that enough?"

"If I agree, will you protect me against these Thakurs from Anantpur?"

"You shall have two stout tenants of ours with quarter-staffs at your house by day and another two by night," promised Ram Kallan. "But you must make up your mind at once. The police will come tomorrow morning to ask you questions. It will be better if you come with me tonight to the police station and volunteer to tell them what you know."

Prem Badri Nath did not hesitate long. On one side he was offered money with the possibility of trouble with his employers and the police, and the certain enmity of a large landowner near his house. And if he accepted this offer he would be disgraced and perhaps ruined by the revelation of the Dabera affair; while if he accepted Ram Kallan's terms he had nothing to fear but the vengeance of a landowner who lived eighty miles away.

Prem Badri Nath stood up.

"Will you come with me to the police station?" he asked.

Chapter Nine

The Private Affairs of the
Fifth Witness

· ◇ ·

IT was on the fourth day after the death of Pyaran, on February 10th, that Ram Kallan Singh first spoke about Jeharan to Dost Mohammad. Dost Mohammad was sitting in his bus at the time, thinking of his wife. Not that it was really his bus, for he and four others held it jointly from a hire-purchase company, but it was Dost Mohammad who usually drove it. He had made one trip already to the little market-town to which he usually plied from Shahabad, and now he was back again on the bus-stand in the city, waiting till he had a full load of passengers before he started on his second journey. And as he sat and waited, his bus barely half full, he thought with pleasure of his wife.

Few men would have been proud to own as a wife a woman with her history. Once she had been well known to most of the young men of the town, a lady of pleasure, and not one of the most expensive. He had first met her then, and though he had visited her professionally once or twice, he had never thought about her very much, until one day, after such a visit, he had sat talking to her half the night, and had been amazed to find next day that he strangely desired her company again. But he had not given way to the desire, for he was already contracted to go as servant to an English sergeant in one of the ancillary corps of the Indian Army; and that day they had left for the frontier.

He was not a very capable servant, and after six months in which he had patiently accepted a good deal of what he knew to be abuse, though he seldom recognized the language in which it was couched as his own, he had been dismissed for a particularly flagrant neglect of cleanliness. Back he had come to Shahabad, and it was then that he first got casual employment as a cleaner in the pay of a man who owned several buses. He learnt to drive, and was soon taken on as the permanent assistant of one of the drivers. It was after this that he joined up with several friends and became a bus-owner on his own.

He had been back in Shahabad for about six weeks, and was still working only occasionally as a cleaner, when he remembered the girl with whom he had spent the night talking. There had been something in the way she laughed that suddenly stirred him; and their talk had been interesting and somehow curiously intimate and exciting. He had wanted to go on talking to her, and he had felt as though he would never tire of that pleasure, as he had tired of other pleasures. When he remembered this he went to look for her in the street of the ladies of delight. Other houris stretched out their arms to him, but her he could not find; he wandered up and down for some time, vaguely unhappy, dissatisfied at the prospect of spending the night with anyone else. He could not remember her name, and this made it difficult to ask for her; but at last he yielded to the charms of one who reminded him of her a little. He was still more disappointed and wished he had not come; but when he described the girl he was looking for his hostess was able to give him some information.

"Ahmadi Ján, you mean," she said. "She's taken a place with Babban Sahib."

Babban Sáhib was a kind of nickname, familiarly used by everyone, even himself, for a gentleman who lived in the city and owned considerable lands in the surrounding country. His real name was Bashir Háidar Khán, but he never used it except printed on his visiting cards, and even there it was followed by the words "Alias Babban Sáhib." Dost Mohammad knew at once who the girl meant, and he understood that by "taking a place" with Babban Sahib she meant going to live with him as his permanent mistress; and he knew that for him to go to see Ahmadi Ján would be dangerous work. He was a small and rather bird-like little man, his face pale and grubby with gear oil, a figure who to some would seem repulsive, and to a few pathetic, but to none a likely home for courage or initiative. All the same, he showed both when he determined to see the girl he had suddenly remembered, in spite of Babban Sahib and the tenants who filled his yard with their bundles and quarter-staffs every day.

One day when he was not working he went to the house and mixed with the crowd of tenants, beggars and hangers-on who came and went among the regular servants. Two days spent like this gave him all the information he wanted. He knew that Babban Sahib kept her close, as close as a wife; she was not allowed to leave the house, nor to go to market herself, nor to show her face. But Dost Mohammad knew where her window was, and one night he found a way there when Babban Sahib was away and threw in a message.

Ahmadi Jan was surprised to find it. She could not remember the name of Dost Mohammad, if indeed she had ever known it, and the information that they had once spent the night in talk was not enough to recall him; but she was touched that he should remember her. She was unhappy with Babban Sahib. She was left alone most of the day, jealously locked up; and in his behavior to her he was, of course, wholly lacking in respect. He was rough, too; and though a woman gently brought up sometimes admires roughness, mistaking it for strength, to a woman trained in the hard school of Ahmadi Jan it is gentleness and restraint that are pleasing. She knew that he would tire of her soon, and she was often tempted to anticipate the inevitable day when she would be turned out of the house. Only two considerations kept her back, the thought of the money she was earning and saving against the old age she always dreaded and the fear that if she left before Babban tired of her he would look for her and revenge himself. So she stayed, miserable in the present, and with no better outlook for the future than a return to her old trade, hateful in itself and uncertain in its returns.

It was delightful to know that someone remembered her and still wanted to see her, and, dangerous though she knew Babban would be if he found out, she at once threw back a message telling Dost Mohammad he might come. He threw back a pebble with a string and she pulled up the cord he had brought; in a few minutes he was in the room by her side.

When she saw him she almost laughed. He was so small, with his funny little face, as he stood peering at her with his head on one side, like a starling considering whether to peck at a nut. But she managed to change her laugh to a welcoming smile, and soon she made him at home. When they had talked a little she began to remember him, and she found a simple gaiety under his nervousness that pleased her. When he went, she said he might come again, not only because it would give her change and interest in her loneliness, but because she felt sorry for him and because she wanted to hear more of him.

Her window was about twelve feet from the ground, at the back of the house, looking on to a small orchard of guava trees and mangoes. To get there he had to saunter casually, as though he had nothing to do, down a lane which led to the back of the orchard. The entrance to the lane had houses on either side of it, and he was always afraid that someone unseen, behind a window, would notice him and follow him, watch him into the orchard and tell Babban Sahib. He had to wait till he could see no one in the lane and then slip over the wall into the orchard. If there was a moon he still felt horribly visible, for the trees were not set close together and did not give much protection to a city-dweller, though a jungle man would have found them cover enough. Then to the house wall, across a little open strip of moonlight to the satisfying shadow below the window; he was terrified of that open space, where he felt that a hundred eyes were watching him from the windows of the house. But they never were, for there were few windows at the back, and they small and high in the wall.

Dost Mohammad hated the adventure of going there; a boy, or a more robust and adventurous man, might have enjoyed it, but to so timid a little fellow it was all fright and misery. Yet he went, for this was the only woman he had ever met who could talk to him in that curiously intimate and exciting way about himself, and about herself, and who could stir him with that sudden exhilarating trill of laughter. But he was still half afraid of her, for her character was stronger than his and her experience much wider.

She too was always frightened now; Babban Sahib was jealous enough at any time, but if he heard of this, she really believed he would kill her. She was sure that sooner or later he would know, for such things cannot always be hidden, yet she let Dost Mohammad come. She had never met anyone whose interest in her was so personal and who showed her such respect. He seemed to bring out the best in her, the most amusing and lively side of her wit, the softest and gentlest side of her nature; she loved talking to him, and her affection for him grew with every visit.

For some time he made no plans for the future; he thought only that he would come to see her whenever Babban was away, and he shut his mind to the paralyzing thought that some day they would be found out. He did not at first consider what would happen when Babban ceased to support her; but gradually there was born in his timid and unambitious soul that desire for exclusive possession, for unconditional and permanent ownership, which to some seems so foreign to the spirit of love, but which is still the basis of human society. He began to find the thought of Babban Sahib intolerable; and then one night she made a re-mark about that return to her old life which she felt was some day inevitable. He said nothing at the time, but after he had left her the thought lay heavy against his heart. To share her with a hundred others, to go to her home to see her, and there find her so hatefully employed! No, it was not to be borne!

"I will marry her!" he said.

She was as surprised when he told her this as she had been when first he came to see her. No one had ever asked to marry her before. Who ever heard of two adult persons arranging a marriage between themselves! And to marry a woman of her profession! No one had even thought of such a thing. She could not believe he really meant it; she patted him on the back and smiled at him kindly. But he did mean it, and gradually she came to believe him, with a great thankfulness and a new happiness.

Even then, however, she would not make up her mind to escape and to brave the revenge which Babban Sahib would take. She persuaded Dost Mohammad that before long Babban Sahib would tire of her and turn her out, and then she could marry without offense. But one day the landowner came to her in a towering rage. He was a stocky man, thick of neck and brutal of face. He had heard that a man had been seen climbing into the orchard from the lane, and though it did not occur to him that Ahmadi Jan would have dared to let him into the house, he was sure that it was for her that he had come. He left her sick and weeping, her back cut to pieces, sure that she would be killed if he knew all the truth; and he set two of his tenants to guard the orchard.

Dost Mohammad did not come that night, for he knew Babban was at home and his visits were only safe when the landowner was away looking after his villages. It was as well he did not, for during the first two hours of the night, the two stout Kurmis prodded each other into vigilance; but they were cultivators, hard-working folk who were used to reaching their fields as dawn broke and laboring all day on their little patches of land. They were never awake for long after dark, unless at a wedding-feast or some such conviviality, when there were bright lights, and sweets to eat, and drums thudding, tapping and roaring all round, so that sleep was impossible. After two hours, the task of staying awake became increasingly difficult, and by midnight both were sound asleep. It was about two in the morning, soon after the moon set, when Ahmadi Jan dropped a bundle of clothes from the window and followed, herself, with the classical help of a sheet. She stood breathing heavily, in the darker shadow of the house, for there was still a faint radiance where the moon had set. Then she moved cautiously from tree to tree till she came to the lane; but all her care was unnecessary.

She went to the street she knew best, where once she had lived; she found an old companion who gave her room to sleep on the floor, and next day she went to the garage where Dost Mohammad worked; she did not know where he lived.

Frightened though they both were, they were married; and because they had no other means to keep them alive, they stayed on in Shahabad where Dost Mohammad had work. Babban Sahib never saw either of them; but one night Dost Mohammad was attacked in a lane by three men with sticks. He was knocked down and beaten, but by the merest chance a constable on his rounds turned the corner, and Dost Mohammad was persuaded that only by this was he saved from death. No attempt was made to repeat this form of assault, but they had not yet been married long, and both were sure that Babban was only waiting for an opportunity.

All the same, it was with delight that Dost Mohammad thought of his wife. She still stirred his spirit with her laughter and her intimacy, and it was still a pleasure and an excitement to come back to their home and find what she had cooked for him and hear what she had thought of while he was away. He was still thinking of her, with a happy smile, when Ram Kallan Singh spoke to him.

"Dost Mohammad," said the Thakur.

Dost Mohammad said good morning.

"Good," said Ram Kallan, "I have something to say to you. May I sit by your side?"

It was quite a good place for confidences, for the front seat, where the driver sat, and the two seats beside it, which were more expensive than the rest and therefore usually empty, were shut off from the rest of the bus by a partition of glass and wood, and there was a great deal of noise all round; there were a dozen cars waiting for a full load before they started, and their passengers were all talking at the top of their voices. There were hawkers, too, trying to sell fruit and nuts and tea and cigarettes and pan, all calling their wares; and over all was the squalor that seems always to accompany an agricultural community turned suddenly urban.

Dost Mohammad opened the door with a feeling in his stomach that something unpleasant was going to happen. Ram Kallan climbed in and sat down.

He asked Dost Mohammad if he remembered that four days before a Brahman had come to his bus, early in the morning, just as he was starting out on his first trip, and had put inside a Brahman woman, explaining that she had no money but that she was a servant of Thakur Sahib Singh of Galthana, who would pay the fare when she arrived at the house. Dost Mohammad, he said, had agreed to this proposal, for he seldom had many passengers on the first outward trip. At Galthana he had been stopped at Sahib Singh's house, and Sahib Singh's son-in-law, Bhola Nath Singh, had paid him.

Dost Mohammad did not answer directly whether he remembered this. He was quick-witted, and he guessed at once that he was expected to give evidence.

Dost Mohammad did not like the idea.

"I am nervous," he said, "and frightened of clever men who know more than I do. I should get confused when lawyers asked me questions. I should spoil your case."

Ram Kallan said that he would have to say no more than he already knew, and that he would be very carefully prepared for it.

Dost Mohammad said that he did not want to be involved in a case which would attract a great deal of attention.

"I have enemies," he said, "and I do not want to add to them. And I want to keep quiet. I do not want to be much in public."

Ram Kallan Singh said that his master quite understood that, and he was prepared to compensate him for the inconvenience.

Dost Mohammad opened his eyes when he heard the sum mentioned. That was certainly a consideration, and probably sufficient to overcome his scruples. But he would like to know first who was the opposite party in the case. If it was to be Babban Sahib, he dared not do it, for he was convinced that if he added a second offense to his first, he would be killed. Ram Kallan's eyes narrowed, and he looked at Dost Mohammad very carefully as he explained that the other party was not from Shahabad but from Ramnagar.

Dost Mohammad sighed his relief. Then there would be no difficulty, he said; but he would like to consult his wife before he actually pledged himself and received his instructions.

Ram Kallan Singh said he would send someone to see him next day.

Next morning Dost Mohammad had a holiday, for another of the partners was to drive the bus till noon. Quite early a Thakur whom he had never seen before came down the lane to ask for him, and at first he thought it was the man Ram Kallan Singh had sent. Indeed, he asked if this were so.

The stranger gravely shook his head.

"No," he said, "I am Hanuman Singh of Anantpur. I see from your question that you can guess my business, for if you have seen Ram Kallan Singh you know why I am here. I have come to ask you to disappear from Shahabad for six months, telling no one where you have gone."

The inducement he offered for this was three times what Sahib Singh had offered, for the old man at Anantpur had realized at last that things were serious. Dost Mohammad was lost in calculations. In the first place, he was convinced that if he appeared in a trial he would attract the wrath of Babban Sahib; he felt obscurely as though he were in a storm, safe as long as he crouched in caves and holes of the ground, but certain to attract lightning and the thunderbolt if he stood out on a high point in all men's sight. Further, once you ventured into a Law Court, you were bound to do something wrong; and if you had rich and powerful enemies you were bound to suffer. They would watch you and wait till you tripped, and then lay on to you the whole pack of lawyers and police. Hanuman Singh offered him an escape from this, and he offered him sufficient money to pay the initial deposit for a bus of his own on the hire-purchase system somewhere else. And there was nothing he wanted more than to be able to escape from Shahabad, telling no one where he had gone. Then at last he would be free from this fear of Babban which haunted him. And he would have a bus that was all his own. He talked to Ahmadi Jan, and they agreed that they would do as Hanuman Singh asked and vanish. They would go that very afternoon.

Soon after this had been decided and Hanuman Singh had left, a second Thakur came down the lane. He seemed to know his way, and the questions he had to ask of the neighbors were more concerned with Dost Mohammad's visitors than with himself. When he reached the house he had found what he wanted to know, for his step was swifter and more determined. It was Ram Kallan from Galthana and he asked Dost Mohammad if he would come at once with him to make a voluntary statement at the police station.

Dost Mohammad seemed nervous and undecided. He shifted from one foot to the other and offered his visitor a cigarette.

"Will you come?" repeated the Thakur.

Dost Mohammad seemed suddenly to make up his mind.

"We've decided . . ." he began, but a shapely brown arm came out from behind a curtain, grabbed him by the shoulder and dragged him inside. There was a long whispered conversation. Dost Mohammad reappeared.

"I am afraid that just now I can't come to the police station," he said. "I have business. But I will meet you there this afternoon at four o'clock."

Ram Kallan Singh replied that that would be perfectly convenient, but that meanwhile he would wait in Dost Mohammad's house. And he would come with him to the police station in case he lost his way.

"But I am not going to stay here," said Dost Mohammad, "and it seems inhospitable to leave you alone."

"I will come with you wherever you go," said the Thakur kindly.

Dost Mohammad protested that he could not think of troubling him; he was only going down to the bus-stand to speak to his partner and explain that he could not drive that afternoon. His guest, however, insisted; nothing would please him more than a walk to the bus-stand.

At last they started; as they stepped into the street the Thakur raised his hand to adjust his turban, and a countryman a little further down the lane seemed suddenly to remember something he had left at home; he started off in a hurry to fetch it.

As they went through the city Dost Mohammad, who was nervous and excited, and therefore inclined to hurry, found his companion strangely inclined to linger. The Musulman dared not resist a man who was a head taller than himself, and he was not suffered to walk on ahead; yet down the long narrow lane between the windowless backs of houses they walked more and more slowly, like city idlers taking the air at night. The sides of the lanes were like cliffs of red brick, stained here and there by long trails of filth from privies on the first floor which emptied straight out of the house into the street, in defiance of municipal by-laws; the brick paving of the road surface sloped inwards to a runnel in the middle that was choked every day by noon, although it had been flushed in the early morning by the municipal water-carriers with their goat-skin bags. It was not an inviting place to loiter and there was no one about at midday, yet the

man from Galthana would not be hurried. And when they came
to the bazaars he must stop and look at every shop: the pan-
seller, where the broad green leaves were spread out invitingly
between big black pots and jars of water and boards displaying
packets of cigarettes and matches; the cloth-merchant among
bales of cotton stuff, white and black and red, drawing meditatively at his water-pipe; the grocer sitting in a scent of mummy
that tickled the nostrils, with his grimy little packets of dust-
colored spices, sage and turmeric, dried garlic, pepper, carda-
moms and scarlet chilis; the sweetmeat-seller among great pyramids of golden balls, and thickly bubbling pans, giving out a
scent that is the soul of India, the richness of boiling sugar with
smoke and buffalo-milk and drifting dust behind, a scent so
heavy it seems a taste, unforgettable, unforgotten; water-pots of
brass, saucepans of aluminium; shallow cones of grain, wheaten
flour, ground whole in stone querns, barley, grain, dried peas,
millet; tins of sour-smelling ghee; all that is in every bazaar of
northern India; at each the tall Thakur stopped and looked and
questioned. It took them twice as long to reach the bus-stand
as Dost Mohammad usually spent on the journey when he was
alone.

The bus had just come in and was still unloading passengers
and strange bundles of vegetables and sugar cane, brought as
country offerings to relations in the city. Dost Mohammad went
to talk to his partners, wondering whether the Galthana man
would keep by his side, but the Thakur, though he watched him
carefully and stayed within easy distance, did not insist on shar-
ing the conversation.

Four of the partners were there, Dost Mohammad and another
to take over, and the two who had just finished their morning's
work. There were usually two to work the bus, one to drive
and one to swing the starting handle and collect the money. Dost
Mohammad found the other three and began to explain that he
must suddenly leave Shahabad. There was no money to change
hands, since they owed more on the bus than it was worth, and
there was no question of his recovering any of the share he had
contributed to the initial deposit. In fact, it was in itself rather
a good stroke of business to leave the partnership, since, like most

bus-owners, they were several months in arrears with their monthly payments; the takings were not really enough to support so many capitalists. This, however, the others did not think of; each began to calculate how much he would gain on the monthly distribution of profits.

They were thus engaged, and Dost Mohammad was still puzzling how he would be able to escape from the Thakur, when two Hindus of the clerkly class, one looking rather nervous, and the other, to hide his nervousness, very pompous and arrogant, approached them and began to talk. The partners knew who they were, for the agents of the hire-purchase company had been to see them before. The difficulty of collecting installments, and the large staff necessary for the purpose, was one cause of the enormous amount which the hirers had to pay before the bus would become theirs, and this firm, being a small local one, had to charge even more than the big companies. The arrogant Hindu spoke first:

"We have come about our installments. When are you going to pay us? You must pay at once, now; there must be no more delay."

"Who ever pays installments before the end of the month? Why do you ask us anything so foolish?"

"You know very well that I mean your installments for the month before last, and the month before that, too. Why do you not pay?"

"Give us a little time and we will bring some money early next month," said Mahbúb Khán, who had just finished driving.

"No, no, you must pay at once."

"Well, we won't."

"Then I shall seize the bus. It belongs to us, as you know, and I shall resume possession. I call everyone to witness that I resume possession of this bus." He walked importantly to the bus, and put in his hand to take the switch-key. He had some difficulty, for he was very stout, a fact which he had not sufficiently considered when he chose his costume, open khaki shirt and khaki shorts, to show his education and his knowledge of English.

Mahbub Khan glared at him for a second, seething with fury. Was he to be bullied by a miserable Hindu, stinking of cow-dung and ghee, an idolater, he a Pathán, a conqueror? His rage boiled up in him uncontrollably, a mist before his eyes, his veins thickening; for a moment he was no more responsible for his actions than a drunkard or a madman.

He flung himself on the Hindu, shook him, flung him to the ground, snatched the first thing that came to his hand, and began to beat him. Fortunately it was only a light cane that the Hindu had been carrying, but Mahbub Khan would not have stopped if it had been an iron bar. Dost Mohammad and one of the others seized the more timid clerk, who had tried to run away, and held him fast.

The assault only lasted for a moment. A number of country-men detached themselves from the crowd and secured the four partners; others attached themselves to several members of the crowd whom they detained as witnesses.

The Thakur from Galthana stepped forward, and began to speak to Dost Mohammad.

"I think you should know," he said, "that all the rights in this firm have been bought by Babban Sahib. It was quite a good in-vestment at the price, but in this particular matter he will not regard his money. He is a friend of Sahib Singh and at Sahib Singh's request he will forgive you the injuries you have done him, and this assault on his servants, if you will give the evidence you know of. And you will get your price from Sahib Singh. All these men are tenants of Sahib Singh or Babban Sahib, and you will be released and hear no more about it. But if not, if you refuse to give evidence, the bus will be confiscated, and you will all be prosecuted for this assault. Nor is it likely that ven-geance will stop there. And it will be no use running away, for the police will look for you, and no one can escape from them for long."

Dost Mohammad thought what it would mean, the long de-fense against prosecution, with not only the police but a rich man's influence behind; and the endless troubles even when it was over, trouble with the police, for once they know you they never forget, more trouble with Babban Sahib, trouble with Sahib Singh. There would never be an end that way, and it was true, it would be no use running away.

"Tell me again exactly what you want me to say," he said, "and I will come with you to the station at once."

Part Three

THE TRIAL

•✧•

THE case against Gopál Singh for the murder of his wife first came before a magistrate for inquiry; it was his duty to commit the accused to the Sessions Court for trial if he considered that a fair case had been made out. He found that, at least at first sight, the prosecution had made out a case which required rebuttal, and he committed Gopál Singh for trial.

On the day of his trial before the Sessions Judge the space before the Courts was thronged with people. Very seldom does the Indian Press stir up the interest in a murder trial that is so common in England, but there is bound to be local interest when the affair is a test of strength, as it was here, between two important families. There were villagers from Anantpur and the neighborhood, and some from Galthana, brought at Sahib Singh's expense in case they might be needed. There were country landowners who knew one family or the other, idlers from the town, young lawyers and their clerks, and all the riff-raff that hangs about the Law Courts. As many as could manage it thronged into Court, and the rest stayed outside, responsive to the waves of garbled information that from time to time pulsed outwards from the center.

Inside, all was cold neatness and order. The Judge with his assessors sat on a dais, raised high at one end of the room; the prisoner stood in the middle, fenced from the world in his narrow dock. Before the Judge's table, on a raised step, stood the witness.

First came Constable Rúp Singh. He spoke with a nervous stolidity, gazing at the right-hand end of a beam in the roof, giving a wealth of detail as to date, time, and place, with complete absence of allusion to manner and emotion.

He had come to Anantpur village in the usual course of his rounds, at about half-past three in the afternoon of February 6th. He had heard while in the village that Thakur Kalyan Singh's daughter-in-law, the wife of the accused, had died that day. He had gone to see Thakur Kalyan Singh and express his condolences. Kalyan Singh had met him and said she had died a few hours before, very suddenly, of pneumonia. Rup Singh heard later on that she was burnt on the same day, that very evening. This was most unusual, and he had then remembered the common rumors that she was on bad terms with her husband. He had thought it worth while mentioning these curious circumstances to his Sub-Inspector.

The Government Pleader, white lawn tabs on his collar, black of coat and gown, bowed to the Judge.

"The evidence of this witness is almost entirely formal, your Honor. I do not wish to ask him anything else."

But the counsel for the defense wished to question him on one point. The Anantpur Thakurs had decided after long discussion to employ as leading counsel not an Anglo-Indian barrister from the capital of the province, but an Indian from the next district with no very startling qualifications or degrees, but a deservedly high reputation in the neighborhood for success in criminal trials. He was a little man, and might at first sight have been called insignificant; but no one of discernment who had watched his face when he was speaking would have forgotten him. Ajúdiya Parshád was his name. His voice was gentle but very clear, every syllable being pronounced; and it was his manner to address his witness, however rude or hostile, always with the most scrupulous politeness, and sometimes with ingratiating flattery. He seemed to say: Forgive my taking up your valuable time, but one rather stupid little point which has just this moment occurred to me is worrying me, and no one but you can tell me the answer. Even the most suspicious witness was usually caught by this in the end. Today he was backed by four juniors.

"If you will please listen to me for a moment, sir," began Ajúdiya Parshád deferentially, "I should like to ask you about just one point. The disease which Kalyan Singh mentioned to you—is it not one that makes a body decompose very rapidly?"

"I know nothing about that," replied Rup Singh, puzzled, "I am not a doctor."

"Ah, then will you please be very kind and tell me what you do know about this disease?"

"I know it often kills people."

"Consumption?"

"No, pneumonia."

"But what do you think is the difference between consumption and pneumonia? And shall we say influenza?"

"Consumption is very slow."

"And you have heard of influenza?"

"Yes."

"What is the difference between influenza and pneumonia?"

"I don't know."

"But you can be quite sure Kalyan Singh said influenza, when you asked him what his daughter-in-law died of?"

"Yes, I mean no. It was pneumonia."

"You can be quite sure he said pneumonia?"

"Yes."

"But why are you sure? What idea do you attach to the word pneumonia? Only that of death? You know that people die of it, that is all?"

"Yes."

"And to influenza only that of death?"

"Yes."

"Nothing more in either case?"

"No."

"Then it was only a word for a disease you remembered when you made your report?"

"I remembered it was pneumonia."

The Judge intervened.

"I think you have stressed that point sufficiently," he said. "Is there anything else?"

There was nothing else, and the next witness was the Sub-Inspector, Ghulám Husain.

Ghulam Husain was in uniform; leather gaiters, khaki breeches and tunic, Sam Browne belt, revolver, and scarlet, gold-fringed turban. His manner, like Rup Singh's, was outwardly stolid, but concealed an inner nervousness. For an official witness, he was inclined to be reticent. Everything had to be dragged from him by questions, a fact which added impressiveness to his evidence.

When he had taken the oath he recounted how he had been informed by Rup Singh of the rather peculiar circumstances in which Gopal's wife had died, and had decided that it was his duty to make some investigation. Early in the morning of February 7th he had gone to Anantpur.

"I went to Thakur Kalyan Singh's house. I found him at home and told him I must hold an inquest. I asked to see the woman's body. He informed me that she had been burned the night before. I asked him if it were not unusual to burn a body on the same day as death occurred. He said that it was not very unusual and would be quite normal in a case like this where death was due to an infectious disease. I asked him what was the disease of which she died. He said cholera. I asked him to repeat that. He repeated that death was due to cholera. I confirmed from Rup Singh that he had said pneumonia the day before. I asked if I might see Gopal Singh. Kalyan Singh said he had gone to Agra to see some relations. I thought this was suspicious. I had heard nothing of it in the village, and I should have been told if he had really gone away. I had been told that people in the village had heard a shot fired the day before."

Ajudiya Parshad was on his feet.

"Your Honor, I would like to ask if it is proposed to prove this point."

"I was about to ask the same question myself," said the Judge.

"Your Honor," explained the Government Pleader, "I regret that it is impossible to prove this point, on account of the influence of the accused and his family in the village. I would not have brought it out at all, except to explain the action of the witness. I submit respectfully that in so far as it explains the action of the witness it is relevant."

"All right," said the Judge. "You may go on, but remember that it is only so far relevant."

The Government Pleader bowed his thanks. Ghulam Husain went on:

"I asked if I might see Gopal Singh's gun: I only asked about the gun because I had heard this story about a shot. Kalyan Singh said at first that he did not know where it was. When I pressed him, he admitted that it was in Thakur Nannhe Singh's house. We went there. We found the gun and some cartridges. Kalyan Singh identified the gun as Gopal's. I recorded in writing that I took possession of the gun and cartridges, in the presence of two witnesses. The gun was clean."

Ghulam Husain identified the gun in Court, and later two witnesses came to verify that it had been found in Nannhe Singh's house.

Ajudiya Parshad declined to cross-question this witness.

Next came the Thákuráni from Galthana, the mother of Pyari and the wife of Sahib Singh. She was carried into Court in a litter by four men; although she spoke from behind curtains, and her evidence was occasionally illogical and contradictory, she held everyone's attention from the moment she began to speak.

"Gopal Singh married my daughter. Yes, he deceived us all. He was very well-behaved at first. But later on he became impossible."

"One moment, Thákuráni Sáhiba. When your daughter was first married, did she go alone to live at Anantpur?"

"No, she went with her husband. Oh, that I ever allowed her to marry such a villain."

"No, but except for her husband, did she go alone?"

"Why would she go alone? Was I to send her out, to strange people she'd never seen in her life, with no one to look after her that she knew?"

"Do you mean that you did send with her someone that she knew?"

"What else do I mean?"

"Who did you send?"

"Who would I send but her old nurse?"

"What was the nurse's name?"

"Jeháran her name is. And no sooner was she there than those two old crows were scheming to have her sent back."

"How long did she stay there?"

"As long as my daughter was alive, of course. Was I to leave her alone among people I'd never seen, with no one to tell me how she was treated?"

"Did Jeharan stay there always?"

"She came home when Pyari came. And then after the quarrel she came alone."

"How often did she come?"

"How should I know how often she came? She came when I sent for her."

"And when did you send for her?"

"I sent for her this year, in January, and she stayed a week."

"And last year?"

"She came soon after Daséhra [the autumn festival]."

"And before that?"

"I don't remember exactly."

"Did she come between Holi [the spring festival] and Daséhra?"

"Oh, yes, she came once. She used to tell me the news, and bring me messages from my daughter."

"Then she came this year in January, last autumn and once during the summer?"

"Yes. Haven't I just said so?"

"And what were your relations with your son-in-law?"

"Excellent. I was very fond of him."

"But you said something about a quarrel?"

"*I* never quarreled with him."

"Then did he always behave well?"

"Behave well? He behaved abominably. He deceived my husband and tried to swindle him: he tried to poison me. He was unfaithful to my daughter; and he murdered her. He murdered Pyari."

The old lady's voice had been shrill with indignation, but it dropped at the last to a hopeless resignation; and then she began to cry. When she was calmer the examination went on.

"When did you first cease to be friendly with Gopal Singh?"

"I never did. I was always most friendly. No one could have been kinder to him."

"I mean when did Gopal Singh begin to behave badly?"

"The first time Pyari came home. He came to take her away

and he tried to swindle my husband into leaving him all the money."

"Then what happened?"

"He tried to poison me, and I was very ill. Then he ran away with Pyari and we never saw either of them again."

She began to cry once more.

"Then Pyari only came home once?"

"Yes."

"And after that, did you get any news from Anantpur?"

"Only from Jeharan. Jeharan used to send me word."

"She could write then?"

"No, but I sent a man to the village, and Jeharan slipped out to talk to him. *They* never knew."

"You mean that Kalyan Singh and his family never knew?"

"What else should I mean?"

"And what news did Jeharan send you?"

"She said that Gopal was behaving badly."

"What do you mean?"

"He was behaving like a bad man."

"In what sort of way?"

"What sort of way should I mean? Don't I speak clear enough?"

"Your Honor, I think it is clear what the witness means, but in order to make it perfectly clear on the record, I respectfully request permission to ask a leading question."

"You may," said the Judge.

"Do you mean that he had relations with other women?"

"Of course I do. What else?"

"Thank you. Did Jeharan say if your daughter knew about this?"

"She said everyone knew except my daughter."

"And neither you nor Jeharan told her?"

"No. What would be the good of that? She had enough to bear of her own. She was miserable enough without that."

"But if she didn't know that, why was she miserable?"

"Was she to be happy when she wasn't allowed to come home?"

"Ah, she wasn't allowed to come home, I see. Now will you

tell us please how you first came to hear of your daughter's death?"

More tears, then.

"Jeharan came and told us. She came one morning and said—"

"Never mind what Jeharan said. Did you actually see her arrive?"

"No, Ram Kallan came and told me she had come, and said—"

"Never mind what Ram Kallan said. But can you remember the date when you first heard of your daughter's death?"

"I can remember that. I shall never forget it. It was—"

The old lady gave a date according to the Hindu calendar that corresponded with February 10th.

"And before that, although she died on the 6th, had you heard from Kalyan Singh or Gopal Singh?"

"Not a word. Of course I hadn't. Would they write and tell me they'd murdered my daughter?"

"I see. Thank you. That is all I have to ask."

The defense did not deny that bad relations existed between the two families. In fact, they stressed the point more heavily than the prosecution, alleging that only because of these bad relations had the Galthana Thakurs trumped up the story Jeharan told. Therefore, since the value of the Thakurani's evidence lay chiefly in showing that this estrangement had arisen, Ajudiya Parshad had decided to question her on one point only. He left this task to one of his juniors, who rose and said:

"Will you tell us, please, how long it takes a letter posted in Anantpur to reach Galthana?"

The Thakurani said she could not remember; it was a long time since she had had a letter from Anantpur. The most she would say was that sometimes delivery was quicker and sometimes slower, but that there was always an interval of two days at least.

"We shall call evidence, your Honor, to show that a letter posted in Anantpur on the afternoon of February 6th would have reached Shahabad on the 10th and Galthana on the 12th."

Ajudiya Parshad looked across at the Government Pleader. He himself had realized from the first that this was a dangerous point, because it was two-edged. His clients had persuaded him to put the question, against his better judgment, merely to show that they had not been so callous as might be deduced from the fact that they had not told the Galthana family of Pyaran's death. But the point touched on the margin of one of the most crucial questions in the whole inquiry. Jeharan had gone to the police station in Galthana on the 10th; it was now clear that no one there could have heard the news by post so soon. If, therefore, as the defense asserted, Jeharan herself had not gone from Anantpur to Galthana to carry the news, someone else must have carried the news, with a good deal of convincing detail. Who that someone else had been was a question the prosecution was bound to ask, and Ajudiya Parshad felt he was not really running a risk in provoking it now. He could indicate a possible answer, but unfortunately he could not prove that a messenger had actually gone. He looked at the face of his adversary, and saw that most of these considerations had passed through his mind, too.

"One more word, your Honor"—the Government Pleader was up again. "Did you, in fact, Thakurani Sahiba, receive a letter from Anantpur on the 12th?"

"Haven't I said they never wrote to me? Would they give themselves away, a pack of murderers, like that?"

She was borne out in triumph by her litter-bearers; and the Judge needed all the respect due to him to prevent a round of applause.

The next witness was Sahib Singh, who confirmed what his wife had said: only on one point did his evidence reveal anything new. Cross-examined by Ajudiya Parshad, he admitted that he had been tricked into signing a document leaving all his land to Pyari and Gopal Singh.

"Then if you died before Pyari, Gopal stood to get all your land, but if Pyari died first Gopal would get nothing?"

Sahib Singh said he was not a lawyer, and had never thought of that.

"But it is at least true that Gopal expected something from you on account of Pyari, and he would no longer expect it if Pyari died first?"

"Yes, I suppose it is."

The Government Pleader returned to the charge.

"The document you signed. Did not that provide, not only for your leaving the land to Pyari on your death, but for your giving them an allowance at once?"

"Yes."

"Yet it was never put into force?"

"No, never."

"Why not?"

"They knew they could not prove the paper in Court, because I had been tricked."

"How long is it since you signed it?"

"Nearly a year."

"Then it was really of no value to them at all?"

"No."

"And in point of fact, after the quarrel, would you have left them anything?"

"Yes. One rupee," said the old man bitterly.

"Thank you, that is all."

But Ajudiya Parshad was satisfied that, quite apart from the document signed at Hardwar, he had established a point of some importance, in that by the death of Pyari the Anantpur family had been disappointed in reasonable expectations.

Next came Ram Kallan Singh. His evidence dealt only with his meeting Jeharan on the morning of the 10th, when she came into the house, and with his taking her that afternoon to the police station. In his case, too, the only new point came in cross-examination.

"You used to go to Anantpur to get news of Thakur Sahib Singh's daughter?"

"Yes."

"Did you stay at Thakur Kalyan Singh's house?"

"Only the first time I went. After the quarrel I used to sleep at the station and walk over to the village."

"And you just picked up what information you could get in the village?"

"Yes. But Jeharan told me all I wanted to know as a rule. Only when she had said all she knew I used to ask questions in the village to see if there was anything else."

"From anyone you met, did you ask questions, or from anyone in particular?"

"From anyone I met."

"You didn't know anyone in Thakur Kalyan Singh's house, besides Jeharan?"

"Yes, I knew them all."

"But there was no one you knew specially well, whom you met after the quarrel?"

"Yes, one of the servants I knew well. I used to meet him after the quarrel, always."

Ajudiya Parshad sighed with satisfaction. By putting the question as though he wanted the answer he really feared, he had established a means by which the news might have left Kalyan Singh's house, if Ram Kallan had been there to pick it up. He did not expect Ram Kallan to admit that he had been there, but he thought it as well to suggest to the Court the line he meant to take, and he went on:

"And when were you last in Anantpur?"

Ram Kallan Singh's reply indicated a date in November.

"You weren't there at the beginning of February?"

"No."

"Ah, how very interesting. Thank you. Then will you tell us where you were on February 6th, please?"

"At Galthana."

"And the 7th?"

"Galthana."

"And the 8th and 9th?"

"Galthana."

"The whole day on the 9th?"

"Yes."

"In short, you didn't leave Galthana from November till the day when Jeharan came?"

"I went to Shahabad, and to villages near by."

"But you didn't go away by train early in February?"

"No."

"Then will you tell us, please, the name of the place from which you came back by train on February 9th?"

Everyone was interested. It would indeed be a score if the

defense could prove that Ram Kallan had arrived from somewhere by train on the morning of the 9th.

"There was nowhere; I had never been away."

"Thank you, thank you!"

Ajudiya Parshad's voice was gentler than ever, but he gave the impression that he had got exactly the answer he expected, human nature being what it was; and that in spite of his sorrow at Ram Kallan Singh's infamy, he could not help feeling elated at the advantage to his case that he had gained.

Thakur Bhola Nath Singh came next, Pyari's brother-in-law. It was he who had paid the bus-driver for bringing Jeharan to the door, and his evidence was not of much interest. Ajudiya Parshad allowed a junior to question him, as he had questioned Ram Kallan Singh, on the exact position of various things and people in the yard at the moment when Jeharan arrived, but when allowance had been made for the fallibility of memory and powers of observation, their accounts tallied remarkably well. There was a stir when the next witness was called, Jeharan.

She came into Court with her head down and hands meekly folded, submissive, slight, a sad-colored sari drawn neatly about her, the hood pulled over to hide her face, quiet, dark and insignificant. But when she raised her eyes to meet the Judge, and allowed the sari to part before her mouth, her face was lean with purpose.

She gave her name, caste, and occupation, and took the oath. Her evidence followed consecutively, quietly and deliberately spoken, prompted only by an occasional question; it seemed that the whole matter was one of which it was such sadness to speak that she was brought to it only by the will and knowledge that it was her task that she must do.

"I was Pyaran's nurse when she was small," she said. "I nursed both the girls, but Pyaran especially was always my care. When they grew up I stayed with them and sewed for them, and cooked little things they liked and gave them medicine. Then when Pyaran was married I went with her to live at Anantpur. I went there and did not come back until Pyaran came home for the first time. Even before that the wives of Thakur Kalyan Singh wanted to send me away. They wanted to have her alone, so that they could be unkind to her when there was no one to protect her. Perhaps even then they wanted to murder her. They were very unkind to her; often she cried and I used to comfort her. But in those days Gopal Singh was kind to her.

"Then we all went back to Galthana. I went first with Pyaran. She was happy at Galthana. Then Gopal Singh came to take us away. But instead of taking us away at once, he went on a pilgrimage with Thakur Sahib Singh to Hardwar. When they came back there was some trouble. Everyone could see it. The master had always been cheerful, smiling at everyone, but now he seemed dazed and frightened. He went about the house as if he were ill and never noticed whom he met. It came out that Gopal Singh had tricked him and made him sign a paper, saying he would leave him all the land when he died and give him a lot of money every month now. There was a great quarrel. The Thakurani Sahiba said they would never pay. Gopal Singh ran away in the night and took Pyaran with him. Next day the Thakurani Sahiba was ill. She said Gopal had tried to poison her. She said I had better be at Anantpur to help Pyaran; she would need me more than ever now. So that evening I went to Shahabad by bus and by train to Ramnagar, and then by train to Anantpur. I got out there and walked to the village, to Thakur Kalyan Singh's house. They let me in. The wives grumbled more than ever, but just then Gopal was pleased with Pyari and so she was allowed to keep me. I don't know why he was pleased with Pyari just then, but I could see it in her face, and besides, she spoke to me about it. But gradually he became less pleased. Who can tell how things are between a husband and wife? She was glad that he was pleased with her, but there was something. There was something in her heart, some anger against him. And all the Anantpur folk were very bitter against Sahib Singh and the Thakurani Sahiba. Pyari was not allowed to go home. Yes, I was allowed to go. I went in January, and I went soon after Dasehra; and I went once between Holi and Dasehra. I used to stay at Galthana for a week or so and tell the Thakurani Sahiba the news, and then I went back. I did not stay longer, for I knew Pyari would miss me. She had no one in the house to take her part but me.

"Then Gopal Singh began to go with other women. First, there was a servant in the village, and then there was another servant-girl at Kaimuan. Everyone in the village knew, of course; people always do know things like that. And we knew in the house, all but Pyari. Thakur Kalyan Singh was angry with Gopal Singh, I know, and spoke to him for disgracing his caste and his family, but he took no notice. No one in the house but me would have dared to tell Pyari, and I thought it better not to speak. What was the use of telling her? She had enough to bear. I told the Thakurani Sahiba at Galthana, and she said I was right to keep quiet about it. Pyari did not know when I came back from Galthana in January. Then a slut of a Kahar girl told her. She would not have dared, but Pyari had scolded her that morning, and she was cross. Pyari slapped her, very hard, for saying evil of her master, but she did not ask me if it were true. She must have suspected it before, and now she knew it was true. She would not have asked the servants about a thing like that.

"I heard what happened from the servants. I knew my child would be hurt. I went to see her. Usually she told me all her troubles, everything, but she could not speak about this. She would not speak at all. She sat still and said nothing. She was unhappy and very angry. She was the same for a week. She would not talk at all, except to give an order. or answer a question from Kalyan Singh's wives. Gopal Singh was angry. He had not been pleased before, because she had been suspicious for a long time, and he knew he was wrong. But he could not help being angrier now.

"One day Pyaran was sitting upstairs, spinning. She was sitting on the veranda outside her bedroom. There is an inner room, then the veranda, then the open roof. We sat on the veranda. It is not very light there. I was sitting at the end towards the stairs; Pyaran sat at the other end, by the door of her bedroom. Gopal Singh came in. He brought some kurtas. He gave them to Pyaran, and asked her to hem them. She looked at them, and said they were women's clothes. He said they were for his sister at Kaonla. She began to abuse him. She said they were for the girl at Kaimuan. She abused him for going with a girl of a lower caste. She said:

"'Are you sure, Thakur Gopal Singh, that your father was really a Thakur? Can it be that your mother sinned with a skinner of dead cows, or an eater of jackals?'

"He was very angry. He told her to be quiet and to do as she was told. She said he asked her to do this because his whore had laughed at him and said he would not dare; but she would show that he really was afraid of his wife. She would never do it. He said he was her husband and he ordered her to hem the clothes at once.

"'I'd rather die,' she said. 'I'd rather you shot me. If you were a man, you would have shot me already for the things I've said to you. I'd be quiet then. But I won't be quiet now. I'll tell you whenever I see you that you're a cur.'

"Then he slapped her face.

"'That's right,' she said. 'Hit me again if you like. That's more like a man. Why don't you shoot me? That's what a real Thakur would do. It's the only way to make me quiet. But you wouldn't dare. You're afraid, because your father was an eater of carrion. I'd dare anything because I really am the daughter of Thakurs. I wouldn't run away. I won't be afraid. Shoot me and show that you're a Thakur.'

"When she said that, Gopal Singh ran into the inner room. He came out with his gun in his hand, putting in a cartridge as he came. He was very angry. She said: 'You daren't shoot me! You're afraid.' He pointed the gun at her and fired. He was standing about as far away from her as that wall"—she indicated a distance of about three or four yards—"He only fired once. He was not standing on the veranda but on the roof outside. She fell down and I ran to pick her up. She had three wounds, in the stomach, the breast and the eye. She died quite soon, within half an hour; she only spoke once, when she asked for a drink of water. I gave it her; I wouldn't let anyone else. They would have poisoned her, those people.

"When she was dead they took me to Thakur Nannhe Singh's house. It is very close; the two together are like one house. They shut me up in a room on the ground floor, just off the central court. It was a small room, with a barred window. They locked the door, and only opened it to bring me food. Twice a day they brought food, cooked by a Brahman, and there was always plenty of water. I was there that night, all the next day and night, all the third day and night. There was a bed, and I was allowed out in the fields to relieve myself, but someone always went with me. There was a man who slept on the veranda outside my door. He used to go with me when I had to go into the fields.

"At first I was so sad I could think of nothing but my poor mistress. All the first night I cried. But the next day, towards evening, I began to wonder what would become of me. I knew they would not dare to let me go free, because I would go back to Shahabad and tell my old mistress what they had done to our child. But they would find it difficult to keep me always locked up. I began to be afraid that they would kill me too, and so I began to think how I could escape. And I had a great desire to tell my mistress of those evil men and to bring punishment on them. I thought that perhaps if I asked to go into the fields very early, before it was light, when it was cold, no one would come with me. Early next morning, before light, I hammered on my door till it was opened, and asked if I might go. But the man on the veranda came too. I kept him there as long as I could, because I hoped that next time he would remember that it had been cold and be too lazy to go.

"Next morning, too, before it was light, I woke him again. He was very angry. When I told him I had to go into the fields, he was angrier still, but he began to get ready to come. But when we stepped outside and he felt the cold, he told me to go alone and come back soon.

"I went straight to the railway. It is quite close to Anantpur, and I had always come by train, so that I knew where it was. And you can hear the trains always from Kalyan Singh's house. I hurried as fast as I could, while it was still dark. I knew the man who should have been with me would not come to look for me for a little because of the cold; and that when I didn't come back he would first look for me by himself, because he would not dare to tell anyone else that he had let me go alone. When I reached the railway I turned south along it towards Ramnagar. I thought that they would look for me on the road, and that was why I kept to the railway.

"I walked on as fast as I could. I had only ten annas with me. When I had gone a good way—I do not know how far,—and it began to get warm, I was very hungry. I left the railway and went to where the road crosses the river. I could see the place from the railway. There was a man sitting there, a hillman. He sold me some parched peas for two annas. It was enough to last me till evening. I went on without much rest, till late in the afternoon, when I came to Ramnagar station.

"There I went to the waiting-room. I remembered I had only eight annas and the fare to Shahabad was more than that. I was very tired. I thought of my dear child and was very sad. I began to cry. A man came to me and asked what was the matter. I said I had seen my mistress murdered and the murderers had shut me up for three days. Now I had escaped but I had no money to get home. He told me to be careful and not to speak so loud. He asked where I lived. He said that as he was a Brahman and I a Brahmani, and as he lived at Shahabad and had heard of Sahib Singh, he would take me there, and lend me the money. He bought my ticket and took me to Shahabad where I spent the night at his house. He and his wife were very kind to me. Next morning the Brahman took me to the bus-stand and put me in a bus. He told the bus-man to drive me to Galthana and Sahib Singh would pay. When we got there, Bhola Nath Singh came out and paid the bus-man. I went into the house and told them my story. I told it to the Thakurani Sahiba and Sahib Singh. The Thakurani Sahiba sent me to the police station. She sent Ram Kallan Singh with me. I made a report at the police station. I made a statement before a Magistrate, once in Shahabad and once again in Ramnagar. Yes, that is my report, and that is my statement. They are true, every word, in the sight of God, as what I have said today is true. I saw her killed."

Then began her cross-examination. Since so much depended on her evidence, she was questioned mercilessly on every point.

"You say that even before Pyaran went back to Galthana for the first time, Thakur Kalyan Singh's wives wanted to send you away?"

"Yes."

"Why was that?"

"So that they could have her alone to do as they liked with. How do I know?"

"And yet when there had been a violent quarrel between the families, so violent that Pyaran was not allowed to go home, and when you had been left behind at Galthana, you were admitted to the house and allowed to stay?"

"Yes!"

"Did no one protest?"

"Thakur Kalyan Singh's wives grumbled, but they grumbled at everything and no one took any notice."

"And did not Gopal Singh try to send you away?"

"No, he was pleased with Pyaran just then, and glad that she should have company."

"And when he became less pleased?"

"I suppose he did not think of it then."

"Yet you were allowed to go home to Galthana, though Pyaran was not?"

"Yes."

"And to come back again afterwards?"

"Yes."

"Was it not very curious that you should have been allowed much more freedom than the daughter of the house?"

"I don't know."

"Are you asking the witness her opinion?" said the Judge.

"I am afraid I was, your Honor. Perhaps it would be more suitable if I put the question in another form. Have you ever heard of any other large landowner's house in which the daughter-in-law was not allowed to go home, but her servant was?"

"I have never heard of another house in which the daughter-in-law was not allowed to go home."

"And there was never any difficulty about your coming back after your three visits to Galthana?"

"No."

"Not even after your third visit in January, when relations between Pyaran and Gopal were getting worse?"

"No."

"Your Honor, I am not quite sure of the propriety of my next question. Have I your Honor's permission to put it?"

"What is it?"

"I should like to ask if the witness can give any explanation of this very curious fact, that she was allowed to act as a go-between when the two families were on such peculiarly bad terms. Your Honor will remember that it is my client's contention that the witness never returned to Anantpur after her first return to Galthana with the deceased Pyaran."

"I think it is a fact which does require some explanation. You may ask the question."

"Can you give any explanation of why you were allowed to return to Anantpur after your visits to Galthana?"

"It was Kalyan Singh who said I might go. I expect it was he who said I might come back. Perhaps he wanted to make friends with Sahib Singh again."

"Thank you. Now will you please try to remember the day on which you say that Pyaran was killed? You say you were sitting at the end of the veranda by the stairs?"

"Yes."

"A person could come on to the veranda by three ways, from the roof, from the bedroom or from the stairs?"

"Yes."

"And the way from the stairs is at one end of the veranda, from the bedroom at the other end?"

"Yes."

"How wide is the veranda?"

"About as far as to that chair." She indicated a distance of about eight feet.

"Then anyone coming on to the veranda from the stairs would pass close to you?"

"Yes."

"Did Gopal Singh notice you when he came on to the veranda?"

"I expect so."

"Yet he never told you to go when the quarrel began?"

"I expect he forgot that I was there. I had often been there before when they quarreled."

"And even when he went to fetch the gun, he did not remember that you were there?"

"I suppose not."

"You kept perfectly still, perhaps, and that was why you did not attract his attention?"

"Yes."

"You neither moved nor spoke from the beginning of this quarrel till the end, till Pyari fell dying?"

"No."

"And has it not occurred to you that if you had screamed out for help, or even spoken to Gopal Singh, you would have saved your mistress's life?"

"How could I have saved her? I am only a woman."

"If Gopal Singh had known you were there, he would not have shot her before a witness, and when he had time to think he might have repented."

"I did not have time to think of all that."

"But it must have been a little time from the moment when you first heard mention of shooting till the moment when the shot was fired?"

"It was very quick."

"But however quick it was, you knew what they were thinking of, for you remember their actual words; yet it never occurred to you to scream?"

"No."

"Yet suppose that now, here in Court, I, Ajudiya Parshad, raised a pistol slowly, thus, and pointed it at you head. Suppose I did that, even without warning, and said: 'I am going to shoot you.' Surely you would scream?"

"What good should I do by screaming?"

"Perhaps none here, but you might have brought help to your mistress by screaming."

"God knows if I should have done."

"And it simply never occurred to you to move or scream?"

"No, I was too frightened."

"Ah, you were too frightened. Why did you not mention that reason when I asked you before?"

"I thought you would understand that it was a very frightening thing."

"You were too frightened to scream, yet you were brave

enough to walk all that way to Ramnagar, when you might have been killed if you had been caught?"

"I should have been killed if I had stayed behind. There is nothing brave in running away."

"And although at the time of the quarrel you were so paralyzed with fright that you could not scream you can now remember the actual words used?"

"I am not sure that they are the actual words."

Ajudiya Parshad paused for a moment to consult a colleague and Jeharan took advantage of the pause to ask for a drink of water. A court servant stepped forward to give it her, but she waved him aside. She would accept water from no one except one of the Galthana party.

"I am a Thakur, she is a Brahmani," exclaimed the servant indignantly. "She can take water from me. Am I likely to poison her, in your Honor's presence, after serving the Government for thirty years?"

But no less a person than Bhola Nath Singh, son-in-law of the house, had to draw the water himself and pour it for her. It was the Thakurani's order; Jeharan was to touch no food or drink except from their own hands until the trial was over. Whether she had also been told to ask for water in Court, in order to impress the judicial mind with a sense of danger she ran, was not revealed.

Ajudiya Parshad resumed.

"Gopal Singh went indoors to get the gun. When he came out of the bedroom he passed close to Pyaran?"

"Yes, very close."

"But he did not shoot her at once?"

"No."

"He walked out on to the roof to shoot her?"

"Yes."

"He went right away from her to three or four yards' distance, and then turned round to face her?"

"Yes."

"And then shot her at once?"

"Yes."

"He did not say anything?"

"No; she spoke to him. She said: 'You daren't shoot me. You're afraid.' "

"I see. There was bright sunshine on the roof?"

"Yes."

"And it was dark on the veranda?"

"Yes."

"I see. Can you perhaps explain why he did not shoot her at once, why he walked away to a distance, to a place from which he could only see her with difficulty?"

"Perhaps he hoped she would be frightened and say she was sorry."

"That might explain why he paused, but not why he went to a distance. You cannot explain that?"

"No."

"Thank you. Now I am afraid this question will be rather distressing for you." Although his voice was sincerely solicitous, Ajudiya Parshad expressed by a glance round the Court his conviction that this statement should really have been put as a condition dependent on the hypothesis that the witness had really been present. "Will you please recall and describe as clearly as you can the actual wounds on your mistress?"

"She was wounded in the stomach, the breast, and the eye."

"Were the wounds all of equal size?"

"I did not feel them with my fingers."

"But as far you could see, were they all about the same size?"

"I think so."

"Was not one of them noticeably smaller than the others?"

"No."

"The wound in the stomach. Where was that, high in the stomach or low?"

"It was below the navel."

"And the second was in the left breast?"

"Yes."

"I suppose both were covered by clothes?"

"Yes."

"And you did not remove those clothes?"

"No."

"But between the two wounds there was a space where the clothes did not seem to be torn or pierced?"

"Yes."

"And where there was no blood?"

"There was blood everywhere."

"I mean that, in that space between the two wounds no blood seemed to be coming out?"

"No."

"How wide would you say that space between the wounds was?"

"I have told you. About the distance from the navel to the left breast."

"It would be more than so much?" He indicated a distance of six inches.

"I suppose so."

"May it please be recorded, your Honor, that the distance was more than six inches? I submit that, in the absence of medical evidence, the point is important."

"Yes, that may be recorded."

"Now, the wound in the eye. Will you please recall that? Will you say how serious that was?"

"The eye had gone."

"I am afraid," interposed the Judge, "that that phrase must be explained to me a little more fully."

"It is a very colloquial vernacular idiom, your Honor, it means that the eye was completely destroyed. The learned Government Pleader will no doubt bear me out."

"I see. Will you go on, please?"

"That is all on that particular point, your Honor."

Ajudiya Parshad again consulted a junior, and resumed.

"When you were locked up, you were allowed out into the fields to relieve yourself, but a man came with you?"

"Yes."

"You never tried to scream or attract anyone's attention who might rescue you?"

"No. It would have been no use. Everyone at Anantpur is the tenant of Kalyan Singh or Nannhe Singh or one of their relations. No one would have helped me."

"I see. Now let us come to your journey along the railway. Had you ever walked so far before in your life?"

"No, never."

"Had you ever walked further than from Anantpur to the station, half a mile?"

"I had walked from Galthana to Shahabad, about eight miles."

"But do you not always go by bus?"

"We do now, but I had walked before, when my husband was alive."

"How long ago is that?"

"Twenty-five years."

"So that for twenty-five years you had not walked more than half a mile, and yet that day you walked twenty?"

"Yes. I am strong, but I was very tired."

"You must have been," said Ajudiya Parshad solicitously. "Now tell me, please, if you will, whether you knew before that you would find a grain-seller where you did?"

"No, I did not."

"Yet he is a man who sits there always, isn't he?"

"I don't know. He was there that day. I had never been there before except in the train."

"You simply guessed he would be there and left the line to look for him?"

"No, I could see him from the line. It is only a little way off."

"I see. Now will you tell us, please, whether there were many people in the stations you passed through?"

"When I saw that I was getting near a station I went into the fields and went round. I was afraid that if anyone saw me they would tell the Anantpur folk and I should be caught."

"I see. And who else did you meet that day, besides the man who sold grain?"

"No one else, till I came to Ramnagar."

"You did not speak to anyone in a party of men working on the line?"

"I saw a party working on the line ahead of me, and I went into the fields and went round, as I did for the stations."

"But when you got near to Ramnagar, there were no fields to go round?"

"No, but when I got to Ramnagar I thought I was safe from the Anantpur folk, and besides, I was too tired to think. I just walked straight on."

"But the line runs through Ramnagar for—let me see, how far before it comes to the main station?"

"I was too tired to notice."

"What did you see by the sides of the line?"

"There were many people."

"But did you not notice anything else, any small station, any line of trucks waiting, any big building, anything of that kind?"

"I was too tired to notice."

"You have no recollection at all what you passed?"

"It is all confused. There were many people, and it was very noisy."

"Thank you. May I remind your Honor that I am calling evidence to show that she would have passed through one station in Ramnagar city and would have passed the woodyards, where piles of wood are stacked and where there are big cranes she must have noticed?"

"Thank you. I see what you mean, but your point is hardly conclusive. If her story were true, she would undoubtedly have been in a state of considerable exhaustion."

"Yes, your Honor. Thank you. Now, Madam"—Ajudiya Parshad habitually used to his witnesses terms of address to which their social position would not ordinarily have entitled them—"when you reached Ramnagar station, you went to the waiting-room, where you met this Brahman, Prem Badri Nath?"

"Yes."

"And where exactly were you in the waiting-room?"

"On a bench, crying."

"Was the bench in the middle, or against a side wall?"

"Against a wall."

"Which wall?"

"The south wall."

"In the middle of the wall, or a corner?"

"In a corner."

"Which corner please?"

"The south-east corner."

"Thank you. Did anyone else speak to you?"

"No."

"It so happened that the first person who spoke to you happened to come from Shahabad, and happened to be a Brahman, and happened to be ready to lend you money?"

"Yes."

"It was pure coincidence?"

"I don't understand."

"It was entirely by chance? You had never met before?"

"No, never. We had never met. I don't know about chance. It was our destiny."

"Of course. Thank you. And did he get the ticket, or you?"

"He did."

"And no one else spoke to you?"

"No."

"There was no one else, of all those hundreds of people on the platform, who spoke to you, or whom you would remember, or who would remember you?"

"No, no one else. Why should they?"

"And at Shahabad station you saw no one you knew?"

"No."

"And spoke to no one."

"No."

"Nor on the way to the Brahman's house?"

"No."

"Nor in Shahabad next day?"

"Only the bus-man."

"Now on the way to Shahabad where did you sit? In a third-class carriage?"

"Yes."

"On a bench in the middle, or at one end?"

"At one end."

"In front or at the back?"

"At the back."

"And at which end of the bench did you yourself sit? Or did you sit in the middle?"

"I sat in the middle."

"With the Brahman on your left or on your right?"

"He was on this side"—indicating the right.

"In the middle of a bench at the back of the carriage, with the Brahman on your right. I see. And in what part of Shahabad is his house?"

"I don't remember. I just followed him."

"But don't you remember next morning the way to the bus-stand?"

"No, I just followed him."

"Now, will you tell us please where you sat in the bus?"

"I sat by the driver's side. The Brahman put me there so that the driver would look after me."

Some questions followed about the courtyard at Galthana when she arrived, the position of the carts standing in the yard, the number of bullocks there, the names of the people there. These questions Jeharan answered in much the same way as Ram Kallan and Bhola Nath Singh. Then Ajudiya Parshad went on:

"I see. Thank you. Now I should like you to think of those days between Pyaran's first visit to her home and her death, when you say you were at Anantpur."

"I was at Anantpur."

"Were you at Anantpur when the census was taken?"

"I don't know."

"You have heard of the census and know what it means?"

"Yes."

"I have here the census records for Galthana. Your name is shown in the household of Sahib Singh. Can you perhaps explain that?"

A sigh of admiration and excitement went round the Court. He had got her at last!

"Perhaps they counted the people at the time when I was staying at Galthana. When did they count the people?"

"It was in January."

"I have already said that I stayed in Galthana in January."

Another sigh went round the Court, but Jeharan permitted herself no sign of triumph. Nor did Ajudiya Parshad show any disappointment; his voice continued, gentle and even.

"Now will you think please of the roof outside Pyari's bedroom?"

"Yes."

"You must have been there often?"

"Yes."

"Do you remember whether any green stuff was growing there? I mean, at the time of Pyaran's death?"

Jeharan considered for a little.

"I do not remember any," she said.

"Thank you. I shall lead evidence, your Honor, to prove that that is incorrect."

"Even so, it is not conclusive. It is a small detail and she may not be observant."

"She remembers the words of the quarrel very accurately, your Honor."

"I see that; but again I do not see how you can prove irrefutably that green stuff was there at the time of the girl's death. However, we shall see. Will you go on, please?"

"Now, Madam, we are speaking of the summer and autumn of last year. During that time you were living at Anantpur, looking after Pyari."

"Yes."

"Was a child born to Pyari during that time?"

"Yes."

"Then you helped to look after the child?"

After a moment's pause—"Yes."

"Was it a boy or a girl?"

"A girl."

"In what month was it born?"

Here Jeharan paused for still longer. At last she said—"I don't remember."

"You don't remember the month," said Ajudiya Parshad as though that were only to be expected. "Do you perhaps remember the time of the year? Was it the hot weather, or the rains, or the beginning of the cold weather in the winter?"

Jeharan thought again.

"I don't remember," she said.

"You don't remember the season; then would you be able to tell us how old the little girl was when her mother died?"

"Less than a year," Jeharan answered.

"But exactly how old you cannot say?"

"No."

"Now, you would naturally not go to stay at Galthana when the child was to be born?"

"No."

"And so you were at Anantpur when it was born?"

"Yes."

"Where was it born?"

"In the little room off the central yard, on the left as you go in."

"Ah, yes, the traditional place. And when was it born, in the day or the night?"

Again the pause—"I don't remember."

"You don't remember whether it was by day or night?"

"No."

"Who went to tell the Thakur Sahib that it was only a girl?"

"I don't remember."

"I suppose a midwife came in from the village?"

"Yes."

"What was her name?"

"I don't remember."

"I suppose a Brahman came in for the first ceremonies?"

"Yes."

"What was his name?"

"I don't remember."

Ajudiya Parshad turned to the Judge.

"I think those answers speak for themselves, your Honor. I shall not question the witness further."

When Jeharan had left the witness stand, the Government Pleader rose to explain the circumstances which had led him to take the peculiar step of calling the District Magistrate as his next witness.

"Both points on which Mr. Tregard can give evidence," he said, "are dealt with in his reports, which are before your Honor. They are not essential to the prosecution, but I have thought it better to set them before you, to give your Honor a complete picture of both sides, for it is my duty, not to secure a conviction, but to display the truth. Further, these reports could be proved without Mr. Tregard's presence, but I understand that counsel for the defense wish to question him, and that I have thought it more suitable that the prosecution should request his presence than the defense."

"I see," said the Judge. "Will you please question him?"

Although he was himself to be a witness, Christopher Tregard had been allowed by the consent of both parties to be present during Jeharan's evidence. He was sitting on the Judge's left hand, and gave his evidence from that position.

"You are District Magistrate of Ramnagar, sir?"

"Yes."

"Are these two reports yours?"

"Yes."

"Will you please explain how you came to make them?"

"When I first heard of this case, it struck me that it was one of peculiar interest and difficulty, and I followed its progress with great care. When I read, in the statement made by the last witness, the woman Jeharan, before a Magistrate in Shahabad, that there were three wounds in the body of the deceased, I was puzzled to know how they could have been made by one shot from a shot-gun. I accordingly conducted the experiment described in my first report. Later, I received a petition from the relatives of the accused, asking me to inspect the scene of the supposed crime. I carried out an inspection, described in my second report."

"I should like to ask a question, which is in no way intended as a criticism, sir, but which will perhaps make the way easy for any explanation you may wish to give."

"Please do."

"Would it not have been more usual to have deputed a subordinate magistrate for both these tasks?"

"You are quite right. It would have been more usual to have deputed the Sub-Divisional Magistrate, before whom the formal inquiry took place which ended in commitment to this Court. That Magistrate, however, happens to be unused to firearms, and hardly seemed a suitable person to carry out the first inspection. I therefore did it myself, and I did the second myself, partly because I had done the first, and partly because I was very interested and wanted to see the place." Christopher smiled disarmingly.

"Will you please explain your experiment?"

"I should begin by saying that when I read Jeharan's statement I was puzzled to know how one shot from a shot-gun could have hit the deceased in three separate places, so far apart as she described. I should have expected that at three or four yards' range the charge of shot would have made one very ugly wound about three or four inches across. I decided to test this, in the interests of justice, and, I must add, to satisfy myself of the truth of my own ideas. I had a sack stuffed with rags and paper, and sheets of white paper pasted over the face of it. I propped it up against an earthen bank, and set myself at a distance of eighteen feet. That is four and a half yards' range, the greatest distance that would square with Jeharan's three or four yards, and incidentally the greatest possible in the place where the death is said to have happened. You will see from the plan that the veranda is eight feet wide, the roof ten feet. There are arches on big square pillars between the roof and the veranda, so that his line of fire must have been more or less parallel with the edge of the roof. In short, he could not have been more than eighteen feet away. Is that clear?"

"Quite clear, thank you, sir."

"Now the cartridges recovered from Nannhe Singh's house were apparently all that Gopal Singh had, except one or two unopened boxes which cannot have been used. They were in a leather cartridge belt"—this had already been produced in Court by the Sub-Inspector, Ghulam Husain—"and they were all of some age. You can see that all these are last year's cartridges, if not older. You can see, too, that the belt holds about thirty cartridges when it is full, but that now there are about twenty, and ten empty spaces. There were six empty spaces before. I used four cartridges. It seemed a fair assumption that the cartridge which killed Pyaran came from this belt. There was no other store of cartridges from which it could come, though of course one odd cartridge from another box which had been destroyed might have been lying about. I therefore chose four cartridges from the belt, two with a large size of shot and two with a small size. You can see that they are a very mixed lot, of different makes and different sizes of shot."

"One moment, sir. Will you please explain what is meant by different sizes of shot?"

"Roughly speaking a cartridge consists of the powder, the wad and the shot. The powder is here, at the brass end. Next comes a cylinder of felt, called the wad, and then this much"—he pointed—"of the cartridge, at the end, is full of shot. This is graded in sizes, according to the size of the grain or pellet, and of course the smaller the pellet the more there are in one cartridge. In this belt, the smallest shot is No. 8, which is suitable for small birds, snipe or quail. There were five No. 8 cartridges, of which I took two. I should guess that there would be about two hundred pellets in a No. 8 cartridge, but I may be quite wrong. No. 8 shot is rather like round grains of rice—smaller than wheat. The largest size of shot in this belt is marked S.G., which are about the size of a pea when cooked, or a little larger. I think there are seven or eight in such a cartridge. They are meant for small animals like hog-deer or barking-deer, but I believe that up to twenty yards they are deadly even against a panther."

"Then it would really be more suitable to take S.G. for a murder?"

Christopher smiled. "I have often seen tables showing the size of shot you should use for different game," he said, "but none of them dealt with human beings. I can be quite definite that at four yards' range it would make no difference what shot you used. The smallest would be as deadly as the largest. But I do think that a person used to shooting who wished to murder some one might instinctively take a heavy shot, without considering the range at which he proposed to fire.

"There were nine S.G. cartridges, of which I used two. You will see that there are seven left, and that they are fairly old. I fired one S.G. and one No. 8 cartridge from each barrel of Gopal Singh's gun. I fired from each barrel because as both are clean it was impossible to say which had been used."

"Would it make any difference which had been used?"

"Yes. The right barrel is a cylinder; that is to say, perfectly cylindrical inside. The left barrel is a full choke; that is to say, the barrel is slightly narrowed at the muzzle. This has the effect of keeping the shot together when fired, so that there is less spread from the left barrel."

"Is there much difference?"

"Very little at four yards' range. At twenty-five, the usual distance at which a shot-gun is used, there is a noticeable difference."

"Will you tell us the results of your experiment, please?"

"I fired four cartridges. In each case, all the holes made by the shot could have been covered by a round plate six inches across. The No. 8 cartridges made, as I had expected, a jagged hole about three inches across, with isolated punctures scattered round it, but, as I have said, a six-inch circle would have covered them all. The result from the left barrel was slightly smaller. The results from the S.G. cartridges were more surprising. In each case, four or five slugs had struck the mark so close together that they made a hole not much bigger than a rupee [about the size of a half-crown] while two or three others had made a second hole, smaller, about two and a half to three inches distant. That surprised me. I was also surprised to find that at that range the wad was thrown with such force that it pierced the paper, in every case at a distance of from one to two feet above the hole made by the main charge, and a little to the right from my point of view."

"Would a person accustomed to shooting naturally use the right barrel or the left when firing one shot?"

"He would be more likely to use the right barrel, which is usually fired first, before a bird has had time to go any distance."

"Then suppose Gopal Singh had taken an S.G. cartridge which he fired from the right barrel at a range of eighteen feet, he might have caused two wounds in the body, three inches apart, and the wad might have flown up and hit the deceased in the eye?"

"It is possible. But your suggestion contains three assumptions."

"Thank you, sir. I suggest, your Honor, that it might be convenient if the counsel for the defense questions the witness now on his first report, while it is fresh in our minds, before I turn to his second."

The Government Pleader sat down and Ajudiya Parshad rose to speak.

"I have very little to ask, sir. I would only ask you to explain a little more fully what you have said. First, if Gopal Singh had been less than eighteen feet away, or if he had used the left or choke barrel, the distance between the wounds would have been less than three inches?"

"Yes."

"While if he had a smaller shot, there would only have been one wound?"

"There would have been one main wound and a number of tiny punctures. The other shot in the belt are much more like No. 8 than S.G. You may say that there could have been two wounds only if he used S.G. or a similar shot."

"And in any case the two wounds would be closer together than the distance from navel to breast?"

Christopher smiled. "I have conducted no experiments on that point," he said, "but I think they would always be considerably closer together than six inches, which the witness said was the minimum distance."

"You said the wad was thrown with sufficient force to pierce the paper. Could it have been thrown with sufficient force to put out an eye, to justify the expression—'Her eye was destroyed'?"

"I should not have thought so, from the state of the paper and the sacking. As I have said, I was surprised to find it was thrown with so much force as it was. You really need a doctor and a gunsmith to answer your question. I can say however that, even after my experiment, I should be surprised to hear that a wad could cause as much damage as that at such a range."

"Thank you, sir."

The Government Pleader rose again.

"Now, sir, will you please describe your second report?"

"My second report describes an inspection made after Jeharan had stated before a Magistrate that she remembered nothing green growing on the roof where the shot was fired. I inspected the place and found a number of kerosene oil tins, containing earth. In two of them were growing some marigolds, in two some herbs of a kind which I am told is used for flavoring certain kinds of cooked food. There was nothing to show for certain how long these tins had been there; but it was pointed out to me that there was dust and cobwebs between them. The tins certainly appeared to have been there for three or four months at least, and the dust and cobwebs appeared to be natural. I could not however be certain that it had not been prepared. I do not think it was."

There were no questions, and Christopher's evidence was ended.

Next came Prem Badri Nath, the Brahman who had met Jeharan on the station platform at Ramnagar.

"On February 9th," he said, "I had been in Ramnagar city on business connected with the temple which I serve. I finished my business and went to the station to wait for the four o'clock train to Shahabad. About half an hour before the train was due to arrive, I was sitting in the waiting-room when a woman came in. She looked like a Brahmani. I noticed her because she seemed utterly exhausted, hardly able to walk. She sat down on the floor by a bench; then she put her arms on the bench and began to cry. I thought it was my duty to help her. I went to speak to her. She said she had seen her mistress murdered, and she had been locked up by the murderers; she said she had escaped and had walked twenty miles. She said she did not know what to do next. I told her not to speak so loud; I was afraid someone might hear and if the murderers were about they might want to kill me for helping her. I asked her if she had anywhere to go. She said she wanted to go to her mistress's family at Galthana, near Shahabad. I asked their name. She told me Thakur Sahib Singh; I had heard of Thakur Sahib Singh of Galthana and I knew he would repay the money if I took her home. I said I would take her with me to Shahabad and send her on next morning to Galthana. I went to buy her ticket. It cost fifteen annas. I took her with me in the train to Shahabad and she came home with me. My wife looked after her. Next day, early in the morning, I took her to the bus-stand. I knew one of the men who drive buses on the Galthana road. I went to him and told him to take this woman to Galthana. I said that Sahib Singh would

pay him when he got there. I told him to look after her carefully.
That is all."

Ajudiya Parshad rose to question him.

"You spoke to this woman from pure benevolence?"

"Yes."

"You had never seen her before?"

"No."

"Would you have done as much then for any woman you
had seen in distress on the station platform?"

"Not for any woman. But I thought she was a Brahmani before I spoke to her."

"Then you would have helped any Brahman woman?"

"I would have spoken to her. I do not know if I should have
lent her the money if I had not known the name of Sahib Singh."

"I see. Now you are a man of affairs, and are often in the Law
Courts, as a collector of rents?"

"Yes."

"Principally in the Revenue Courts, in order to sue for rents,
I suppose?"

"Yes."

"But I suppose you have sometimes been in the Criminal
Courts, prosecuting for trespass or perhaps assault?"

"Very seldom."

"But still, you have prosecuted in the Criminal Courts?"

"Yes."

"And you will agree with me that every villager, even the
most ignorant, knows this much about criminal procedure, that
if an offense is committed, the first thing he must do is to report
it to the police with as little delay as possible?"

"Yes. But in this case—"

"Excuse me, Pandit-ji, but if you will forgive me, I must ask
you to confine yourself to answering my question. You agree
with me that every villager does know this?"

"Yes."

"And you know the importance of an early report to the
police even better than the ordinary villager?"

"Yes, but in this case—"

"Again, Pandit-ji, I must ask you to answer only my question.

Then this woman told you that she had been the witness of a horrible crime, which would obviously not have been reported to the police. You were helping her and advising her, yet you took her away from the district where the crime had been committed without her having made a report to the police. Did you advise her to make a report at once in Ramnagar?"

"No."

"Will you please explain why not?"

"I was frightened that the murderers might have followed her. If they were in Ramnagar they would have followed us to the police station and probably killed us both. And in this case there had already been three days' delay, so that one day more could not make much difference."

"If there had been three days' delay, there was all the more reason for seeing that there was no more."

"I am sorry. I did not look at it like that."

"And you must have known that the police of the district where the murder was committed were concerned with it?"

"Yes, I did know that, but I was frightened."

"You were frightened that you might be followed through the streets of Ramnagar, but not that you would be followed home to Shahabad?"

"Yes. I did not think they would come to Shahabad."

"Yet if these murderers were desperate enough to kill you and the woman in the streets of Ramnagar to prevent your telling what you knew, surely they would not be too lazy to follow you to Shahabad and kill you there?"

"I did not think of that. I felt safer at Shahabad than at Ramnagar."

"I see. Now will you tell us, please, exactly where the woman was when you found her?"

"She was sitting on the floor with her head on a bench, crying."

"In what part of the waiting-room?"

"She was in the south-east corner, against the south wall."

"I see, thank you. Now, did you meet anyone at Ramnagar station whom you knew?"

"No."

"And at Shahabad station?"

"No."

"Yet you must know many people in both cities?"

"I know hardly anyone in Ramnagar, and not very many in Shahabad, although I live there. My work is most of it out of the city, in the villages."

"I see. But still it is surely unusual for you to pass through the station at Shahabad without seeing anyone you know?"

"I don't think so."

"And I suppose Thakur Sahib Singh sent someone to pay you what you had spent for Jeharan?"

"No, he sent me the amount by money order. It came through the post, ten days later."

"I see. Now during this train journey from Ramnagar to Shahabad, where did you sit?"

"In a third-class carriage."

"At the front, or the back, or in the middle?"

"At the back."

"And where did you sit and where did Jeharan sit?"

"On the back bench: I sat on the right and Jeharan in the middle of the back bench, on my left."

"I see, thank you. And in the bus next morning. Where did you put her?"

"On the seat next to the driver."

So it went on; in every detail, his story agreed with Jeharan's. He was followed by Dost Mohammad.

"On the morning of February 10th," he began, "quite early, about half-past six, I was sitting in my bus waiting for it to be full enough to start. There are usually very few passengers on my first journey out, and I start when there are six or seven as a rule, so as to get out in good time and fill up with a big load coming back. Pandit Prem Badri Nath came to me with a Brahman woman. He said that she was a servant of Thakur Sahib Singh of Galthana, and that if I would take her to Galthana, to Thakur Sahib Singh's house, I should be paid by the Thakur Sahib. He asked me to look after her, as she had had some trouble and was very sad and tired. I put her next to me in the front seat; it is really a more expensive seat, but I did not charge extra for it."

"Did anyone pay you for bringing her?"

"Yes; Thakur Bhola Nath Singh, Sahib Singh's son-in-law, came out from the house, and paid me."

"How did you let him know you had come?"

"I sent the woman in and waited, and Bhola Nath Singh came out. He had been in the courtyard before."

Ajudiya Parshad began to question him.

"Tell me please, Miyán," he said, using the polite form of address for Musulmans, "tell me, if you will be so kind, why there was so much enmity between you and Babban Sahib?"

This was delivered with such solicitous gentleness that it took the little man completely aback. He shuffled and fidgeted, hesitated, looked at the floor.

"I don't know," he mumbled.

"But there was enmity between you?"

"I had no enmity for him. How could I? He is a very big man. I am a very poor man, of no importance."

"But he had enmity for you?"

"I don't know. I never spoke to him."

"But you had heard that he was your enemy?"

"I—yes—no—I don't know. No, I had not heard that."

"Your Honor, I would ask you to note the demeanor of this witness."

"Yes, I have made a note of it."

"Thank you, sir. Now, Miyan Dost Mohammad, you drive a bus?"

"Yes—" with evident relief at getting away from the subject of Babban Sahib.

"Of which you are part owner?"

"Yes."

"But you still owe most of the price to the hire-purchase company?"

"Yes—" with reluctance.

"And it is true, is it not, that Babban Singh has lately become the owner of that company?"

"I don't know."

"Your Honor, I shall bring evidence to that effect. Now Miyan

Dost Mohammad, are you not in arrears with your payments to that company?"

"Yes, we are."

"For how long?"

"For four months."

"Yet no action has been taken to make you pay?"

"All the bus drivers are in arrears."

"Will you please be so very kind as to answer my question? Has anything been done? Have they taken possession of your bus?"

"No."

"Thank you. Now, is it not true that Babban Sahib is a friend of Sahib Singh's?"

"I don't know."

"Your Honor, I shall prove that this is so, and therefore that this man is under the influence of a man who was formerly his enemy, who is still a friend of Sahib Singh's and who is not taking, against the witness, action which he legally might. I think the conclusion is obvious."

On this triumphant note, Ajudiya Parshad sat down.

The Government Pleader would have liked to produce a few witnesses from Anantpur, who would swear that they had seen Jeharan at Kalyan Singh's house up till the time of the murder; but he had to accept the report of the police, that this was impossible because no one who had had any legitimate business in Kalyan's house would give evidence against the family. The chief consolation was that no one who had had any legitimate business in Sahib Singh's house would be prevailed on by the defense to say that he had seen Jeharan in Galthana during the critical period. The prosecution therefore came to an end with a string of formal witnesses who identified the various exhibits and reports that formed part of the record of the trial.

Gopal Singh himself stood to the story he had told Christopher.

The quarrel had taken place much as Jeharan described it, the words used being many of them identical with those she had described; the difference came when he had slapped his wife's face. Then he walked out of the room and out of the house, across the lane to Nannhe Singh's house, and there he had heard a shot. He ran back, and went upstairs. He found his wife lying half on and half off the bed. She was wounded in the body, and his gun was lying by her side. It appeared to him as though she had sat on the edge of the bed, holding the gun between her knees. All Indians are accustomed to using their toes, as Europeans use their fingers, and it would not have been hard for her to pull the trigger.

It was a case which must stand or fall by the prosecution story, and there was little room for a positive defense. Without any belief in their value, therefore, Ajudiya Parshad called four witnesses, tenants of Kalyan Singh's who came constantly to the house, who had always seen Jeharan during the period before the fatal visit to Galthana, but who since then had looked for her in vain. It was entirely useless as evidence, because they were tenants, but Kalyan Singh insisted that they should be called. The next witnesses for the defense proved the points to which Ajudiya Parshad had referred when cross-examining the prosecution witnesses; for instance, the association of Babban Sahib with Sahib Singh in various enterprises, Babban Sahib's declaration that he would be revenged on Dost Mohammed, and his ownership of the hire-purchase company. These were followed by three witnesses who had been at Shahabad station on February 9th and had seen Ram Kallan Singh arrive from the direction of Ramnagar; but as they all lived at Anantpur and had no very plausible reason for being at Shahabad, and as furthermore they were all tenants of Thakur Kalyan Singh, no one paid very much attention to their story. When the evidence closed on the third day of the trial, the defense had really brought to light nothing new. It was still a question of whether or not you believed Jeharan.

Judgment and sentence were to be pronounced next day. In the evening, when the Court had risen, Khan Bahadur Mohammad Altaf Khan came to see Christopher. It was a time when no ordinary visitor would have dared to call, but the Khan Bahadur was privileged. He had earned by his courage a consideration to which no one else could lay claim. Christopher was glad to see him, for now that the case was entirely out of his hands, when he was a mere spectator, he could discuss it more freely than before. He explained this.

"Now, Khan Bahadur," he said, "the matter is finished as far as I am concerned. Even if you told me something most important now, I could not put it before the Judge. He would not listen to me. So I ask you tell me, as a friend, what really happened."

"I am to tell you as a friend, Presence, not as District Magistrate?"

"Yes. It is only for my own interest in the people that I want to know."

"Then I will tell you, Lord, as one man tells another man. They quarreled, the husband and wife, just as Jeharan says they did. Then Gopal Singh slapped her face, just as he says, and went away in a temper. She shot herself and he ran back and found her dead. They burned her that day so that the doctors should not see her body; and the Constable found out. Next day, the Sub-Inspector came. You have seen him, Presence. You know him. I am telling you as a friend."

"Yes, I have seen him and I think I know him. He asked for money, I suppose."

"Yes, Kalyan Singh was ready to give him some money, but he asked for more. He asked for more than Kalyan would give, for the old man is mean. In the end they quarreled, and the Sub-Inspector got nothing. He had asked for two thousand rupees."

"Two thousand!" Christopher whistled.

"Yes, Lord, two thousand. And he got nothing. So he went in a very bad temper. That is how the case began."

"But I don't quite understand. How did the Galthana people come into it? Where did Jeharan get her story? Because, Khan Bahadur, one thing stood out in that trial. Jeharan's story and Gopal's are so much alike that there must be some truth behind which is close to both. Where they agree, they must be telling the truth. If what you say is true, how did the Galthana lot get to know so much, and who took the news? It can't have gone by post."

"No, it didn't go by post; I am telling you as a friend, Lord?"

"Yes."

"Then I will tell you everything. The Sub-Inspector caught a Kahar from Kalyan Singh's house. He made him tell the truth."

"How?"

"Oh, they put the legs of a cot on the backs of his hands, and other things. All the things the police do. He told them what really happened. Then the Sub-Inspector sent Rup Singh, the Constable, to Shahabad. He went by train, in plain clothes. He told them everything that had happened, and left it to them. They were as angry with Gopal Singh as if it had been murder, because they thought he had driven their daughter to kill herself."

"He sent a constable! Surely, Khan Bahadur, that was a very extraordinary thing to do. A constable! I could have believed that he sent anyone else."

"He dared not write anything, Lord. If he had written anything and the paper had come to an enemy he would have been ended. And he could not trust anyone else to give so long a message properly. He had plenty of men who could carry a paper, but to give so long a message correctly, he had to have a constable, and a clever one, too."

"Yes, I see his difficulty. Not the sort of thing you'd put on a post-card. And when the news got to Galthana, what did they do?"

"Presence, do you know what they did? Do you know why their story was so clever? The wife of Sahib Singh, her brother, is a barrister, trained in England. They sent for him before they made up their story, before they went to the police."

Christopher laughed at the idea of calling in a barrister for consultation before you composed your lie, but he admitted that it was a wise precaution.

The Khan Bahadur went on:

"And that was why, Presence, they had thought beforehand of the answers to so many questions."

"Ye-e-s," said Christopher, "you do explain, Khan Bahadur, the chief difficulty in believing Gopal's story. But there are still a good many difficulties both ways. First of all, how do you know all this?"

"Everyone near Anantpur knows. Everyone knows."

"Then why didn't they come into Court and say so? What was the sense of inventing a story about Ram Kallan being seen on the station platform when they had a true story to their hands?"

"Presence, it was Kalyan Singh. He said that if they told the true story the Judge Sahib would be angry with them for speaking evil of the police, and he would think everything they said were lies."

"Well, it was very silly. If only people would stick to the truth! Again and again I have heard a true story in a village, and then when they have got into Court they have told some stupid lie."

"I told them that, too, Presence. But they would not listen."

"Then again, Khan Bahadur, I find it very difficult to believe that an Indian woman would shoot herself with a shot-gun. We know how often a village woman gets hysterical, loses herself in a passion, rushes out of doors, and jumps into a pond or a well; we've had those cases often, and I have heard, too, of women hanging themselves. But I never heard before of one choosing a gun."

"But, Presence, this was not a village woman. That kind become mad; they do not know what they are doing, and it is over in a minute. But this was a woman of good family, a Thakurani, and one used to giving orders. It was not just the idea of a minute for her; and you will remember that during the quarrel there had been this talk of shooting. She had not spoken to her husband for a week; she must have been thinking to herself of suicide, and when she quarreled so bitterly and asked Gopal why he did not shoot her, perhaps she thought that would be the best way. She wanted to show she was not afraid, and she may have wanted too to bring some trouble to her husband."

"Which she certainly has done," said Christopher. "But how did she know how to load a gun and fire it? How many Indian women can do that?"

"True, it is not usual, Lord, but she may have asked her father or her husband to show her some time."

"She might. But another thing, if she put the gun between her knees and fired with her toes, why did she shoot herself in the body? They both say she did, so I think it must be true. It would be more painless and much easier to have put her chin on the muzzle. I've tried myself; I'm bigger than she can have been, but I find it difficult to get the muzzle lower than my chest."

"But she need not have held it tight between her knees. She had only to reach it with her toes. She may have pushed the butt forward, along the ground."

"I see what you mean. But a more serious difficulty. If no one was there during the quarrel, how does anyone but Gopal know the words they used? How did the Kahar know enough to tell the police?"

"Lord, the servants in a house always know what has been said. If they did not hear these words the first time they were uttered, they will have heard Gopal repeat them to Kalyan."

"Well, that may be true. All the same, I'm not sure I believe your local rumor that it was suicide. I think the odds are that he shot her; but I'm not at all sure that I believe this story of Jeharan's—it's my turn to speak as a friend, Khan Bahadur, not as District Magistrate. And what I think, even as District Magistrate, makes no difference now."

"Then you think, Presence, that he will be acquitted?"

"Oh, I won't go so far as that. I don't know. He may be convicted. Some of her story was most convincing. But I don't think that I'm convinced myself. In the first place I don't think they'd have had her back at Anantpur after the quarrel. But they may have done. It's odd that Gopal should have murdered his wife with someone in the room. But murder is odd anyhow. I agree with Ajudiya Parshad that it's surprising Jeharan didn't scream or call someone, or even speak to Gopal or Pyari. They seem to have acted as though they were both bewitched, and a word might have called them back to themselves. But Jeharan may have been too frightened, as she says. Most of all, I think the wounds she describes are very surprising."

"Yes, Lord, that story was invented by someone who had never fired a gun. It is a clerk's tale or a woman's."

"But on your own showing, Sahib Singh was there when they made up the story. He must have fired a gun. And if they knew the words used, they'd have heard where the wounds were. If the wad had happened to hit her eye, and he'd used a large shot, and the result had been rather loosely described, the result might have been rather like she said. But it was odd. And it does not really prove much either way, because there can really be no reasonable doubt that she was shot—whether by herself or someone else. And so the wounds are incomprehensible either way. Then again, do you think, Khan Bahadur, she could have walked so far?"

"Presence, it is impossible. She was a woman of the woman's side of the house. How could she have walked so far?"

"Well—a special terrific effort, at a great crisis—it's surprising what people can do when they try. But it's odd she met no one on the way but one old man who can't be found. You might say it was odd she knew of his existence, but if you assume she was lying, you must assume that she had very accurate information from Anantpur, and that would be part of it. Personally, I find it most difficult of all to believe that she walked all the way into Ramnagar, through all that complication of sidings and branch-lines, standing trucks, cranes, and the rest, without meeting anyone. And then on the platform, there can have been only one man, of the thousands there must have been in the station, who was of her own caste and her own town, knew her master, and was ready to help her. That one man, of those thousands, was the only man who spoke to her!"

"It is incredible, Lord."

"Well, not incredible, but very unlikely, Khan Bahadur. Then the green stuff growing on the roof—well, that may have been faked when I went, or she may not have noticed it; I don't myself think that's very important. But I do think it's important about the child. Aren't I right in thinking that purdah women, shut up by themselves, talk and dream of children more than anything else?"

"Quite right, Presence. Two things are more important than anything for them, children and weddings. What else have they to talk about?"

"And the girl she had nursed and was so fond of! She could not remember the month when her first child was born, nor

even whether it was in the day or the night! It's impossible.
Whenever else she was at Anantpur, she can't have been there
then."

"Then if she was lying in that, Presence, her whole story would
be rejected?" The Khan Bahadur leaned forward eagerly.

"Well, I don't know. If you always acted on that principle,
no one in this country would ever be convicted; but I must say,
when it's a case of hanging, and the whole case depends on one
person's word, and you find that person's lying on one point—
However, it's not for me to decide."

Secretly Christopher was wondering why the stout old man
was so keen a partisan. Probably, he decided, Kalyan had promised to desert Nannhe Singh and come over to the party of
Hukm Singh and the Khan Bahadur if by their influence they
could help. The belief of every Indian in personal influence is
pathetic. Or perhaps the rest of the Anantpur Thakurs had sworn
to destroy Hukm Singh entirely if Gopal was convicted—and
that would drive a fatal wedge into the Khan Bahadur's system
of local control. Not that it was Hukm Singh's fault, but they
might think it was.

"You must remember, Khan Bahadur," he went on, "that what
seem to us convincing arguments one way may mean the opposite to other people. That business about the census, now. To
me, that made Jeharan's story more doubtful. She had her answer
so pat: she knew just what was coming, and if you're honest,
you don't prepare as carefully as that. That barrister of yours—he
must be a clever man to have thought of so much. I must admit
I was lost in admiration when that came up. I thought: 'These
people are too clever for me!' Then again all this exact correspondence of position, where they met, and where they sat—I
don't like that either. I don't think people do remember things
as clearly as that; but of course to the Court these points may be
convincing. They may find that for them they clinch the story.
And there is one outstanding point, which you have explained
to me, but which was never explained in Court. They are bound
to ask: 'If Jeharan was not there, how does she know so much?'
That question may outweigh everything else."

Apparently it did, for next day Gopal Singh, son of Kalyan
Singh, Thakur, of Anantpur, was found guilty of the murder of
his wife and sentenced to death.

It was April when they led him out to die. The light of early
morning had not yet taken on the coloring of the full-grown
day; it was still fresh and sweet. There was a sparkle of dew in
the flowers and vegetables of the prison garden, a savor of dew
in the air, a million points of dancing light in the smooth grass
of the lawns. Within the high walls of mellow sun-warmed brick,
an avenue of laburnums smiled in the happy sunshine, the tender
green of their light-winged foliage breaking into a foam of delicate blossom, palest gold against the green, rejoicing in the sweet-
ness of the sun. Beneath that avenue came the procession of death.

Gopal Singh walked between two policemen, with two more
in front and behind. He was wearing prison clothes, knickers
and shirt of a sort of coarse white cloth. He carried himself
straight with his head up, but his face was gray. "Ram, Ram,
Sita, Ram," he said over and over, quietly to himself, that he
might die with the names of the divine lovers on his lips. The
procession reached the entrance to the gallows enclosure; there
it halted, and the jailer stepped forward. He was a little man,
and his brown face was old and twisted. All his life had been
spent in watching over unhappiness and the fruit of crime; his
mouth was straight and thin and his eyes small behind steel
spectacles. He carried a tall twisted stick of dark wood, as high
as his breast; his left hand rested on this, while in his right he
held a warrant for the death of the tall young man to whom he
spoke.

"You are Gopal Singh, son of Kalyan Singh, Thakur, of Anantpur. You were condemned to death by the Sessions Court of
Ramnagar, and the sentence has been confirmed by the High
Court. Today has been fixed for your death. Is that right?" His
voice was sharp and dry.

"Yes. Ram, Ram, Sita, Ram."

"March."

They moved on, and turned between fixed bayonets into the
gallows enclosure. There were no flowers here, but a square of

grass within high brick walls. In the middle an earthen ramp led up steeply to the foot of the gallows, an iron cross-bar on two iron uprights. Three nooses hung from it above three separate traps.

By one of these the hangman stood waiting for Gopal. He was a Dom, an outcast, a disposer of dead bodies, unclean as his brothers the jackal and the vulture. He stood with downcast eyes, his dark face sullen and ashamed, in a prison suit of dull green sacking; but his hands were nimble when Gopal came to him. Quick as a lizard, they bound his arms, pulled over his head a drab bag marked with the red line of a Government factory, drew tight over that the knot of the noose; he looked to the Superintendent of the Prison. His face white as his clothes, the Superintendent raised his hand. The hangman jerked a lever. Gopal Singh had gone.

That April Christopher Tregard was in camp. It was past the regular camping season and a tent was hot at midday, but he had gone out to inspect some work which he thought had been scamped. He had been riding till ten in the morning, and he lay down to rest at midday. After his rest he went through the day's mail which had been sent out from his office. The last item was a formal report of the execution of Gopal Singh.

Christopher laid it down and went out of the tent. He was camping in a grove of mangoes by the gigantic ruins of what had been a city two thousand years ago. He climbed the ramparts of shattered brick, and looked out across the plain to the high snows. In the velvet warmth of the April evening the earth was paying back the heat it had borrowed by day from the sun; brick and dust and scrub gave out a breath like an extinguished furnace. The light had not yet faded, and the plain lay before him in minute detail like the background of a Renaissance portrait, the trees, tiny, dark and glossy, standing up among fields bare from the harvest.

Christopher thought of the waste of two lives. He saw the roof above Anantpur village, the blazing noonday sun, the day Pyari died. He saw the flies busy about her blood: almost he smelt it in the sun. He saw the lean face of the viperine Jeharan;

and there came suddenly over him a despair of his work, a contempt for the sand of his daily plowing, a baffled feeling that he was on a surface beneath which he could not see, playing always with guesses to which he never knew the certainty. Passionately he longed for England; he wanted to deal with people who would say what they thought and who were not the slaves of passion and intrigue; he wanted to feel beneath his feet a soil that was friendly to man. Softly he repeated to himself the names of English trees: oak and elm, chestnut, beech and ash, their names as English as the quiet certainty of their growth. He remembered days in England: the clear light of the north, shifting patterns of cloud on the bold sinewy limbs of sunlit fells; a Cornish headland, where the bright heather of the south, scenting the air with honey, lay in brilliant banks against the glossy green of bracken, and where the sea wrapped the rock in amaranthine coils of palest jade and wine-dark purple; a Dorset meadow on the chalk before the hay was mown, where the flowers chimed to the eye as prettily as their names to the ear, rest-harrow and bettany, hawksbit, centaury and scabious. Dearest of all he remembered the softness of twilight and the scent of the lanes in the evening; and then his eyes dropped to the tawny scrub before him, where there sprang up like a shout the vivid splendor of flame-of-the-forest, bright as a story of pain and love in a world that goes to the office at half-past nine every day.

Christopher stood up and laughed and ran down the hill. A few days later he had a letter from the Superintendent of Police at Shahabad. "By the way," it ended, "you will be interested to hear, à propos of your Anantpur murder, that the woman Jeharan was found poisoned two days ago. So far there is no evidence at all against anyone."